To Sue

Best wishes

enjoy the read

X

# Unidentified:

## To the Moon and Back ... and Beyond

by
J. D. Crawford

Cover concept: Art Dione

Cover images: Creative Commons License (Public Domain)

ISBN: 97988337846915

In Memory of the men who inspired me to write this book: Gerry Anderson, Ed Bishop, George Sewell, and Michael Billington. And to my father, Joe Crawford, who died at the age of 46 Years old and sadly never lived long enough to see my achievements.

# CHAPTERS

*At the age of eleven in the 1970's the Television screening was just beginning to broadcast in colour. Previously it had been in black and white and consisted of three channels BBC1, BBC2 and ITV. Saturday evenings were by far the better night for viewing the best shows and UFO was one of these. My fondness for the show found me ready each week to watch one of the twenty-six episodes and again in later years with its repeat series. It was escapism at its best and an imaginary world of heroes who fought for good against the bad. In later life I was sad to learn of the passing of the main characters and of course the creator of the show Gerry Anderson. I had always wished for more episodes and so decided to ignite some new life into this visionary realm in my own way.*

   - J. D. Crawford

# Introduction

In the late 1960's the successful landing on the Moon infused the obsession of UFOs and Aliens. It had almost become a fashion. Although the Moon and Mars were both barren there were many planets out there that we were uncertain if like us they had life forms. Television programmes were arrayed with stories of UFOs and aliens in the form of TV series and films. There were even songs written about space and fashion statements were made with space in mind.

Of course, there were the conspiracy theories and the so called "X files." People who were missing were thought to have been abducted by Alien beings and some even claimed to have been taken and later released from these crafts after being experimented on.

However, these visits from UFOs were never seen by the masses, making it questionable. Some suggested that Aliens were of a higher intelligence and may have shown ESP potential and yet these same beings apparently never wanted to share their knowledge with us and communicate. They were often perceived as the bad guys who were an aggressive race intending to conquer our World. Except, if this was so, what was stopping them from doing this?

As the Alien obsession declined, we accepted that at least in our solar system no other life-form existed and any that did would be too far away with a very, long journey that even with advanced crafts would take a lifetime to reach.

By 2020 the solar system and space along with NASA and many scientists continued to show interest in furthering the search for life on other planets that could aid in our quest of how we as humans came to really be on Earth. Evolution is a science that proves the progression and making of man but was there something else that made our planet special enough to bear human life or did we journey from another Universe to make Earth our home?

# Saunders

Harry Saunders was born in New York, America in 1987 to a family of Military Airforce pilots. He too followed his ancestor's path by attending Military college and later taking a degree in Astrophysics. He learned to fly as soon as it was possible and eventually became an astronaut working closely with NASA. He was dedicated and passionate about his work and for him Space was heaven, peaceful, still, and quiet. With the bright lights of the stars, he looked down at Earth and considered himself to be exceedingly fortunate. Harry's younger brother John followed in his footsteps and they would often work together in space. Satellites were always needing astronaut's assistance and the Moon offered an endless supply of rocks and soil specimens for the scientists that were forever being requested. They had also surfaced Mars too, though this was under wraps for now.

It was during one of these trips in 2010 that Harry along with his brother John was making a return journey to Earth when Harry had his first real encounter with a UFO. There had been suspected sightings before, but he had always been given vague excuses by the Military authorities about these and they had been dismissed without any thought. Harry was a person who worked on facts not a maybe and so never pursued them any further. Yet this time, there was no doubt and when the UFO attacked their craft, Harry contemplated that he would not see the light of day ever again.

They had landed heavily in the sea and the rest was just a blur. This was also to be Harry's first contact with General Samuel Grant a Canadian born General who would change the destiny of Harry's life forever. He was a tall upright man who looked uncompromising but was sincere. He had worked hard as a Black man to gain his ranking and because of this had taken longer than usual to achieve his position. He had a good instinct of what was good and right and immediately saw the potential in Harry.

He took no prisoners but his desire for the truth was key to him battling on and at forty-five years old he had seen many changes in the Military over his time, some for the better and some not so good. He had witnessed first- hand the torn and mutilated bodies that had been found with little explanation and although there had been possible signs of UFO landings this was never enough to give solid proof. It was his job to clean up and destroy evidence to avoid any suspect theories that did not fit with the Military, but recently he had been feeling that he was spending too long hiding the truth from enquiring families and the public.

So many aircraft attacks were blamed on terrorism when there was every possibility that these were the result of Alien violence. He was sure there was so much more and had managed to finally convince the authorities that if he could show evidence without any doubt that UFOs really were at the root of these attacks then they would be willing to fund an organization to defend Earth. To do this he needed the right people in his recruitment that he could rely on to bring this together and whilst reading Harry's files had recognized that same determination and qualities in Harry.

When Harry woke, he found himself in a Military hospital with General Grant at his bedside. Standing over him was a strange looking man with a Russian accent who he later learned was a psychiatrist and surgeon Vladimir Ivanov.

He was top in his field of medicine, a true eccentric but, nevertheless a genius at what he did. It was then that Harry discovered that his brother John had not survived and died in the crash. Harry had two broken legs and several fractured ribs but they would heal, whereas the death of his brother would stay with him forever.

General Grant visited Harry every day whilst in the Military hospital and they discussed in great detail the events of the crash. Harry found it refreshing to talk with someone especially of his rank about UFOs.

"You know, you can never tell anyone what you witnessed, Lieutenant Saunders," warned the General. "In any case, no one would believe you and you would never work for the Military again if you persisted." The General was direct and straight to the point. "So, why are we even having this conversation then?" asked Harry. He was angry and still grieving for his brother's loss and was being informed that he could never relay what really happened to John, to his parents and friends, when all he wanted to do was seek revenge on the UFOs. The General looked Harry in the eyes. "I could do with a man like you on my team." Then the Doctor began to speak "You have determination, enthusiasm, a thirst for knowledge and truth and a vendetta to right your brother's wrongdoing. We need compelling evidence without any possible doubt to convince those in authority in order for them to support us in our fight against these attacks". The General sighed "but it will be a long, dangerous, and a hard road to follow. So, are you in Lieutenant?" asked General Grant. "Yes sir," replied Harry, "you can count on me, for sure." At 23 years of age Lieutenant Saunders was a handsome, six-foot- tall guy with a pale complexion and blonde hair. His vivid blue eyes were distinct, and he had an air of confidence about him that was unusual for someone so young, making him extra popular with the ladies. Though his relationships never lasted long as he was always too busy with his work and gave his dates little attention. He was a fact finder and to Harry it was either black or white there were no in-betweens. Still there was a softer, romantic side to him that as yet had not been kindled.

Meeting with Lieutenant Carl Peters at the Cumbrian Military base would lead to a long and lasting friendship. Carl Peters was a Londoner whose Grandparents had been Jewish refugees. He had been fascinated with flying from an incredibly young age which meant he was destined for the RAF but unlike Harry he was not an astronaut. He had flown just about every kind of aircraft available and in the last two years had worked in the Military intelligence. He was much more rugged looking than Harry but still had an attraction about him with his dark hair and blue eyes. Lieutenant Peters was older than Harry by one year, being born in August 1986 and was from quite a different background but they complimented each other perfectly. Carl's work in intelligence required a tough and cool manner, yet his eyes were warm and sensitive, and he had a gentle and calming voice that suggested a caring man. Though, Carl also had an air of mischief about him and when things became tough, he always had something to say that would cause a smile. He could also be charming to the ladies yet he never actually got far with them as he came over as being too forward when in fact, he was anything but, it was all an act to hide his disappointments. His shoulders were broad, and he too reached six feet in height. Carl was dependable, trustworthy, and loyal to the end. He was also Harry's voice of reason and would eventually become his second in command.

# Sara

Sara Croft was born in 1989 to a Military RAF Colonel and his wife Maria who he met late on in life at the age of forty. Maria had begun her career as a dancer. She was a descendant of a Swiss family who emigrated to England and later moved to Cumbria with her husband. She was a stunning woman with all the curves in the right places. Her ash blonde long flowing hair cascaded onto a beautiful face with green eyes and long lashes. Colonel Croft was smitten with his future wife from the onset and once Married Maria slipped into Military life by becoming a schoolteacher at the Military Base that her husband James was commissioned to in Cumbria.

James Croft's family were Cumbrian farmers for over a hundred years and he was expected to follow suit but the RAF base nearby was much more inviting to him and when his parents Passed away, he inherited the farm and land but showed little interest in farming. He had decided to rent out part of the land and the adjacent buildings and used the rest for chickens and horses. Although the colonel and his wife spent most of their time at the Military base, they still chose to live at the Croft family farmhouse.

Sara's love for animals began in this instance, perceiving the animals not as food but as creatures to be respected and cared for. Sara was a gentle and kind child and the apple of her daddy's eyes and wherever her father was Sara was never far behind. Mum used her teaching skills to educate Sara as soon as she could and found her very receptive to learning early on and Sara was soon top of the class at her school. She was a pretty child with her mother's looks of blonde hair and green eyes, unlike her father who had thick dark curly brown hair with brown eyes. He had a strong, powerful, appealing look which signified that Sara would become a striking young woman. Her father was an excellent pilot and it was not long before Sara developed a shared interest with her father for flying, especially as he often took her with him on flying trips which was to her delight.

Mum was fun loving and would often dance and sing around the house with Sara in tow and was adored by the children she taught at the school. There was never a dull moment with her mother whose zest for life was coveted by all those who were lucky enough to be around her.

Sara was indeed a fortunate child, with both their incomes and renting part of the farm to a local, the crofts were financially stable. This being so allowed for some family luxury items. For James's and his love for flying led to the purchase of his own light aircraft, that was often seen flying in the area and around the nearing countryside with his young daughter. At eight years old dad had made a makeshift steering and control panel for Sara so she could pretend she was flying the aeroplane herself.

His motto during flights was something that Sara always remembered "It is easy to fly, but harder to crash safely" and had insisted on going through many scenarios of how to crash safely and become unscathed as he himself had survived four crashes and lived to tell the tale. She would appreciate this motto later in her life.

At ten years of age came the biggest tragedy of Sara's life when her mother, returning from a school trip with five children was victim to a terrorist bomb attack. The explosion left nothing not even charred bodies for a funeral. Her mother was gone from there life and her father was never the same after this day. James argued with the Military authorities for a full investigation for his wife and the five children but it was deemed a closed case. No one was ever brought to justice for the crime and he never received a full explanation of what really happened.

This eventually led to Colonel Croft leaving the air force two years after his wife's death exhausted from fighting for justice and taking a position as a commercial pilot instead. At this time Sara was posted to a private boarding school in the Cotswolds, and only visited home on weekends where her father continued to let Sara pursue her love of flying and by the age of eighteen to her father's immense joy, she had her Flying license. However, he was saddened to learn that Sara would not be following a career in the RAF as she could not forgive the Air force for the way they had been with them over her mother's death.

To her father's dismay she enrolled on a Bachelor of Science honours degree in Psychology at Lancaster University which meant that she could commute daily and be at home with her father in the evenings as he had become lost and lonely these days. Whilst continuing her studies she had also applied for her helicopter license and was soon flying high with her newfound interest. Up in the sky was where she felt the happiest and safe and had decided to put her skills to effective use by volunteering with the mountain rescue. The helicopter was a life saver for anyone who needed their help and Sara got to do what she enjoyed the most, helping people whilst airborne.

When Sara graduated with a first-class degree her father was delighted, especially as she had received the highest marks in the country and led her to a master's degree in Parapsychology. Her father knew she was bright and intelligent as well as being kind and caring, just like her mother and could not have asked for a better daughter. Though, he was unable to share her enthusiasm for her subject of choice but he supported her, nonetheless. Sara had only just completed her master's degree when her father sadly passed away with a heart attack. Her father's death was unexpected and sudden and now Sara was alone in the large Farmhouse dealing with all the legal affairs left behind but Sara picked herself up and battled on as her father and mother would have done. The choices were sometimes difficult for a young person alone in the world but Sara had a will to make good of her life and never give in.

After selling the farm Sara found a pretty cottage just outside of Lancaster in a semi- rural area suitable for her to begin a new life. She had been fortunate to be in a comfortable position with her finances due to her parents, but she still wanted to achieve and offer others her help when she could to those who needed it. There was a drive within her to always do right to others. She had recently begun her PHD in ESP or Extra sensory perception which included several commutes to Edinburgh University and travelling to such a beautiful city for Sara was all part of the excitement. Also, with her love for animals Sara became involved in volunteering and rescuing dogs and cats from European countries where animals were in danger of being killed if they were stray or part of the cruel meat trade. She would fly over to the chosen country in her father's light aircraft and collect the animals, bringing them back to rescue centres in the UK besides, this helped to keep her flying skills and license intact too.

After completing her PhD, Sara tried to follow in her father's steps by flying as a commercial pilot but found it meaningless and was met with arrogance and sexism at her being a female pilot. Thankfully, after a few years she was able to work in a much satisfactory career as a helicopter pilot for the Lancashire police force. It was only two shifts a week and she spent another day a week lecturing in Psychology at the Local University where she had previously studied to make the hours up but she enjoyed both professions equally.

# All Systems Go!

They finally had it, the proof they needed filming: photos and documentation containing evidence of recent UFO disturbances including sightings, attacks, and the disappearance of individuals. They did not know why the UFOs came or where they came from, but they were becoming an international threat. Now all they had to do was get the funding.

The international conference was to be held at the Cumbrian Military RAF base. Leaders from all over the world were gathering and were briefed on the findings, but this was a difficult operation to conduct with so many leaders and such secrecy surrounding the event. They would need a complete media shutdown for this meeting if it were to be a success and although this was a vigorous task, it was achievable with the correct professionals on board.

General Grant and Lieutenant Saunders travelled from their office to the conference to present their findings to the Governors of the Earth, who were shocked at the reality of increased visits and attacks by the aliens. There was now a realization that unless a defence was imminent then the preservation of the human race would be in great danger. It was 2015 and the vote was accepted unanimously by every leader and funding's would be made available for this multi-billion-dollar project with affect.

The USA President addressed the board. "I have a question for the General and lieutenant Saunders. Now that you have your organization, who will command this brave team of defenders?" Harry looked towards the General and responded. "Of course, Sir there can only be one-man, General Grant." General Grant shook his head. "It will take years to bring this organization to fruition and by then I would be much too old." He continued: "It needs determination, dedication, and the vigour of a younger individual. Lieutenant Saunders you are that person. You can refuse the position but if you do it must be now as there will be no turning back later." Harry was surprised as he had always believed that it would be the General who would lead them in this battle but he also knew it had to be right and therefore he had to accept and be willing to sacrifice everything he had known in order for the organization to work. It would take a further five years for the whole organization to be completed as this was a mammoth undertaking. Finally in 2020 the defence against Alien forces was finalized and ready for operation and its name was SHEALD Special Headquarters for Earth's Alien Legion of Defence.

Commander Saunders was now heading the defence and would be responsible for every part of the department, even the building work would be overseen by him. A base was built on the moon with quarters for staff, offices, a control centre, medical unit, canteen, gym, and a rest room. It also had a docking station for a shuttle to commute staff to and from the Earth and Moon with three launch pads and Interceptor armed spacecrafts including several Lunar buggies to travel around the surface of the Moon. There was a satellite with the latest technology to detect any UFOs in the space area heading towards Earth or the moon. Naturally, Commander Saunders helped to install the satellite defence system into space. SAAM or "Sam" as they called it, which was the 'Space Alien attack monitor' was the first response to any Extra-terrestrial visitors.

There were also specially equipped submarines around the world in several oceans with an underwater jet attached to them that was capable of swooping from the seas into the sky. SEASKY was supersonic in speed and the Jet could be in the air within seconds, entering another country in minutes. If the Lunar interceptors missed their aim, then SEASKY would be the next port of call and then it would be up to the Land roamers to search on land. These were usually brought in a transporter which could fly them swiftly to their destination with several vehicles at a time allowing a quick and safe landing. There were Planes, jets, and helicopters which were all part of the crew available to SHEALD when and if needed. The main operations and headquarters were to be in the

12

North of England and Cumbria was determined as the ideal spot. With its surrounding hills and vast countryside there were plenty of woodlands to keep the base hidden well. An underground unit was suggested as a safer option for HQ offering a better defence against any attack. The latest and most superior computer systems were fitted with radar and radio transmitters and manned by the most experienced controllers. This would be the home of SHEALD and Commander Saunders.

General Grant still had some involvement as he would join the committee who oversaw all SHEALDS spending and other military costs. General Grant was Saunders main contact when needing finances and although billions of dollars had already been spent on the set up of SHEALD Harry was always demanding funding for a new project or devices that he saw as vital to their performance or for the defender's protection. Grant was not always obliging to Harry as he felt that Harry had more than his "lion's share" of the budget.

His first staff recruitment as Commander was to find his second in command. He had already met Lieutenant Carl Peters whilst in Cumbria and they had hit it off straight away though they were both hugely different in personality. Harry being an American who was serious and confident, and Carl was the jovial Londoner who was happy to be in the background but they both shared the same loyalty and determination to the organization and with the two opposites they would become an unbeatable force for the good of mankind as these two men's lives were now entwined forever. "General Grant may I introduce you to my first recruit and second in command colonel Carl Peters," said Harry as Carl offered to shake hands with the General. "Ah, a wise choice," replied Grant. Neither of the men had any idea of the true scale of what they had let themselves in for, but they both had the motivation, loyalty, and passion to do justice to the job.

Harry and Carl had been through endless military CV's and the best of the best had been sifted out. They were checked and checked again for their suitability with IQ, Psychoanalysis testing, combat training and physical fitness as just some of their requirements. They would never settle for second best in the recruitment process and were eventually left with a handful of candidates but they were the right people and a vital tool to the organization. There would also be a lengthy training programme for each and every member that would take months to complete but there would be no compromising for anyone and everyone would undergo the same training whoever they were.

After the many years of challenging work, building, recruiting, and installing, SHEALD was up and running. Staff had been trained to the highest standard through a gruelling and lengthy enlistment and the underground headquarters was complete becoming a thriving working centre. Any UFOs passing through space near to home were identified and alerted by SAAM with "Red alert" which was a definite sighting and possible attack. The radar would follow their path and was capable of predicting the termination of where they could be heading. With the interceptors at the ready they could be launched in minutes on Lunar base giving chase to any trespassing UFOs detected. These interceptors carried an explosive missile that could fire at the UFOs preventing them from landing on Earth and avert any attack but on the odd occasion the UFOs managed to avoid the missile attack and escape out of the Lunar bases range and into Earth's atmosphere the search was able to continue with SEASKY and the Land roamers. Eventually the UFO would be caught and usually destroyed.

Even so, it had been the desire of Commander Saunders to capture an alien for interrogation and particularly to confiscate a space craft for investigation, but this was improbable as once the ships entered Earth's atmosphere they would disintegrate shortly after, meaning that at present this was near to impossible to do. However, they had fallen lucky on one occasion when they captured an alien who was brought back to headquarters and taken to the medical centre. Saunders had tried everything to make some kind of contact with the being but failed and sadly the alien, died in a short time of arriving at the centre. Saunders was frustrated that he was unable to gain any further knowledge from these Extra-terrestrial's after so long as he had imagined by now that he would be partial to many answers relating to alien life. Though they had prevented the UFOs from entering Earth undetected and possibly saving many lives and for some that was enough, but not for Saunders as he wanted answers.

Colonel Peters was much calmer and always able to make Harry see the positives of what they had taken from the events. Harry would rage at staff if they were not up to his high standards, leaving Carl to comfort them. Peters did most of the organizing and training of new staff with his softer, more welcoming approach. Carl's approach to staff was friendly and supportive but he was no push over. At the end of the day, he had been trained to kill the enemy on command without a second thought and Harry trusted Carl with his life and visa-versa. Harry gave everything to his profession even his marriage which had failed within months due to his absence at home. Harry's sacrifices were huge and Carl understood that but hoped that one day he would find more than the organization to love.

Colonel Tom Green was a later recruit who quickly rose up the ranks. He was younger than Harry or Carl but showed enormous potential. He had been trained in the RAF but had diverted into becoming a test pilot more recently. Where he had also experienced a UFO attack first hand during his work. He had insisted on pursuing his experience of UFOs until the authorities believed he was becoming a threat and suggested him as an Ideal candidate for the defence team. Both Harry and Carl had put him through his paces before accepting him into the team and instantly realized his capabilities were immense. He soon became part of the SHEALD family and with such qualities and skills he was hastily identified by Carl and Harry as third in command.

# Attack!

It was a cold and windy day when Sara set off from the air-port with her light aircraft. On her way out of the cottage the scruffy black three- legged dog followed her. "No Jack, I'm sorry I can't take you this time, go!" She pointed to the sofa in the living room. He often joined her on the rescue flights but this time there were so many dogs to bring back that there would not be enough room for Jack. He whimpered with his head down sulking at his disappointment.

Sara smiled. She loved her little dog; he too was a rescue from Spain and had been in such a bad state when she had first seen him with little fur on his body that was covered in sores and he was painfully thin too. She just had to take him and help him and since that day he had become her loyal companion. Her life was busy with work and her volunteering but that was how she preferred it to be. She had little time for dating, as the men she had met had been quite boring and predictable. She blamed it on her father who was her role model and such an interesting person to be around, no one could ever match up to him. In any case most men were scared away by her intelligence and independent ways. She was very pretty and feminine in her looks, but she was no femme fatale by any means.

She landed at the Spanish airport and was met by two volun-teers who would join her on the journey home. They loaded up the dogs and set back to the South of England where the dogs and helpers would part ways with Sara and continue their journey to a local rescue centre who were waiting for them. Luton Airport seemed quieter than usual so, it was not long before the dogs were unloaded. The dogs were tired and frightened so there was a silence that hit the room and made an uncomfortable entry. It was nine O'clock in the evening, dark and still raining and it had been an exhausting trip and she would be glad when she was home, in her warm and cosy cottage.

It wasn't far now, just another twenty minutes and she would be landing and in her car on her way home. The aircraft was cold and breezy but at least she was well wrapped up. She always wore her flying suit and had a chunky woolly hat and a scarf wrapped tightly around her face to keep the warmth in. That was the only problem with the old light aircraft it was very draughty indeed.

Lunar base had alerted Headquarters that the UFO had outrun the interceptor's shots and was on its way down to Earth. "What's the predictive projective determination Lieutenant?" asked Harry.

"Sir it's heading in your direction, Cumbria," replied Lieutenant Leah Rose. "Don't worry Leah, we'll get it Colonel Carl Peters and Colonel Tom Green are out in the field around that region on the roamers. I'll get them in place in case it lands and SEASKY are already on their way." Harry was confident they would apprehend it.

"Sir, Sir," interrupted the HQ Control operator Paul. "I've located it but there's another aircraft directly in its path.

"Paul" asked the Commander "what type of aircraft is it, is it Military?" Paul shook his head. "No sir, it's a light aircraft, civilian by the looks of it." Harry Sighed.

"Damn, that's all we need. Tell SEASKY to try and miss the aircraft but at the end of the day we can't lose the UFO so if it gets in the way then he still has to shoot." Paul nodded to the Commander and relayed the message to Captain Lu Lee in the SEASKY jet. "Roger, will do my best Commander." He knew how important his orders were and so had to do them with precision.

Sara could not see the UFO but sensed someone was on her tail. Within seconds she heard firing and the plane shuddered. "Was someone shooting at her?" Then she saw a bright flashing light and an explosion behind her which blew her plane off course and now she was dipping in a downward motion and lost control of her plane. She had been hit by something. "Mayday, mayday!" she called on her radio, but the radio did not respond. it must have been damaged in the attack. She was desperately out of control. "Come on dad, help me," she muttered as the plane went down and She held on for dear life. "Remember!" She shouted to herself, "control it, you can do this!" "Commander it's a direct hit, UFO destroyed," informed Captain Lee. "What about the other aircraft?" asked Commander Saunders. "I'm afraid it's taken a hit too Sir." Harry banged his hand down on the desk, loss of any life was always personal to him. The idea was to save life, not destroy it, but sometimes he had no choice.

"Commander" It was Colonel Peters on the ground with the mobile roamers. "We can see the aircraft falling it's very near and it's not completely out of control, whoever the pilot is, must be very experience." Carl and Tom were watching every move the plane made and followed it. luckily, it was an open rural area and mainly fields and seemed to be heading for a particular field that had Hay bales packed in long rows, "very clever," said Carl. "a crash landing into bales of hay, they could be lucky" added Tom. Sara's mind was working overtime now, "It's easy to fly but harder to crash safely." She kept repeating her father's words over and over to herself as she hit the bales of hay hard. "Boom!" For a short time, she had lost consciousness. Carl jumped from the roamer vehicle towards the crashed aircraft and looked inside.

"I think the pilots still alive," he shouted to Tom who was just getting out of the vehicle. Carl ripped open the door of the plane grabbing the pilot's arm and pulled them from the aeroplane. It was very dark, and he only hoped that no one else was in the plane as it set on fire. Carl dragged the body further away from the wreck as he heard Tom Shouting, "Get down Carl, it's going to blow." Carl's survival training kicked in and he threw himself over the body and lay on top with his head down to avoid the explosion debris.

They were safe. As Carl lifted his body in the black of the night the woollen hat and scarf fell away from the pilot to reveal a beautiful face peering back at him. Her blonde hair rolled over her pretty pale face as she caught her breath. Carl was beyond surprised as he found himself sprawled over her, he turned to look towards Tom saying, "well now, I didn't expect that!" Tom nodded "Yeh me, neither." Carl awkwardly got to his feet and held his hand out to help Sara stand. "Can you walk?" he asked. Confused and bewildered by the events Sara took his hand. "Yes, I'm ok, I think?" She felt safe and at that moment she knew Everything would be alright. Then she felt a sharp jab in her arm but before she could react, she had fallen asleep.

When Sara woke, she was in a hospital bed with a doctor and nurse standing over her bed. She was groggy but aware.

"You are safe and well, don't worry, try to get some sleep and we will talk in the morning." He had a strange accent but in her present state she could not work out where the accent was from as she drifted back to sleep. In the morning she heard talking but she instantly recognized this voice, it was the guy who had rescued her from the burning plane.

"How are you feeling Sara?" "I'm surprisingly well thanks," she replied. He had a kind smile and pulled up a chair.

"My name is Colonel Carl Peters, but you can call me Carl. You are in a Military hospital as you engaged in a rouge Russian aircraft attack that had been flying over the area unannounced. We had to shoot it down and unfortunately, you were caught in the crossfire."

He paused for a moment, "That was an impressive flight, you held that plane really well, how you managed to land as well as you did was something else. There are a lot of pilots I know would never have been able to do what you did." Sara answered Carl.

"My father was an excellent RAF pilot and he taught me everything I know about flying and crashing." Carl listened. "I'd like to meet your father some time, he sounds quite a man." Sara dropped her head. "I am afraid he's dead." Realizing he had put his foot in it, he rapidly changed the subject. "So, the doctors say you're well enough to go home tomorrow, that's great news, isn't it? and don't worry we'll arrange transport home for you too." Sara seemed a little more serious and he was concerned to what she would say next. "Carl, could I ask a favour please? It's my dog he's been on his own at the house." He stopped her, "You mean Jack? we sent someone round this morning. You were quite persistent last night you even gave me the keys from your pocket." He smiled and gave her the keys back.

"He sounds very cute with his three legs." She laughed. "I can't even remember saying that," said Sara "but then I was probably a bit concussed. Thank you so much Carl, you are so kind." He proceeded to leave the room and gave her a cheeky wink. "You are welcome anytime." Sara liked Carl he was easy to talk to.

Tom was already in the commander's office when Carl arrived the following morning. Harry was in a rush as usual and giving his orders out for the day to the staff. He had a dozen reports on his desk and the phone calls were just starting to come in. He looked at his to do list for that day, as usual it was long. He was due to meet the pilot in the hospital and had the report with all the information on, but he hadn't had time to look through it yet. He would just adlib as he went along, he was good at that.

"I'm off to see the pilot before he goes home to check everything is ok." Carl tried to speak before he visited Sara, but Harry was in too much a hurry.

"We can speak later Carl, I'm sure it can wait." Carl opened his mouth to speak but Harry was gone. Tom grinned at Carl and shrugged his shoulders.

"He's going to put his foot in it" said Tom and they both laughed.

As Commander Harry Saunders arrived at the hospital room, he still had the information on Sara in his hand, but his confidence got the better of him. "Good morning, good morning I'm C...." He finally looked up and stumbled on his words. She was stunning and not at all what he was expecting. He felt his heart miss a beat and he realized he had made rather a fool of himself. By now Sara was getting used to the reactions to her being female.

"Yes, I know you weren't expecting a woman," she replied sarcastically. "Sorry to disappoint you." Harry tried to pull himself out of the embarrassment.

"No, no, your right of course, I wasn't expecting a woman but your wrong it definitely isn't a disappointment." Sara could feel her cheeks blushing as she looked up at his bright blue eyes staring at her and her stomach felt strange. He was handsome and his American accent made him sound even more confident. Yet he stumbled from foot to foot in nervousness of this attractive woman he had just insulted. "I believe you are going home today?" He asked. "Yes, in the next couple of hours. I've left my poor dog, he will be fretting," said Sara. "Yes, yes, I imagine so," he replied. He could not take his eyes off her, "I will arrange for a ride home for you," he added. He smiled as he left and somehow a calmness rippled over him.

When he entered the office both Tom and Carl were grinning. "I tried to tell you Harry," teased Carl. "She is very attractive, don't you think?" asked Tom. Harry played it down.

"I suppose she is," Carl smiled.

"You suppose she is? I tell you, when I first realized who was underneath me the other night, I almost wished she had stopped breathing." Harry made a disapproving face. Really Carl?" He questioned. "No" Explained Carl, "then I could have given her the kiss of life." Tom and Carl fell about laughing but Harry ignored the remark but as he left the room, they saw a smile on his face. Carl turned to Tom. "Well, you would, wouldn't you?" Tom nodded and they both laughed again.

As Harry was leaving, he shouted back to them both. "Oh, by the way," he said smugly, "I will be out of the office for a few hours later as I will be driving Miss Croft home." The two men looked at each other. "What a sly fox," taunted Carl. Harry smirked, now he was having the last laugh at them. He liked being in command at times like this.

Sara and Harry chatted all the way home. He had been a little anxious at first but now he was easy to talk with and intelligent, she found that incredibly attractive in a man. As he stopped at the cottage Sara asked him if he would like to join her for a coffee to which he accepted. As they entered the house Jack bounded over to Harry, Harry bent down and stroked him and Jack wagged his tail. As Sara went to make the coffee, she was glad that Jack liked Harry, it was always a good sign when someone got on with Jack. If he liked animals, he had compassion and that was a good enough excuse for Sara to like Him.

As Harry left, he went back into his professional mode. "I'll be in touch with all the details and compensation soon and a few witness forms for you to sign too. May I also please ask that you do not involve the media with this event, it can make life exceedingly difficult if the media start stirring things up. We like to deal with these issues in private with the appropriate people." Sara drew her finger over her mouth. "My lips are sealed." Harry smiled at her again and her heart melted. His eyes seemed even bluer in the daylight. "Thank you," he replied. Sara hoped he would be in touch soon, she really wanted to see him again. She needed not to worry about seeing Harry again as he was already planning his return on the way home.

It was several days later when they met again. Sara was lecturing at the University on ESP. The lecture was always a success with the students. As the last student left, she noticed Harry walking towards her. Sara hadn't seen Harry enter the lecture theatre and wondered how long he had been there. "That was a very interesting lecture, I must say," he pronounced as he came closer to Sara with a handful of papers. They sat chatting in the University café for what seemed like hours and she found herself opening up to Harry and telling him all about herself. Now she wanted to Know all about him. Was there or had there been a wife and children at home?

To her surprise he spoke openly of his short marriage and divorce. There were no children just a disgruntled wife who was left at home night after night whilst he worked long hours with his job. He explained how it had been difficult to have a relationship when dedicated to long hours and the secrecy of his profession. He described how his work was in Military intelligence and that there were many aspects of his job that he was unable to discuss with anyone outside the organization. In a strange way the mystery of him was more attractive and she

23

found that she was beginning to become truly fond of Harry but for now she was playing it cool.

Back at Headquarters Harry was on his third visit to see Sara with yet more forms for her to sign. After Harry explained to Carl where he would be and why Carl turned to him saying, "for goodness' sake Harry, just ask her out, how many more forms can she sign?" He could always rely on Carl to be truthful with him, being his Commander made no difference to Carl, Harry was his boss, but he was also his friend and that was why Carl was his second in command and he knew his friend was right and would always encourage him to do what was right. "She is an intelligent and very attractive woman; you would be a fool to not start a relationship with her. If I had the chance I certainly would." "Yes Carl," Harry smiled. "We all know what you would do." He waved at Carl, "I will see you later."

As Harry left Carl shouted, "Good luck!"

Sara quickly signed the forms, sadly she was in a rush as she was about to start her twelve hours shift with the police helicopter and did not want to be late. Though she wanted to stay just a bit longer with Harry. Harry sensed she was in a hurry and made his excuses, ready to leave. Then he stopped at the door of his car.

"It was now or never," he thought. "I don't suppose you would join me for dinner sometime?" He waited for an answer. Sara tried not to sound too keen or excited "Yes, thank you, I would like that very much." Harry's face lit up. "Great! I'll call you then, would Saturday be good?" Sara agreed as he shut the car door. She could hardly contain her excitement and was already planning what to wear for her date with the handsome Commander.

When Harry arrived at the cottage to take Sara for dinner with flowers and treats for Jack, Sara knew the night was going to go well. She felt nervous and giddy when she saw him. Harry on the other hand was calm and confident and as always, a complete gentleman. She found this wonderfully endearing about him. She had never met anyone like Harry before and never previously felt the way he made her feel, but it was early days in the relationship and Sara did not want to rush anything and ruin what they had.

The restaurant was small and cosy but decorated tastefully and to a high standard. They were shown to a table at the back of the restaurant with a large window that overlooked the sea. It was perfect and allowed them to talk freely. During the meal they found that they both had some similarities; they were both vegan and neither of them drank alcohol. It was a relief to both as at least they did not have to explain or justify themselves for being different. However, Harry did have a reason for not drinking. He said that he "liked to be in control of his actions and feelings," and Sara guessed it was probably the same for her too but she had never questioned it before. The meal was outstanding as was the company and Harry listened intently to every word that Sara said. She found Harry fascinating, although there was a great deal that Harry could not tell her he was able to talk openly about his trips into space and his friendship with Carl.

He asked Sara about her studies in the paranormal. "So, Sara do you believe in UFOs then?" He asked. "Well," said Sara, "I think it would be arrogant of me to think that only Earth had life on it but I do believe that they are so far away in the Universe that it would take forever to visit. Also, we always assume that they would be more intelligent than we are and capable of better things such as space travel through the Galaxy, when they may even be further down the evolutionary stages than us. If they were these 'little green men' visiting our planet, I think we would know about it by now." Harry smiled. "You are quite right Sara." It was interesting to hear what Sara thought of the whole UFO scenario and at least he knew he had nothing to fear from her uncovering his real job. Sara turned to Harry. "Well, if anyone should know, it would be you Harry, being an astronaut and working in space, surely you would be more likely to have an encounter. So, what are your thoughts on the subject?" she asked. "What, little green men with space suits and flying saucers? Well, what can I say?" He shrugged his shoulders and laughed and so did Sara." If only she knew the truth," he thought to himself.

25

On their return to Sara's cottage, they sat talking with coffee, they had so much to talk about and neither of them wanted the night to end. Harry's phone began to ring and he answered straight away, "Saunders," (she guessed it must have been work). It was half past ten in the evening, but Harry had to go as there was something he had to attend to immediately. She did not question him as he had already explained how it was with his job. She would learn to accept this as part of Harry's life if she wanted to be part of his and she knew she did. Harry made his apologies to Sara and left. As he walked through the door he turned back and kissed her gently on the lips. It felt as though she had been kissed all the way through her body. He was special in every way to her and she felt contentment that he was in her life. "Can I see you again?" he asked. "Yes, I would like that," she replied. Harry pondered a moment. "Why don't you come over to my home and I'll make you dinner next week, let's say Wednesday?" Sara agreed happily. As he rushed down the path of her cottage, he mimicked with his hands, "I'll call you." She waved to him and he was gone. She sighed heavily. She had not felt this good in a long time.

As Harry drove back to SHEALD he pressed a button in the car and spoke, "I'm on my way, keep the line open for me so I know what's happening Carl." Carl felt bad that he had interrupted his date with Sara and began to apologise. Harry stopped him, "Its fine Carl, don't worry, I think she understands the situation." Carl continued to explain that SEASKY had shot down a UFO and had managed to find an alien body and they were conducting an autopsy back at the medical centre and he thought Harry would want to be there.

"Yes, you did right, calling me Carl." They had only once before had the luck of an alien body being available and an autopsy was vital in their quest to find out who they were and why they came to our world. Harry hoped that maybe next time they would capture one that stayed alive long enough for him to question properly and maybe get more answers.

"The green tinge to the skin is due to the oxygenated Bio fluid that was in the helmet and is used whilst flying at vast speeds, over long distances for long periods of time. They use eye lenses to protect the eyes from the liquid. The body is humanoid like our own human bodies and as with the last autopsy there are signs of organ transplants. These are from people on Earth, His heart and left kidney belong to a human who was reported missing five years ago. The alien can also breathe our oxygen once the bio fluid is removed safely," said Doctor Ivanov. "Thank you doctor I appreciate your findings and look forward to the full in-depth report tomorrow," said the commander. Carl knew what he had to do. This was part of the job that he really hated but it had to be done. The organs were removed from the alien and tissues samples confirmed them to be the missing person they had suspected. They were then returned to the family with a fictional story. At least it allowed them to have some sort of funeral and closure for the family. It was hard to see the families breaking down after such a long wait with uncertainty and then to receive a small box with small parts of the family member. Carl quickly moved on to other thoughts, he knew that tomorrow Harry would be on the warpath to Lunar base, wanting to know why the interceptors had missed their target. The commander would want answers and the interceptors would be given more training. He could be hard with his team and required a one hundred percent performance and nothing less, yet he would die for any of them if he had to and defend them to the end to anyone else.

SHEALD was a hive of activity night and day. There were Computer experts and radio transmitters, everyone to the highest of their ability, specially chosen by the organization. Each member of the team underwent months of gruelling training and needed a good psychological profile that required a higher-than-average IQ, skills, and experience in their field to the highest standards and be physically fit, enabling them to attend gym sessions several days a week with a supreme medical. They would have yearly medical checks were heart, lungs, kidneys, and liver functions were monitored with body scans that were regularly carried out. Whatever the position all staff had combat training and shooting sessions with target practices monthly. Everyone had to be able to use a gun and have a reasonable aim should the need arise.

The exception to some of these aspects was allowed only to one member of the team. Lieutenant Paul Gordon was a radio controller and expert in Radar and Information technology, and a wheelchair user. However, Gordon was quite able to bring down any intruder or alien attack with one shot. He had one of the best aims in the organization and attributed it to years of playing computer games as a child when he was sick and confined to the house. He could also move at speed with his wheelchair and was known for doing "wheelies" all around the office when the Commander was not there. On some occasions this was encouraged by Colonel Peters who was responsible for the personnel of all the staff. Carl was not as serious as Harry with a much lighter attitude to staff and was often caught joking with his colleagues to try and improve the office atmosphere. Although, he always made sure that Harry was nowhere to be found, Harry was Military old school through and through.

The introduction of robots was a useful asset for the domestic labour. Employing domestic staff in a top-secret Military establishment was always difficult with all the security checks they would need to do so it seemed like the best solution to have the androids. General Grant did not see it this way and complained endlessly about the cost of robots to clean and serve in a staff canteen but Harry had argued that the security of the building was necessary if they were to protect the nation there would be no short cuts or short-changing the lives in the SHEALD organization.

Harry usually got the funding he needed for SHEALD and more. The food available in the canteen was also manufactured through machinery and needed to be of superior quality, nutritious and available twenty-four hours a day, every day of the year, due to the long hours and shift patterns that members of SHEALD would do. This was especially so for those on Lunar base who could be living on the base for many weeks. The menu choice needed to be cosmopolitan as staff recruitment was worldwide and therefore had dishes from every country, needing to be inclusive to vegetarians, vegans, pescatarians and those with food intolerances. It was a huge menu and even the tea and coffee had twenty choices.

The Committee had accepted the large costs of the security buildings of SHEALD and Lunar base and its equipment and expensive vehicles, rockets, aircrafts, helicopters, submarines and much more but it never ended. Harry was always back in front of the committee with another project or piece of new equipment that they could not do without. They didn't even argue with the high salaries of the employees as these were the best of the best and so the salaries needed to match their value. Harry was also granted extra funds as Commander towards his home so that it would be secure and in a secluded area away from prying eyes. His vehicle was adapted to the needs of the organization too being bullet and bomb proof with all the gadgets imaginable. He boasted that he and Carl were better equipped than James Bond.

A uniform was available for staff at SHEALD that would be comfortable and suitable for the job, but even though, Carl, Tom and Harry had their Military uniforms they were not expected to wear them or the SHEALD uniform whilst working as they were often dealing with the public so wore civilian clothing that was formal, smart, and impressive. The uniforms were different in each area particularly those at Lunar base. The conditions were different to Earth and the staff also spent longer at work, usually several weeks. So, they had brighter stimulated uniforms to help with the mundane isolated life.

The uniform colours were vibrant and pleasing to the eye and according to the Psychiatrist Doctor Ivanov it was believed that "the brighter colours not only effected the senses but encouraged a positive mental state and helped staff morale, whilst keeping them alert."

Harry enjoyed the occasional stay over at Luna base as he loved to look out into space. At his home Harry had a telescope and spent many hours looking up at the moon and stars from Earth but on Lunar base he could do the opposite and look back at Earth. In contrary to Harry, Carl was not keen to stay over on Lunar base and would do anything to avoid an overnight stay. He liked the crew on Lunar base, they were close due to spending so much time together in isolation on the moon and were great fun to be with, but he liked to be on solid ground. He enjoyed being home in his penthouse in Lancaster and especially enjoyed having friends' round for dinner. He had a zeal for cooking and took pleasure in preparing dishes in his fully equipped kitchen that he had specially commissioned before buying the penthouse. Carl was at his best when entertaining and making his appetizing cuisines for his guests.

Colonel Tom Green had an apartment in the same block as Carl which they referred to as their "bachelor pads." Although Tom had been seeing Fiona for some time now and Carl suspected it was getting serious. Tom was young and worked out regular at the gym and had a body to match. He took great care of his looks and dressed impeccable. He had a broad build with dark hair and brown eyes and could have easily been on the cover of any magazine. The ladies swooned after him but recently since meeting Fiona he had been uninterested in anyone else. There were a few other SHEALD employers living in the same building as Tom and Carl due to the fact that it was an easy commute to the office from the apartments, making it a popular place to live. It also had excellent night life being in the city and allowed them to let off steam after a stressful shift.

In the last month Harry had created a new project that he was keen to get passed by the committee for new funding which was to build a defence base on Mars. It would be costlier and larger than Lunar base but with the right people, equipment, and money nothing was impossible. "No, no, no!" said General Grant, "not this time Saunders, you think there is only SHEALD, what about everyone else?" Harry opened the file and place the plans on Grants desk. "Get them off my desk Saunders, now!" shouted Grant, "the door's that way." He pointed to the door. "Out now!" Harry left with Carl behind him. "So, that went well," joked Carl. "I'll get it, you wait and see, just not this time." Carl had no doubt he would get the funding, he usually did. Carl liked the project and saw the potential it had to make the defence for Earth much stronger, but it would be a heck of a job to bring it together, let alone the costing. Then that never fazed Harry. At times Harry was fearless and so focussed it was scary.

The UFO visits were more organized recently and it was obvious that they had been managing to tune into the radio transmissions of late. There had even been an attempt on Harry's life on his way home but thankfully Harry was able to fight off the firing at his car and Captain Lu Lee from SEASKY was alerted and quick on their heels, destroying the UFO in seconds. The aliens were gaining knowledge about SHEALD as they understood that they were their biggest threat to preventing them achieving their goals on the planet.

Nevertheless, the Commander now had some questions answered about the aliens though this was still nowhere near enough. They came to Earth because they were a similar race to humans, but the alien race was dying. They were sick and reproduction was poor so they needed the human organs for themselves to transplant and replace in their ailing and weakened bodies in order to survive. So, they travelled millions of miles to Earth not to destroy the planet but to take what they needed to continue their life. It was cold and callus but sadly a reality and great threat to the human race. If only they could communicate with the extra-terrestrials, then maybe they could help them without such destruction. There had been theories in the past that the aliens could communicate through telepathy, but this was still just a theory and more investigative work would have to be carried out in order to show any proof for Harry.

# The Beach House

Sara checked her hair one last time. "Yes, that would do," she said to herself. She bent down to Jack and kissed him on the head, he wagged his tail in contentment. "Be a good boy and I will be back soon. Check, bag, keys, and satnav programmed." She opened the door and then turned back "Perfume!" she ran upstairs, picked up the perfume, sprayed it all over her and placed it into her bag. She then braced herself in nervous excitement. "Right, let's go!" she muttered to herself.

It took her a while to find Harry's place. The satnav said she was close and Harry had said something about a house by the beach. She could see a beach at the side of the road, but she wasn't sure how to get to it. She gave in and called Harry "Sure, you're here, you see the track on your left, turn down there and you will see a drive right in front of you." Harry stayed on the phone until he could see her car. "Wow!" it was an amazing house and huge with lots of windows at the front of it.

Harry stood at the door waving to her, he looked so relaxed. Sara could hear the sea waves gently beating against each other. "What a place to live," she thought. It even had its own private beach, "How cool was that?" The drive had steps that led to the front door and at the side of the door was an outside seating area leading to a conservatory with a large telescope to view the stars with. Harry kissed her on the cheek as she entered the house. The hall was grand and was as large as her lounge at home. It was as enormous as it looked from the outside and full of light with high ceilings. In the lounge there was an amazing view of the beach and the sea was just about visible. From the side of the lounge was an open plan kitchen which housed every gadget imaginable, Harry would more than likely be a great cook too with all the utensils he had. There was also a utility room that was hidden at the back of the kitchen. The dining room was just off the lounge at the rear of the house and looked onto a small pristine garden. They were separated by an open staircase and Just off the hall was the conservatory that Sara had seen from the outside of the residence.

As Harry led her through the rooms Sara had to make sure her mouth was not left wide open at its wonder. There were four bedrooms that had their own Ensuite's and the master bedroom also had a dressing room. "This was a big home for one man," thought Sara. Sara asked Harry, "why all the rooms?" Harry shrugged his shoulders, saying "You never know." But the best was yet to come as he showed her the Helipad that was present on the top of the roof. "You have an amazing house Harry," complimented Sara. Harry did not look impressed "yes, I am lucky, I guess, but sometimes I find myself rambling around in this big old house and wondering why I'm here, it's just a place I come to sleep." Sara was surprised at his comments, then a house without people and love in it no matter how big and grand could be very lonely and not a home just a house. She knew all about that herself living alone as she did. The meal Harry made was delicious and she hoped that Harry did not expect her to return the favour as she was not the best of cooks. (What Sara did not know was that Carl had actually prepared the meal for his friend and Harry had just warmed it up in the microwave). He had wanted to impress Sara with the meal and would tell her the truth someday about the cook but for now he just wanted the date to be right.

It was getting dark outside. "Lights soft," ordered Harry and the room faintly lit up as did the beach which was looking most inviting. "I usually walk along the beach at night I find it helps me to unwind from the stresses of the day. Would you care to join me?" Harry pointed to the door and they both made their way outside. Harry looked down at Sara's high heeled shoes. "It may be better if you remove your shoes. I find it easier walking barefoot, it's ok, the beach is cleaned every month so its safe underfoot." Sara removed her shoes and felt the sand between her feet, it felt good. "You're quite small really, aren't you?" teased Harry. Sara was five feet four inches tall and compared to Harry's six foot stand she did appear small. "Ah, but I'm a pocket rocket," she jested. "I bet you are," laughed Harry. Harry slipped his hand into Sara's as they walked quietly along the beach until they came to a low fence with a gate. "This is where my beach ends and further out is where the sea begins but I think that is probably enough for tonight." It was getting a little colder and Harry put his arms around Sara and pulled her closer to keep her warm. As they walked back to the house Harry thought how lucky and content he felt. Everything about Sara was right, she was special to him and he was captivated with her beauty inside and out.

On their return from the beach Harry beckoned Sara to the conservatory. "I want to show you what it is like up there with the stars" He directed Sara to the telescope and instructed her on how to use it. Then he pointed up to the Moon. "I've been there many times and if there really is a heaven, then for me it's there. When my time comes that's where my ashes will be scattered." He had a twinkle in his eyes and she could see the passion he felt for space and his work. She understood since she had the same feelings when she was flying. She had never floated in space like Harry or watched the stars whilst looking back at Earth though she wished that she too could do this. Harry had a tight hold around her waist while he showed her space through the telescope and as she pulled away from the scope to turn around, she found herself looking into Harry's deep blue eyes. There was a sadness about them and a need to be loved as he kissed her intensely and Sara knew what heaven felt like. Without any words Harry led Sara to his bedroom.

When Sara woke early the following morning Harry was not beside her. She began to panic at first but then Harry appeared at the bedroom door dressed, with a cup of coffee in his hand for her. He put the coffee down at the side of the bed and spoke softly to Sara. "Good morning beautiful, I am so sorry that I have to leave for work early" Harry pulled a face. "I feel so rude leaving you in this way, but I must go" It did not matter to Sara she had the most wonderful evening with the man of her dreams, nothing could spoil that. "Please forgive me, I really do have to go" apologised Harry again, He did not want to leave this amazing woman, but he had no choice. Harry kissed Sara on the lips and made a sigh, he wanted to hold onto her forever. "Go, go" She laughed, pulling the covers over her naked body, and getting out of the bed. "No, please" said Harry "there's no rush, leave whenever you are ready," Sara sat back on the bed and sipped her coffee as Harry left. This had been a happy time; one she would always remember and most of all she hoped this was the start of something special.

She had always warmed to people and was a great communicator. She was also kind and caring with a beauty that was inside and outside, a rare commodity indeed. Though Sara had lots of friends and was well liked, she struggled to get too close to anyone. She attributed it on the loss of her mother at such a young age and the sad passing of her dear father in her early twenties which had left their scars and created a barrier that had stopped her getting too familiar with others. She had to be strong and independent to get by in life, yet it felt different with Harry. He had gained her trust and her love, maybe, it was time for her to let her guard down. Everyone she had loved had left her, but she was sure that Harry would be there for the long haul.

# Lunar Base

It was training day in the gym for Tom and Carl and Combat was top of the list. When they reached the fire range Carl hit every target, his aim was always first grade, as he and Harry, along with Paul Gordon where the best shooters there were in the organization. Tom had been out late drinking the night before with Fiona and had only got home at 4am so his hits were disappointing to say the least. "Busy night Tom?" asked Carl. "Something like that," replied Tom. He did not even want to talk as his hangover was giving him a pounding head. "Green! You had better improve on that or you will be here all week until you can hit something!" Yelled the trainer. "Gosh, these guys are sadists," whispered Tom to Carl and they both smiled. "No messing around you two or you'll be staying late for extra workouts," threatened the trainer. "Yes Sir" said Tom as he winked at Carl. At least they could have a bit of a laugh together during their arduous training and later he had to get the shuttle to Lunar base for the night shift, if he had enough stamina left. "Note to self," said Tom "do not go partying the night before training."

Harry was speaking to Lieutenant Leah Rose from Lunar base. "Yes sir, I will forward you the report immediately," she replied. Harry had known Leah since the beginning, she was one of the early recruits and second in command at Lunar base. She ran the base whilst Tom was elsewhere which was quite often and she did not disappoint. She was very efficient, and Harry knew how reliable and professional she was, he knew he could trust her with Lunar base. Leah was engaged to the lead interceptor Ali Barbosa who was from Brazil. Ali was loyal and not afraid to be part of any action but, some-times Leah felt he was too fearless and was concerned that it may be his downfall one day. Nevertheless, he had never lost a single member of his crew and his aim was impeccable.

Harry called Ali "The weapon." As he said Ali was "courageous and driven making him an excellent Lead interceptor and a good weapon to have on side."

It could be very lonely on Lunar base so having a special someone to share the time with helped with the monotony of life up there. On occasions it could be quiet for days, even weeks, but then it could be bedlam in a matter of minutes. For the Luna crew the silence was the hardest to take but they tried to keep moral up and motivated by training to perfection and were always poised for action and when it came, they gave it everything they had.

Saphy Mistry was also a radio and radar controller on Lunar base. She was from a Hindu family and had left home early in life to develop her career. She was aware that her parents were pushing her to marry which would not have suited her lifestyle or her sexuality. Whilst working with the Military she had met Jo Nowak her partner who worked with her on Lunar base. They had clicked straight away. Originally from Birmingham Saphy felt she could be herself on Lunar base with Jo and although, Saphy loved her family she felt they would struggle to understand that she was lesbian. Jo Nowak was ten years older than Saphy but they were very much in love and matched well together so, the age gap had no significance to either of them. On Lunar base and in SHEALD people were much more accepting of individuality. If everyone did their job well there was never a problem. That was one of Harry's qualities that he was accepting of all his employees and would defend them to the end. The Commander was highly respected by all but they never wanted to mess up and feel the wrath of him.

As Harry drove home from the office he thought of Sara, "was he falling in love with her? But that was silly as he hardly knew her." He considered the situation, in truth, he knew quite a bit about her as he had read her file after the plane crash and she was as clean as a whistle. She was single, no children, lost both parents, had no debt, no convictions, not even a driving ticket but then she had told him already. At least he knew she was telling the truth. Harry felt very lucky to have finally found someone like Sara, a special person who lit up a room when she entered it. He dialled her number in the car but it went to answer phone. "Hi Sara, Its Harry, I know you are at work but I thought I would just leave you a message. Thank you for a wonderful evening, you are really something... Oh, I wanted to ask you if you would like to join me to our annual Ball at work? I know it sounds posh, but it isn't really. Well, you must dress the part ... you know, all formal and that, but really, it's just a get together for the organization. It helps keep morale up. Sorry, it is work but I think you would enjoy it. It's on Friday next. I could pick you up and you could stay over if you wanted? Bring Jack too and we could take him on the beach for a walk, let me know, I would love you to come and be my plus one... I'm rattling on now so, I'd better go, bye."

Sara did not receive the message until the following morning as she had been working all night with the Police Helicopter. She was thrilled and called Harry to accept the invitation straight away. All she had to do now was go shopping for the right dress and she knew the right place to go in Lancaster City Town centre. She would buy something exceptional for the Ball as she did not want to let Harry down. She would be meeting most of his colleagues, mainly for the first time with the exception of Carl, Tom and the Russian doctor and felt she had got on well with Tom and Carl, especially Carl and he was Harry's best friend, so at least that was a good start. She would buy an evening gown, shoes, bag and have her hair done too and she would even treat herself to some new makeup. "Yes, she was going to relish this."

It was the week before the Ball on a Friday that Jack Sara's old three- legged dog took poorly. Within the hour she had taken him to the vet and he had been put to sleep. Sara was devastated. She had lost her little companion the reason she went out in the evenings and walked for miles. Having three legs made no difference to Jack he still loved his walks. He had suffered a blood clot and had a stroke, suddenly and there was nothing anyone could have done but Sara punished herself believing she could have done more if she had known sooner. Nothing anyone could have done sooner or later would have changed the outcome for Jack but as always Sara blamed herself when life took from her those she loved. She could not take the fact that sometimes fate took over and she was powerless to help.

The phone rang unexpectedly and she was unsure if she should answer in her state of grief but decided it may be of importance. It was Harry who at the off chance, had some spare time and thought he would have a brief conversation with her. Sara could hardly explain what had happened, being so distressed about Jack, but Harry knew enough to know that she needed him and wasted no time in arranging to see her. Carl was surprised when Harry asked if he could cover for him for a couple of hours whilst he called to see Sara. Carl knew then that his friend must be in love with Sara. He had never put anyone or anything prior to his duty before. Still, Carl was more than happy for him, realizing that she was just what Harry needed.

When harry arrived at Sara's he was attentive and kind and he held her sensitively as she wept. Sara was grateful for his presence as in the past she had dealt with her grief alone. It was easier knowing Harry cared but she understood that he could not be with her for long. Though, she was happy he could be with her just for that moment and with time and Harry she would heal from her sudden sorrow.

# The Ball

Her hair was slightly pulled from her face with a wave as the shiny blonde hair showed off her gentle features. Tonight, she would wear the red lipstick to give her pale complexion a lift. She had even treated herself to a new perfume which she sprayed liberally around her body, there was nothing being left to chance tonight.

The dress was outstanding and fit her shape like a glove. She was a slim build with curves in the right places so the long dress outlined her perfect hour- glass figure. The dress colour was beige with a gold thread that ran through the material blending suitably with her complexion and was covered with tiny beads. The length went to her ankles where a pretty pair of golden shoes accentuated her slender legs and was finished with a small matching bag. The cut around the neck of the gown was not low but fell from the shoulders where her mother's gold necklace could be seen. She hoped that her mother would be looking down on her daughter tonight and would be proud. Her mother would have loved the Ball and danced all night with her father until his feet were too sore to continue.

The doorbell rang at the cottage. Sara was excited and nervous at the same time and hoped that Harry would be pleased with her appearance. She stopped, drew a breath, and then opened the door to greet him. The handsome man's large blue eyes grew even wider and his face said it all. "Wow" he could not stop himself from speaking aloud. "You look stunning Sara" He had brought her red roses which she quickly put into water and thanked him before they left. In the car Harry turned and looked at her repeatedly, he could not perceive how this beautiful creature was going to be by his side all night, he was truly blessed. Sara was overwhelmed with so many feelings for Harry at once and did not want them to end.

Harry carried off the formal suit with such ease and genre, he had never looked more attractive as he did in that instance.

When they arrived at the venue, they were later at attending than, anyone else, then they had travelled further. As the large doors opened it led to a large staircase, they could see the ballroom below them and from the top of the stairs everyone could view who was entering the room. There were security guards all around who were trying to blend in as not to cause any concerns and allow everyone to be at ease with the party.

As Sara and Harry stepped onto the staircase, they were visible by everyone below. It was an entrance that caused a stare as normally the Commander attended alone but this time, he had a stunning woman on his arm. Harry felt pride as he descended with Sara and saw the glaring of acceptance as he held her hand tightly squeezing it to reassure her as they walked into the room and towards their table. At the table was Carl and Tom with Fiona who was the only other civilian. The other table guests were Leah, Ali, Saphy, Jo, Lu, and a wheelchair parked on the end with Paul. Tom was sat beside Fiona and to the other side was Carl were there where two empty seats that had been saved for Harry and Sara. As Carl spotted Sara heading towards the table he was in awe of her beauty. "Well, the lucky son of a gun, she looks gorgeous" he muttered to Tom." Leah quickly commented to Carl, "She really is as pretty as you said she was, Harry is a lucky man." "I think he knows that with that smug look on his face," replied Tom. Saphy laughed, "Guys, guys, put your eyes back in their sockets, though it is a pity she isn't gay." Jo nudged her and frowned in disapproval. As Harry and Sara reached the table Harry began introducing everyone before sitting down. Carl was sat on the right side of Sara. "Hello again Sara, you look rather different to the last time we met." Sara was quick with a witty reply. "You mean I'm not horizontal this time?" He smiled, he liked that she had a sense of humour.

The evening went well and there was lots of chatter between everyone and Sara fit in straight away with everyone. Harry had to circulate and speak with his staff. As Commander it was important that he recognized everyone and made the effort to socialize. Sara did not mind as she was in good company with the group on their table. Harry was Happy and Carl was glad to see him this way, it had been a while since he had seen Harry smile properly and he was pleased for his friend, he deserved a break. Sara got up with the girls on the dance floor joined by Paul, Tom, and Ali. Harry was not a dancer so took the opportunity to stand at the bar with Lu and Carl and chat with people as they came along. After a while on the dance floor and lots of laughter they made their way back to their seats, and Harry, Carl and Lu returned from the bar to join them. Sara noticed a tall Black man with grey hair and a stern face walking towards them who spoke to Harry. Everyone else seemed to be slightly uncomfortable by this man's presence and Sara suspected he was someone of authority and importance. Harry turned to Sara, "Sara, this is General Grant." She smiled and shook the general's hand. "Very pleased to meet you Sara, I hope he appreciates how lucky he is to have a beauty like you with him." He had a prominent Canadian accent which was not as strong as Harry's American pronunciation but he also had a much more powerful voice. For a moment she saw her father in the general with his stern military look and yet underneath there was a heart of gold. His handshake had a tough grip but it was warm and she knew he agreed with her. General Grant swiftly moved on to the next table as he was just doing 'the rounds' and showing his face to everyone. Sara felt sad that her father was not able to be with her. There was a full piece band playing on the stage not a DJ or a solo artist with backing tracks, there had been no expense spared for this event. The band leader announced that they were going to change the mood of the music and have some classic dancing for those who wanted a more refined dance.

"Please, everyone, take your Partners for the waltz."

Harry nudged Carl, "Hey Carl, Sara can do all that ballroom stuff that you do, why don't you get her up for a dance?" Carl was taught many years ago when he trained with the Military on how to dance as Balls were often a big part of the Military celebrations. Sadly, these days no one knew how to do this type of dance and so Carl never got the chance normally. It was Sara's mother who had taught her how to ballroom dance but like Carl she had not danced this way in an awfully long time. Carl jumped to his feet and held out his hand to Sara.

"Would you do me the honours madame?" Sara looked at Harry for his approval and he nodded to her with encouragement as she rose to her feet. Carl was an excellent dancer and she enjoyed dancing with him as they chatted all the way round the dance floor. Carl was funny which helped her to relax he had the same sense of humour as Sara so they got along well and as he was Harry's best friend it was important to her that they did.

As she sat down Harry grabbed her hand. "Are you having a good time?" "Yes, I am, thank you," smiled Sara. He leant towards her, kissed her on the cheek, and looked into her eyes with such affection and whispered. "You are so beautiful and there isn't a man in here tonight who isn't in love with you." She squeezed his hand, replying, "I only need the one man to love me." Harry stood up and led her to the dance floor, it was the last dance of the night and as he held her tightly, she hoped he would never let her go.

# To the Moon and Back and Beyond!

They drove back home in silence and every now and then he would look at her and smile. He carried her overnight bag in for her and took it to the bedroom as Sara followed. After making love he kissed her forehead and spoke softly to her "I love you Sara"

It had all happened so fast but she knew she loved him too and told him so as they both fell into a deep sleep. Sara stayed with Harry the whole of the weekend and not once did the telephone ring.

On the Sunday evening they took a walk on the beach holding hands all the way and later they watched the stars from Harry's telescope. He pointed to the moon, "the next time I'm up there I'm going to stand on the Moon and shout to you, "Sara, I love you!" Sara turned to him "and I love you to the Moon and back." Harry replied, "and beyond." This became their special message to each other and Sara would tell Harry that she "loved him to the moon and back" as Harry would always reply "and beyond."

It had been several months since Harry and Sara had been dating. Their love went from strength to strength. Harry had commissioned a gold bracelet specially made for Sara. It had three charms hanging from it, one of the Earth, another of a crescent shaped moon and a tiny star that had a diamond in the middle. Inscribed on it was, "I love you to the moon and back" with "and beyond" on the reverse.

When he presented it to Sara she was thrilled and promised to wear it always and the bracelet never left her wrist from that day on. For Harry's birthday Sara had returned the thought with a silver keyring that also had an Earth and moon on it with the very same inscription as on her bracelet. Harry kept his House and car keys on it so it was always with him. Harry was portrayed by others as being strong and at times a ruthless commander but he had a romantic and sensitive streak that only Sara and those very close to him saw.

They would meet for dinner with Harry's friends and had been invited with the others to Carl's penthouse often whilst Carl cooked them his appetizing dishes. Sara now knew that the meal at Harry's on their first date was made by Carl and they had laughed and joked about it many times. When being invited to Carl's penthouse there was always a different date to be introduced. The women in his life never lasted very long but he seemed happy enough with these circumstances so no one ever questioned him about it. Tom and Fiona had since moved in together and Tom was hoping to buy a more suitable house for them both. Carl would miss Tom but there were still other SHEALD members who shared the same apartment block and Leah and Ali were thinking of buying Tom's old place. Leah and Sara got on well together as they had a shared interest in Astrology and would often discuss star signs of their friends. Sara and Fiona were Capricorn's, Leah, and Carl were Virgo's which matched good together as they did with a Taurus which was Tom's sign. Harry was a Gemini but they did not always get it right, however, it matched his personality, work orientated, youthful and intelligent. Harry would roll his eyes when they started on the subject though he tried to show some interest especially when they mentioned his good qualities and that he was a strong character and intelligent.

Back at HQ Carl and Harry were in the office checking through figures and data for SHEALDS expenditures. Harry got up and poured himself and Carl a coffee. Tom had just left to get the Shuttle to Lunar base and they were catching a rare quiet time as friends. Carl had been relaying some silly story and they were both happily chatting and for a change it was not all about work. "You know Harry you've changed, Sara's been good for you." Harry patted his friends' shoulder, as if to thank him. "You're right Carl, I've been thinking of asking Sara to marry me." Carl was not completely surprised as they made a good couple and it was obvious how much they felt for each other. "It's a big decision Harry for someone in your position." Carl was playing devil's advocate. "But, if you are sure, you have my blessing... not as you need it," he added. Harry had never felt happier and there was no doubt in Harry's mind that he wanted her in his life forever. Carl left the office and Harry finished his coffee and unlocked the drawer in his desk and pulled out the diamond engagement ring that he had bought for Sara. "Yes, it was right," and he was going to ask her tonight.

For the last two days Sara had been feeling unwell. She was never normally sick so, having dizzy spells and having an upset stomach had been a disruption. She could not fly the police helicopter if she was having dizzy spells so for the first time ever, she had to call in and cancel her shift. She had managed to get an appointment the same day with the nurse who had checked her blood pressure, Heart and temperature and took blood and urine samples.

"Yes" she said to Sara. "it's positive, you are certainly pregnant, possibly three months." Sara was in complete shock; they had always been careful but somehow this was happening and she had to deal with it.

She was pregnant with the man she loved not some one-night stand and although it had come as a surprise, she did have a sense of contentment, she was having Harry's baby. She thought about how Harry would take the news and from the times children had been mentioned he had been keen to have his own family in the future. The future was now, and although it was not planned it was a happy outcome, and hopefully, once Harry had time to digest the news, he would feel the same.

Sara rang Harry, "I'll be over around 7pm tonight, Harry... I have something to tell you." "That's great Sara and I also have something I want to speak to you about." He rolled the diamond ring between his fingers; this would be right he thought to himself as he put the phone down, tonight could not come soon enough. It had been a quiet day at SHEALD and Harry decided to take the chance of finishing early for the day as he wanted to get everything right for when Sara arrived. It would be a special night and something they would both always remember so it had to be done properly. He collected some red roses on his way home and ordered a meal to be delivered for 8pm, everything else he could do from home.

Tom was out in the field, training with the roamer vehicles close by in the woodlands of Cumbria with Carl when the call came through. "Lunar base to SHEALD. "Go ahead Leah," replied Paul. Harry's transmitter in the car tuned him into the conversation. Carl and Tom could also hear from the Mobile roamers radio. "Commander, we have three UFO sightings from SAAM, we have 'red alert,' Interceptors on course, the predictive termination is Cumbria Sir." Harry put up the radar screen and monitors in his car. "Interceptors one and two have direct hit on UFOs and Interceptor three also direct hit on UFO. All UFOs destroyed sir," said Paul. "Well done, Ali and team," praised Harry. "Request for Interceptors to return to Lunar base?" asked Ali, "Request granted," replied Leah. The interceptors only got one chance to hit their targets with only one missile on board each ship but they had delivered as usual and destroyed all three UFOs. Harry was surprised to hear of three UFOs at once they were mainly solo attacks. There was something different about this attack.

"What were they up to?" Thought Harry. "Sir, Sir," it was Leah again. "SAAM has detected another UFO, I repeat fourth UFO sighted, red alert!" It was too late for the Inter-ceptors to reload and relaunch and so the UFO was through and heading for Earth. "Damn," Harry banged his hand down on the dashboard of the car. He then noticed a text that had come through on his phone from Sara. "On my way. Love you, Sara xx." "Paul can you give me a more precise predic-tive termination," asked Harry. Paul clicked a few buttons on his computer. "Yes Commander, it's within five miles of your home Sir." Tom and Carl where quick to respond and follow the signals. Harry had a bad feeling about this, the aliens had sacrificed three ships in order that one of them could get through to Earth. SHEALD was already aware that the aliens were possibly able to tune into their radio transmissions and knew about Lunar base, SHEALD and who Commander Saunders was and Harry knew that he was a target for the aliens but to destroy his house when he wasn't even home did not make any sense, it had to be something else and he was sure it was something big. His car was showing on radar the UFOs position which he was following intensely. Carl and Tom and the land team were doing the same but they were much closer and ahead of Harry. Harry put his foot on the cars throttle so he was now doing 120 MPH in order to catch up with the roamers. SEASKY had been alerted and were on their way too. He was not leaving anything to chance. A Heli-copter was already nearby so the area was well covered, they would get the UFO one way or another. Harry was almost home but he could see that the signal was passed his house and much further on as he saw the time in his car, it was six forty-five which jogged his memory of Sara's text she was heading in the same direction as the UFOs signal. Harry pressed control room button on the transmitter. "Paul, you have Saras phone number and car registration?" Yes Sir, you want me to track her?" asked Paul. "Yes, find out how close the UFO is to Sara's car," panicked Harry. "Sir, Sir the UFO has landed a quarter of a mile away from Sara in the woods at the side of the road." Harry's heart was beating faster and he felt a terrible dread. "If they got Sara, they would use her as a bargaining tool after they had tortured her and torn her apart, he had seen first- hand what the aliens could do. "Tom, Carl" shouted Harry, "did you get that?" Carl answered, "Don't worry Harry, we'll get them, we're nearly there."

Sara was unaware of the drama unfolding and was casually driving with the window down and the radio playing. Harry phoned Sara on her mobile phone but Sara never heard the ringtone. There was someone in the road just in front of her that caught her attention as she tried to slow down. She could now see there were two of them in strange suits and helmets and holding guns. She tried to break hard but it was too late they had fired at her car tyres and the wheels of the vehicle lost control and veered off the road, tumbling over and over and time slowed down as she hurled over again, she felt a sharp pain in her stomach and lost consciousness.

"We can see her Harry we're here now shouted Carl." Tom and Carl jumped from the roamer with their guns as one of the aliens ran towards the car. Tom fired and hit the alien, he fell to the ground and was dead, but the other alien had gone around Sara's side of the car and was pulling the car door open ready to pull her from the vehicle. Carl was right behind him and crept up close. "Get your filthy green hands off her." With one shot the Alien was dead but Carl continued with several more shots as Tom shouted to Carl, "Get her out, the cars on fire." Carl grabbed Sara from the car cutting off her seat belt quickly. Sara's lifeless body lay in Carl's arms, blood dripped from her forehead and face as he saw Harry running towards him. Carl lay Sara on the ground and noticed his hands were covered in her blood there was a large piece of metal protruding from her stomach. Then there was the sound of an explosion as the space craft disintegrated in the forest as usually happened. One of the roamers was caught up in the blast and was damaged but thankfully no one else was hurt. Carl put his head to Sara's chest, "she's still breathing." Harry was calm but angry and shouted, "get her to the hospital now!" as Carl handed her over to the helicopter, he called to Harry, "Go, go" Harry jumped into the helicopter with Sara. The journey was quick and Doctor Ivanov was waiting at the entrance to the underground hospital as Sara was rushed in, followed by Harry. She was taken straight into surgery. Ivanov turned to Harry. "I will call you when I have her stable, I will do everything I can, but she is seriously injured," he warned.

Harry waited for two hours in his office with the diamond ring still in his pocket. Today he was going to ask the woman he loved to marry him and now he wasn't even sure she would live to ever hear his words. Time seemed to stand still for Harry at that moment as there was nothing more he could do. He kept on asking himself the same question, "how could this have happened?" He felt he had put Sara in terrible danger, he was supposed to protect her not get her killed! Carl and Tom were now back and stayed with Harry until they knew Sara was out of surgery.

Carl put his hand on his friend's shoulder "Ivanov is the best surgeon you could have, he'll save her, you'll see; he won't give up on her. Harry put his hands to his head. "How could I have been so stupid? I should have known." Carl stopped Harry, "don't punish yourself Harry, you know no one could have seen this coming."

The call came through from the nurse that the surgery had gone well and Sara was in recovery. Tom was relieved to hear she had survived the attack and now he wanted to get home to Fiona, it had made him realize how important it was to have time with those you love as it could always be taken away in a split second. Harry thanked Tom for his part in the rescue and felt blessed to have such friends who risked their lives to save others. Harry walked back to the hospital with Carl and he was greeted with Ivanov. Carl thought what a strange man Ivanov was and yet he was a genius at surgery. "Commander she is out of danger and with time she will make a good recovery." Harry sighed with relief. "I am so very sorry that we sadly were unable to save the baby."

Harry lifted his head up "What? Did you say, baby?" That must have been what Sara wanted to tell him. This was going to be the happiest day of his life and now it was a complete nightmare instead. He felt sick to his stomach, he would have loved that child. It would have been the icing on the cake and he would have been such a proud father watching them grow and be part of his family, but now his baby would never have the chance. Ivanov paused for a moment, "I am sorry.... but there is sadly more." Ivanov explained. "The piece of mental that pierced her body not only killed the baby but damaged her womb so badly that we had to remove it and she will.... never be able to have children again." Harry hit his fist into the wall. "This is not fair, for heaven's sake, why Sara?" His eyes glazed over, "this is so wrong." Carl was lost for words how could he respond to such devastating news and poor Sara who would have made the perfect mother now had that choice of motherhood ripped away from her. "Life could be so cruel and some people got more than their fair share of it," thought Carl.

Harry recollected the last conversation he had with Sara. "I have something I want to tell you." She sounded excited and happy but he never expected her to tell him he was going to be a father. He grasped the box with the ring in his pocket, everything had changed now. Harry felt as if he had been punched hard and was suffering with terrible guilt of what had happened. He had destroyed Sara's chance of ever having a family. Their baby was dead and it was all his fault, "why did he ever suppose that life could be good and happy with Sara with his involvement in an organization like his?" The emotion he was experiencing was the same as of when his brother died, he should have been able to save John but he couldn't, "Sara was better off without him."

Harry sat beside Sara in her hospital bed as she began to come round from the operation, "I'm sorry Harry "she cried. Harry comforted her "Shush, don't you dare apologise, you have nothing to be sorry for," He tried to calm her as Sara was drifting in and out of consciousness from the anaesthetic and she murmured. "I love you to the moon and back." Harry kissed her on the forehead and whispered to her, "and beyond." He rose from the chair and left.

The next morning Carl called in to see Sara at the hospital. Harry was refusing to see Sara as he was convinced that he had caused her enough hurt. Sara, as a civilian had now witnessed an attack from aliens and seen SHEALD in action and had now become a security risk. Harry was more concerned that whilst she had any connection with him, she would always be in danger and sadly, in his heart he knew that his life with Sara was over. Now, they had to decide what to do with her and inside it was tearing him apart. As the commander of an alien defence institute, he had to be strong and show an example to its members. There would be no privileges or special treatment because of his rank, procedure would have to be followed.

"Hi Sara, How's things?" Carl knew it was not the most appropriate way to start this conversation after what she had been through but he did not know what else to say. Tears ran down Sara's face, Carl grabbed a tissue, wiped her cheek, and sat down at the side of her and held her hand offering his support. He wanted to take the pain away but he could not. Sara asked Carl when Harry would be visiting, but he knew that Harry was not coming and he understood his decision but he could not bring himself to tell her the truth, so he lied. "He has had to go over to America on an urgent meeting over the attack and may be there several days." Thankfully, she accepted this. Sara continued. "So, the secrecy around your work is to do with Aliens and UFOs?" Carl nodded, "now you know. Harry feels he put you in great danger and is finding it hard to forgive himself at the moment." Sara shook her head. "I love him and whatever he does I will support him and it wasn't his fault it was just part of the territory that he works in." Carl listened but he felt overwhelmed with the sadness at what had happened and what was to come.

Every day for two weeks Carl visited Sara in the hospital. They chatted about their shared interest of flying and he dropped the odd joke that Sara smiled at knowing that she was only being polite. She normally had an enthusiastic sense of humour but he would overlook it on this occasion. Leah visited with Ali and Tom but Harry never appeared.

Doctor Ivanov got to know Sara too, over her confinement and found her so easy to talk with. She was never fazed by him like other people and excepted him as he was. She found him extremely intelligent and dedicated to his work and he discussed several of the experiments that he had been involved in. He did not always get the answers he wanted but he would always keep trying until he had exhausted every avenue. He also confided in her about his partner Tim Walker who was also a doctor at SHEALD, they did not let many people know about their relationship and he had never discussed his sexuality with anyone before but Sara was different and refreshing. She also had so much knowledge about ESP which he found fascinating as he had suggested that the aliens used telepathy to communicate but had struggled to show any evidence of this yet. He was a private, sensitive, and caring man who was very misunderstood and he found it inspiring that even though she was going through so much and still had more to come she was able to show an interest in other people's lives and be so understanding. He wished that he could have done more for her, he had done what he could to save her life but it was nowhere near enough especially as there was worse for her to endure. He would miss her when she went home and that day was nearing.

# Amnesia

General Grant had made the journey to chair the meeting as Harry would not be allowed to due to his emotional attachment to the person in question. Carl, Tom, and Leah were also present in the boardroom, no one was looking forward to this meeting but it had to be done. Harry could be present as it was him who had called the assembly even though he was not allowed to contribute in any way. When a civilian came into contact with a UFO, they were taken to SHEALD and given a drug that induced amnesia for up to twelve hours. It was highly successful with no side effects. Civilians who were given this drug after a sighting would be checked on a few days later by a SHEALD member who they had spent some time with before and have a brief encounter with them to see if they had any recognition of them. Thankfully, they never did. Doctor Ivanov had an even stronger drug that was capable of wiping out memories of up to six months and could replace the old memory with a new suggestive story. They could then go about their daily life as normal.

The latter drug was the one they would use on Sara. Everything was in place. None of the people Sara knew had ever met Harry and where Sara lived was rural with neighbours at a distance so it would be straight forward. The story was she had met someone and dated for a few weeks but they had parted amicably.

Her memory of Jack dying would stay but the encounter with the UFO would change to a collision from a drunk driver on a country road. There would be no baby just the operation and the fact that she was now unable to have children. The accident and stay in hospital would be a blur and a few weeks later she would wake up in her own home. Some confusion would be explained away by the accident and then everything else would go back to normal. Both of her places of employment had been informed that she had been involved in a serious car accident and was staying in a remote hospital in the Lake district and would be returning after a long recovery. There would not be any unforeseen problems. Harry and the baby would be completely removed from her memory forever and there would be no threat from any alien attacks or abductions this way.

It was time for Sara to meet with the board as Doctor Ivanov led her into the room. She felt nervous as she knew nothing of the plan yet. "Please Sara, come in and sit down. I think you know everyone here, Colonel Green, Colonel Peters, Lieutenant Rose and of course Commander Saunders." Sara smiled and wanted to run over to him but Harry put his head down and stared at the table. He did not want to make any eye contact with her and was extremely uneasy with her presence. She was hurt but more than anything confused by his actions and what she had walked into. She did not understand what this was all about and no one looked pleased to see her. There was a sternness on everyone's face that told her this was serious and not going to be a happy outcome.

General Grant did all the talking as everyone else sat in silence including Harry. The general explained what would happen to her and why this had to happen but Sara was distraught. "You don't have to do this, I will keep what I know about SHEALD secret, you can trust me, tell them Harry," but Harry said nothing. "I'll take my chances with the aliens it's my decision, I don't want to forget, I can't go back to the life before, it was empty and I have all you now." Grant spoke again "I am sorry Sara, but we cannot take the chance, you know too much. If the aliens took you, they would use drugs to get answers and torture, they are ruthless monsters that all of us in this room have witnessed many times. The organization is bigger than the people here in this room. I am afraid that the reality is it is the drug or a firing squad and we have no say in the matter and sadly you don't either Sara. I am deeply sorry as we all are but when you awake from the drug you will have no hurt or upset anymore. Unlike Harry who will have to feel your loss forever more as there is no drug for him. Believe me when I say this is the kindest way and the

best, we can do for you." "Please Harry, do something,"
begged Sara. "Have I not been through enough?" Leah's eyes
filled with tears. Grant nodded to Ivanov and he began to in-
ject Sara.

"Please, don't do this, please... no!" She struggled and then
collapsed in the chair. Two nurses entered the room with a
stretcher and took her back to the hospital wing. Even Tom
and Carl found this difficult to watch. Harry got up and
walked out of the room and followed the nurses back to the
hospital wing where Sara was drifting in and out of sleep trying to fight the drug. Harry asked Ivanov if he could see Sara
for one last time to which he agreed and for a moment Saras
eyes opened and she shouted to him. Harry entered the room
and sat by her side. "Harry, I love you to the moon and back"
she muttered. Harry bent over her. "shh... and beyond," he
said softly as she closed her eyes. He kissed her lips and whispered in her ear, "I will never stop loving you Sara, never."
Sara was gone and into her new life. As Sara was wheeled
away to a vehicle outside Harry noticed the bracelet on her
wrist, he stopped the stretcher and took off the bracelet. She
should have nothing of her past memories as he held it tight in
his hands, he realized that would be the last time he would
ever see Sara and his heart was breaking. Harry returned to
his office, locked the door, unplugged the phone and Buzzed
Paul. "No calls for the rest of the day Paul." "Yes Sir,"
replied Paul. Harry opened the locked drawer and put the
bracelet with the ring in and noticed the bottle of whisky that
was given to him one Christmas that had lay in the drawer un-
touched for many years. He took the bottle out before locking
the drawer and poured himself a drink. He was done with
self-control for today. Tom and Carl left Harry alone for the
rest of the day and later when the office was quiet, they both
carried Harry out of his office and took him home, he had finished the whole bottle of whisky.

Sara woke in bed at the cottage and for a moment she had
forgotten about the accident. She had no memory of the two
weeks in hospital but the doctors had said that it was quite
normal during such trauma to have complete blanks with
memory recall. She remembered she had met some guy but
he was nothing special and the relationship had fizzled out

quite soon. She also remembered the sad day Jack was put to sleep and rolling over and over in the car with the accident but that was it. There was this overwhelming feeling of loss that she had, but she assumed that was most likely down to the operation and not being able to have children anymore. She was grieving for the children she would never have and hopefully it would pass as she just wanted to get back to work and normality.

Finally, she was back in the sky, flying the helicopter. The control room were giving her instructions for the next job. It seemed there were three men who had stolen a car after robbing a Jewellers in the Preston area of Lancashire and were being pursued by the force. They were tracking them closely with the infra-red camera as it was night and very dark. As she looked out for the men, she found herself distracted by the full Moon. It was bright and alluring and she felt drawn into its glow. There was something about the moon that felt special but she could not remember what? She had so many blanks in her memory these days which was beginning to frustrate her. Her co-pilot saw her looking at the Moon, "they say it effects people.... the full Moon, you know .... all the idiots come out on the full Moon," he joked. Sara was back with the co – pilot. She had drifted off again but needed to concentrate, she had never been like this before as she was always so focussed now, she would go off to somewhere else at a moment's notice. She smiled and nodded to her colleague. She had also been having lots of vivid dreams about the Moon and the stars since the accident. Sara had a recurring dream about a beach she walked along at night and when she looked up, she could see the Moon and felt happy and calm. Though, in recent weeks there were times when she doubted her own mental health but she could not let this beat her, she had to fight it.

By the time the sun had risen in the morning her shift was over. She would need to go to the supermarket to get some groceries on her way home but first she would have a coffee in the café. An hour passed by as she checked her watch it was ten o'clock in the morning so she tried to motivate herself to get her shopping and go home where she could go to bed.

As she walked around the isles searching for the items, she needed she felt weak and tired. Suddenly she felt a man tap her on the arm. "Excuse me, I hope you don't mind me asking but my wife asked me to get her some cotton pads for removing makeup and I haven't a clue what I am supposed to be looking for," he smiled. Sara quickly looked on the shelf and found they were directly in front of her. "Here you are," she said and passed them to the stranger with a smile. As she looked at his face she looked into his eyes and thought to herself, "kind eyes." He turned and thanked her. As the man moved away, he turned and looked back at her and Sara felt she knew him but then she could not have known him or they would have acknowledged each other properly.

It was really getting the better of her, all this confusion and the feeling that there was something else, which could not be explained. On her return home she did not make it to bed but fell asleep on the sofa. She was back on the beach looking at the Moon then the man from the supermarket tapped on her arm as her alarm went off, wakening her. "That dream about the beach and moon again. Was she being reminded of something? What did it mean? if it wasn't important then why did she keep having the same recurring dream?"

"How did it go Carl?" asked Harry. "Well, I have some cotton pads for removing makeup if you want them Harry," replied Carl. Harry pulled his face. "Was there any reaction to you?" questioned Harry. Carl sat down. "At first no, but I really am not sure. At one stage she stared at me for a while and I thought she was going to recognize me." "But she didn't?" said Harry, "she was probably thinking what the heck is this strange guy up to? You can look a bit shifty sometimes." Joked Harry and they both laughed. "Ok, ok, Harry that's enough, for that you can make me a coffee," replied Carl. Harry looked more serious as he poured Carl a coffee. "How did she look Carl? did she seem ok to you?" Carl thought for a while before answering, "She looked pale and she has definitely lost weight, but she's still beautiful." Carl changed the subject, "So what other exciting work have you got for me today then?" He could not dwell on Sara it would not be good for either of them. The job was done and that was the end of it.

"This is the latest technology." Paul was demonstrating to the commissioning board. "This was another expense that the commission would be billed for," thought General Grant. "You can be anywhere," said Paul "anywhere in the world yet, you can be having a conference with others in the same room." Harry appeared from nowhere. "I can be here," then Harry appeared at the other side of the room, "or here," and again at the back of the room, "and here." Paul was excited. "This is the future, holograms. They are a terrific way to have a conference with anyone from anywhere even on the Moon and the scope is endless what you can achieve with just a small device like this. We need to keep up with modern technology and this could be crucial for our organization." Harry opened the door.

"Come in Saunders," called Grant and rolled his eyes "Ok the funding is yours and take your IT geek with you." Grant knew when he was beaten, usually when he saw Harry with his briefcase! Harry's phone rang "Saunders." Carl spoke "Harry we have one alive!" Harry suddenly became alert, "I'm on my way Carl."

When Harry got back to headquarters, he went straight to the lab. Carl was waiting and followed Harry into the room. "Same as before but this one is still alive." Ivanov moved back so Harry could see the alien. They had successfully removed the helmet and drained the bio fluid. The eye contact covers were also detached. Harry stood over the alien and banged his fist on the side of the alien as the alien jumped. Harry then went to the other side and went to hit the alien, the alien moved aside. "So" said Harry, "there is nothing wrong with your senses and reflexes then." He began his interrogation. "So where have you come from? and what is the name of your planet?" The alien did not make a sound but moved and wriggled to get away from Harry who was in his space. Ivanov intervened "Their voice box does not seem to be developed. I don't think they are able to talk." "So how do they communicate?" questioned Harry. "Your guess is as good as mine," Ivanov replied. "ESP?" asked Carl. Ivanov shrugged his shoulders, "could be." Harry shouted at Ivanov. "Could be? We don't pay you to Guess! I want answers and facts Ivanov!" The heart monitor on the extra - terrestrial began to bleep a piercing noise. The noise was becoming deafening and then the monitor exploded as the alien screamed and died. Unknown to them all he had picked up a scalpel and stabbed himself in the jugular vein in his neck for a quick exit to avoid interrogation. "He's gone," said Ivanov." Harry was disappointed. "We need to work on other angles of communication ready for next time," said Carl. "We also need to keep them alive longer but I agree with you Carl about doing the contact differently so, I'm afraid it's back to the drawing board," replied Harry.

Back at the office Harry poured himself a coffee as Carl was searching for a pen. Harry's draw was open and Carl checked inside it. His eyes were drawn to a gold bracelet and a small ring box. He felt sad that, this was all he had left of his memories of Sara and that he was still holding on to them. He quickly closed the draw before Harry saw him looking. "That was Harry's baggage and he had no right to question him on this." Harry had never spoke of Sara since and Carl never mentioned her though he knew his friend was still hurting.

It was a lovely sunny day. Sara had bought a new car and was getting used to driving again after the crash. The car radio was playing and Sara was singing along to the tunes. It was just like when her mother was alive accept, they would be singing from the top of their voices. Sara had been driving for a while with no particular destination in mind as she was just testing out her car. She looked around "Where am I?" She could not believe that she had driven unaware for so long. Despite this there was something familiar about the place but she could not be sure. She could see a sign for a village and decided to pull into the village centre, maybe, she had been here with her parents as a child? In the centre facing the village green was a tearoom and restaurant so she decided to have a rest and enjoy a cup of tea. As she entered, she felt drawn to the window in the front of the room where there was a large window to enjoy the view of the Green, "this was nice" and she was comfortable here.

Harry was on his way home and was having a conversation with Carl on the phone when he unexpectedly went quiet. Carl was concerned. "Harry are you alright?" Harry regained his thoughts. "Sorry Carl, I thought I saw Sara sat in the restaurant window we used to go to in the village, I must be more tired than I thought." "These things take time Harry, it's like when someone dies and you start to see them everywhere at first, it can be hard to accept they're gone; you should try some counselling?" Suggested Carl. "No thanks, not with Ivanov." They laughed and Carl imitated Ivanov in a silly Russian accent "We have ways of making you talk!" mocked Carl. Carl always did it, tried to take away the pain with a jest. He was a loyal friend; they had been through so much over the years and had managed to keep each other sane.

Sara's dreams continued and were becoming more distressing for her. The Moon became brighter in the darkened sky and then a spaceship appeared and someone was trying to take her somewhere but she did not want to go. Then she was back on the beach and she was safe and there was a building behind her and a man with her but she could not see his face. Now she was back in her plane and it was falling, falling and she hit the ground with a large bang and woke! She was shaking, hot, and full of panic, "what did it all mean?" The psychiatrist offered her sleeping pills but they were of no use as the dreams persisted. She understood the psychology and that she was suffering PTS but this was more. She had to find out and make sense of all the dreams in order to stop them. She had been involved in two serious accidents in a short time of each other with the plane and car crash and then there was this strong emotional sensation of loss of something or someone.

The village she visited three days ago felt familiar so she would visit it again and drive around the area. "What about the Moon and the beach? and what were their significance in all of this? Could it be connected to the loss of her mother? That would make sense," but there was something else nagging at her but what that was, she did not know. If she could solve this then the dreams and panic would most likely cease.

It was to be another week before Sara tried to find the village again to see if it would reveal a memory. Sara pulled in at the tearoom "No, this was not where she should be but it was close." She sat in the car for a while to think and looked around her. "Where to next?" She pulled away from the village and looked at the road ahead there were only two ways she could go and she had already drove left, up into the village from the Motorway. It would have to be right, onto the road. "Nothing gained nothing ventured," she muttered to herself.

The weather was good at the moment as it was the start of the summer months and the nights were lighter giving her more time to explore. She had not driven far when she had the urge to stop, "Why here? was this a memory?" So much of her memories of this year were missing. The pieces of the jigsaw could be coming together but it was sluggish. She locked the car and continued on foot and began to walk without any purpose. She could hear a seagull screeching in the wind and saw the beach and sea in her mind's eye.

"I am close, I know I am" she said to herself, but there was nothing she could recognize not even any landmarks to help her. "This is hopeless" and she was now getting tired, it was time to go home. She was getting angry with herself; it was silly dwelling on dreams, she needed to move on with her life instead of going backwards, tormenting herself on events that did not exist and were only part of her subconscious mind. As she moved away ready to head back to her car, she noticed a fence and decided to stop to rest by leaning on it. She had become tired easily due to the trauma she had suffered and wanted her energy back. The air felt refreshing and the sun was warm on her face. She closed her eyes for a second and breathed slowly and there it was a road or track hidden at the side of the main road that flashed into her head. "There must be a road of some kind off this one." As she turned her body to her left, she saw the track. Sara could have easily drove down the track but decided it would be better to walk and see if anything else jogged her memory. At the end of the track, it split into two ways and Sara was unsure which path to take. After contemplation she took the second path which led down some steps and onto a beach "This was it! the beach in her dream." It felt right and a sense of peace ran through her.

Up until now she had not seen the "Private" sign, "oh dear, I should not be here, I should go," she muttered. She left quickly and set about the journey home. She knew she would return as she was sure she had found part of what she was looking for and at last it felt positive.

Tom strode into Headquarters with a skip in his step and a large grin on his face. "What are you so happy about on a Monday morning?" enquired Carl. "I can soon wipe that smile off your face" shouted Harry from his office. "Where's that report from Friday, it's late!" Tom smiled and waved the report in the air and placed it on the Commanders desk. "Oh, I don't like this Harry," joked Carl, "he's still smiling." Tom grinned even more. "It's ok you two, nothing can ruin my day," he gloated. "You bet?" Jeered Harry. Tom ignored them both and proceeded. "You see I'm going to be a dad!" Harry and Carl were surprised but pleased to hear Tom and Fiona's news. Carl slapped Tom on the back with fondness. "Well done mate, I'm really glad for you both, I suppose I'll be Uncle Carl from now on?" Harry got up from his seat and shook Tom's hand. "So, what are you still doing here then?" asked Harry, "you have a week's Lieu owed, don't you have baby shopping to do? ... you know, prams, cots and whatever?" "Yes, sir!" said Tom as he hurried out of the room "and thanks," shouted Tom. Harry smiled. Carl turned to his friend. "you're getting soft in your old age." "Maybe I am, hey Uncle Harry! Now that sounds good," laughed Harry.

"Sir, red alert from Lunar base," Interrupted Paul. "So?" Said Harry, "tell them to hit the blighter!" Carl and Harry went over to the radar monitors. "Interceptors have a direct hit sir," informed Leah. "Well done team," praised Harry. "I think this is going to be a good day" said Harry, turning to Paul and Carl. "Let's hope so Sir," said Paul. There was good news at SHEALD and it was something to celebrate at last.

Fiona was due her scan at three months and it was the first scan so it was good to have Tom with her. His time at home was always precious and she took the opportunity with Tom whenever she could to spend time with him. Tom appreciated how Fiona never complained about the long hours he worked and never questioned where he had been. She knew she had to accept this as part of his job and part of him. When the scan revealed they were having twins, Tom looked pale but he soon cheered up when he found out that it was a boy and a girl announcing that, "his family was now complete." Fiona felt lucky and happy with her life with Tom and now there were two little one's that would also be part of their perfect family life. Yes, Tom knew there would be sleepless nights and challenging times ahead but after working with SHEALD anything else was easy.

# Doctor Ivanov

Doctor Ivanov was in the lab conducting one of his many experiments. There were two mice in one cage and a monkey in another and Harry was hoping that there had been no cruelty to the animals. He did not agree with any mistreatment of animals and did not promote animal experiments. "What are they doing here?" asked Harry pointing to the cages. "Don't worry Commander they will not be hurt; you have my promise" assured Vlad. "Hurt one hair on their head Vlad and you will be going to space without the aid of a space craft," threatened Harry. Vlad held up his arms as if to surrender, "I give you, my word." Carl commented as they left his lab. "What's he doing, building an ark? Harry put his hands up to Carl. "Don't even joke about it!"

As Carl and Harry walked out of the lab Carl turned to Harry and spoke quietly. "He gives me the creeps," pointing to Vlad. They had both been checking out the last specimens of the recent aliens picked up by the team and a report was awaiting them in lab two. Harry read the report, passing it to Carl. "So, they have a blood type similar to ours." "Yes" said Carl, "but it says they only have one type A+." Ivanov followed them into lab two. "What about their brain capacity?" Harry turned to Ivanov. "They have a much larger brain than ours and the right hemisphere is considerably sizeable than the left also, the hypothalamus is more substantial, this could suggest ESP and could support the theory of telepathy as a way of communicating." Ivanov continued "Their vocal cords are weak and small so speech would be less likely as we originally thought." Harry still did not have all the answers he needed. "So how are we going to communicate with them?" asked Carl. "ESP is our only chance, but we need someone with the ability to do this well enough and there is not one person in the military who would be anywhere near capable, let alone communicate with an alien that could be very different. You see, I had many a conversation with Sara on the subject as this was her area of expertise." Vlad looked up at Harry and saw his eyes move away, he did not mean to bring up Sara as he knew that Harry was still coming to terms with the loss of her. Harry snapped "We don't pay you all that money to guess and make assumptions, work on it, Ivanov! I want facts not fiction, solid answers and soon!" He yelled. Harry stormed off and Carl followed. Harry was back to being angry again thanks to Ivanov. Harry was still ranting when he got back to the office. "Five years Carl and what do we really know about these attackers? Very little and it is not good enough. If we intend to keep the organization going, we need to come up with much more. I have a world committee to convince we are worth our while and at the moment we have little to prove the benefit of the billions they are spending on us." Carl said nothing and nodded agreeably, when Harry was like this, he was difficult to reason with.

Carl's watch bleeped, "oh sorry Harry I have to leave for the Lunar shuttle for this month's checks. I'll call you when I'm on the base and keep you updated with everything." Harry continued with Carl. "Tell, Ali I want the Interceptors in post sooner than 110 seconds it's too slow. I want them in position at least 90 seconds." Carl waved at him. "Ok, will do." He made haste to the shuttle station just managing to make it on time. He would be on Lunar base for 12 pm, have lunch, do the checks and if he pushed it, he could be home by midnight. No need to spend the night up there. He struggled to sleep on the beds that they had and preferred his own home comforts.

One of the Lunar buggies was out on the Moon when Carl arrived at Lunar base. He could just about make out it was Ali driving and wandered where he was going. Leah was waiting for Carl on his arrival. "Hello Leah, everything ok?" Leah looked flushed. "It is now Sir," she replied. It seemed that a UFO had crashed on Lunar base after being fired at by one of the interceptors and had exploded on landing which cracked one of the windows in the control room and was leaking oxygen and the pressure was dangerously low causing a major incident. It had closed off the control room for two hours whilst the repairs were being made. Everything was back up and running now, but it could have been much worse had the crack spread further. However, Leah had acted quickly and followed procedures for this. She had ordered everyone to be in their spacesuits and use the oxygen available whilst the control room was sealed off until the window had been replaced. "Wow sounds like I missed all the commotion, but of course you dealt with it professionally and to your best ability for all concerned so, well done Leah," praised Carl. "Thank you, Sir," said Leah proudly. The windows were one hundred times strength but it was clear that they needed to be stronger. He would recommend that in future that all Lunar base windows were two hundred times stronger. Carl could not help but think that the General would not be happy with this expense, but it was about priority and the safety for all at Lunar base and the safety of staff would always come first. Carl made himself a note with regards to the window as he needed to do a full investigation and report to cover the incident. Though he could do this at home and then he would not have to spend any extra time at lunar base.

Later Carl reflected on the incident on Lunar base as he travelled back home on the shuttle. It could have been so much worse and it made him shiver, even a change in pressure and small leak could have ended very tragically with everyone losing their lives. People had no idea how they all risked their lives daily to protect them from the UFO forces. To the ordinary person on Earth, they did not even know they existed. They really were the unsung heroes.

His mind reflected further back to the day that Harry had got uptight over the mention of Sara. He was worried about his friend and also considered how Sara was coping with her new life. He hoped she was getting on better than Harry was, she did not deserve what happened to her and he hoped she would find happiness again. He doubted Harry would ever find love and be as happy again like he was with Sara. At least Ali, Leah, Tom Fiona, Jo and Saphy had all found some happiness together so, there could be happy endings for some people and what about himself? "Would he ever find that special someone?" It was unlikely. Then he was doing ok on his own and seeing the heartbreak that Harry had endured it was perhaps better to stay away from relationships. He contemplated on the notion "It would have to be someone very special to make him give up his bachelor life."

"Lunar Shuttle will be approaching Earth in the next ten minutes please prepare for landing" informed the pilot. "Ah, home at last and back on terra-firma" muttered Carl, to himself. He would be back home and in bed for midnight safe and sound, which was just how he preferred it.

# Recall

Sara walked along the beach again, she knew she should not be there, but she could not resist. She felt happy and free when she was here and thought about the recurring dream as she looked behind her and there it was, the house! This house was enormous but inviting. "Why did she know this house? and what did she know about it?" There were steps leading to the front door and without thought she climbed them but as she arrived at the door she panicked. "No, I should not be here," she said to herself and quickly descended the steps, but as she reached the last step a man greeted her. The man stopped in his tracks and they were both startled to see each other. She looked at the tall, blonde figure in front of her and she could not be sure if he was known to her. "Do I know you? she enquired. The man was unsure how to deal with this but challenged her in his American accent. "I don't know, do you?"  A terrible hurt rushed through her and she wanted to run, run far away from here. "I'm sorry, I got lost," she cried, as she ran to her car, not looking back she started the car nervously and sped away. Harry wanted to stop her but was in disbelief at seeing her there. He hastily called Ivanov "You had better get round here now Doc, I have just had a visitor that I think you may be interested in."

"It's impossible, it is one hundred percent successful and it has never failed. It must be a small lapse, somewhere, something must have triggered it. We do not know the circumstances to which brought her here and she did not fully recognize you, did she?" Vlad was trying to offer Harry some reassurance. Carl had been alerted too and was also at Harry's home. "Well, it appears clear to me that she managed to work out how to get to Harry's. So, if she had no memory of that, then can you tell me just how the heck did she get Here?" asked Carl. "Coincidence" suggested Ivanov.

"Some coincidence," said Harry.

"So, what now, do I move house?" asked Harry. "No, no, there is no need to do that I am sure it was just an isolated episode," replied Ivanov.

"We do not need to recall her at this stage," maintained Ivanov. Harry was concerned. "So, what if she remembers? she would be in great danger," said Harry.

"She would be most likely taken out!" said Carl, "they would never let her go as she would be putting the organization in jeopardy. You know how ruthless they are, they make the SAS look like a Nunnery."

"Please, please! you are jumping ahead of yourselves. This may be no more than a freak memory recollect," explained Vlad. "I hope you are right Doc," remarked Harry in a concerned voice.

That night Harry could not sleep as he reminisced on the moments he spent with Sara. She may have amnesia but he remembered every precious, loving second with Sara, her smile, smell, and her warm body against his and it was tearing him apart. The pain of her loss was at times, unbearable, but he had to fight it, she was gone and whatever happened she would not be coming back. His brother John had been killed and gone forever, but Sara was still out there and it seems as if she was suffering, that was harder to take and to know there was nothing he could do to help her.

Sara cried all the way home. The sadness she felt was overwhelming but at the same time she had no idea why she was so upset. She questioned herself "Who was that man and why did she think she should have known him?" Questions, Questions, spinning around in her head. "Am I going crazy? What is wrong with me?

Leave me alone!" she screamed, sobbing, and holding her hands against her head. She was home but could not settle and was pacing up and down in the house trying to get some comfort, but she could not. Once again, the dreams began with the Moon being bright and then it changed into a keyring with the shape of the Earth and Moon hanging from it and then the eyes, they were so blue and loving. It was dark again and she found herself back on the beach but when she turned around this time, she saw her father standing there and she ran to him "Dad, dad help me...I'm falling..."

She woke with tears streaming down her face "Please some-one help me, please!" She cried, but no one heard her, she was alone with this terror and she did not know how much more she could take.

The next day she drove around in her car, anywhere just as long as she kept driving, she did not care where, she just wanted the pain to stop. It was seven o'clock at night now and she was back at the beach. She knew she was losing her mind but nothing mattered anymore. She walked along the beach and near to the house and as she did, she noticed a bench. She needed to rest and so sat on the bench and listened to the sound of the sea in the background. She felt calmer but was still tearful. The tall man with the blue eyes she met last time appeared at the side of the bench. "May I?" he pointed to the seat. She nodded and he sat beside her. "Are you ok?" he en-quired. "No," replied Sara, "I feel like I am going mad. I had this accident and my memory keeps changing and I keep dreaming of this place but I don't know why?" she sobbed. "What's your name?" He had to make it sound real that he did not know her. "Sara" she answered. She did not know why but she felt better now that he was there. He had a kind voice and she felt safe and although she did not know him, she trusted him and knew he would not do her any harm. He spoke softly and calmly "by the way I'm... but he did not man-age to finish his sentence when Sara replied, "Harry, your name is Harry." His eyes widened. "Yes, I am Harry, how did you know my name?" he questioned her but she began to cry again "I don't know, please can you help me, please!" she begged. It hurt Harry to see her so distressed and confused and he knew he could no longer ignore her plea for help, he had to do something. "It's going cold, why don't you come in-side?" she trusted him enough to realize he could help her. He wrapped his jacket around her shoulders and put an arm around her to guide her to his home. She heard something jangle and as he pulled the house key from his pocket and went to open the door, she noticed the keyring. She stopped and touched the keyring in his hand "to the moon and back," she whispered. Harry looked surprised but continued into the house and sat her down. It all looked vaguely familiar. Harry disappeared into the kitchen and appeared with a coffee for her and asked her to drink it "you're frozen, it will help warm you up" He pondered as she drank the coffee. "I have a friend who is a doctor who could help you," he suggested.

Everything was becoming blurry and her head felt fuzzy. She could hear the sound of a helicopter above her and she felt tired. Harry took away the empty cup from her hand and she fell into a deep sleep. He helped her to lay down on the sofa and waited for the arrival of Doctor Ivanov and the nurse. She did not try to fight the sleep; she was too exhausted.

The helicopter landed on the helipad on the rooftop and the doctor and the nurse headed for Sara. She was placed on a stretcher and taken to the SHEALD medical centre. Harry went along in the helicopter, "How is she?" Harry asked the nurse attending to Sara.

"Her blood pressure is low but otherwise she is fine," replied the nurse. Harry turned to Ivanov "I need you to make this right Ivanov, you hear!" warned Harry.

"I will try my best" assured Ivanov. Vlad Liked Sara, she had always been kind to him and treated him respectfully and without any prejudice.

He had never come across anyone who had been so strong and able to fight this drug. It had been processed and used for years with a one hundred percent success rate and yet, they were here with Sara whose emotional attachment was so strong that it could not be wiped away. It was called "love."

While she slept Harry stayed by her side. He stroked her hair and it felt good to feel her hair through his fingers again but he was fearful of her future. If she was remembering she was in grave danger and the charge for this was death. He would have no say in the matter as this was way beyond him and his organization.

Carl charged into the hospital room. "How is she Harry? Harry put his head down and shook his shoulders. "What are they planning to do?" he asked. Harry tried to relay what

Ivanov had told him. They would double the strength of the drug they had used before but there was no guarantee as they had never done this before and it could be dangerous to Sara. She could have a complete breakdown and be in a state with complete memory loss of her whole life that may never return. It was also possible that she would have a resilience even to this and would still have memories and under these conditions it would be a quick exit for Sara.

"For god's sake Harry, you can't let them do this to her!" Harry turned to Carl, "For the first time in my career Carl, I don't know what to do," said Harry. Carl had never seen Harry like this before. He was always the strong Commander who everyone relied on, including him to make the right decision but right now he looked beat and completely defenceless. "You can't give up on her," Carl begged, "there has got to be something we can do?" When Carl left Harry in the hospital room Harry was a broken man. Carl went back to the office as Tom, Leah and Ali arrived, they had heard what had happened and came to see if there was anything they could do to help and to offer some support.

Leah sat beside Ali with tears in her eyes as he comforted her. "I always thought of Sara as one of us with her flying and how she got on with everyone. I could have seen her on Lunar base with me and the girls all working happily together." Suddenly Carl jumped up. "That could be it," Carl muttered and left the office. "What was that all about? "Asked Tom. "I don't know, but I am hoping it could be good news," said Ali.

A meeting was called and General Grant chaired the assembly. Once again due to Harry's emotional connection to the "problem" he would not be allowed any say in the matter. Colonel Peters, Colonel Green, and Lieutenant Rose would also be present as before, along with Doctor Ivanov and Harry. Harry sat with his head bowed, it was intolerable to sit through something as important as the future of Sara and not be allowed to contribute in any way. "So" began General Grant "we have ourselves a situation. The report confirms that Miss Croft has now regained most of her memory involving the UFO attack and information about SHEALD. In short, she remembers everything from the last six months.

There are two alternatives here, neither of which are a positive outcome for Miss Croft but sadly in this case these are the only choices we have to work with. Carl raised to his feet, "I am sorry to interrupt at this late stage but I feel you may be interested in what I have to say." Ivanov smiled they had been busy working and putting files together rapidly, hoping that Carl had found a solution to assist Sara without causing detriment to her. "Go ahead Peters I am intrigued to hear what you have to say," urged Grant. He pushed the file with the report across the desk. "What's this?" The General asked. Carl was to the point. "The third choice Sir for Miss Croft." Harry lifted his head. "It is actually quite evident and was Lieutenant Rose who inadvertently gave me the idea. Sara is a proficient pilot who can fly commercial and light aircrafts, she also flies helicopters and very skilled at crash landing. She has a degree in Psychology, Masters in Parapsychology, and a Doctorate in ESP and as we have recently found evidence that communication with Alien beings could be through ESP this could be favourable to our quest. Sara would be an asset to SHEALD. She is intelligent, physically competent and has already been through our security checks. Yes, she would need to undergo Further checks and the usual training but we have completely missed an opportunity here, Sara would make an ideal candidate for SHEALD." Dr Ivanov spoke. "I too concur this and as part of the team who recruits SHEALD members I would recommend that we give this serious consideration."

The General picked his way through the report and nodded as he scanned the pages. "Well, Peters, you may well have a point, are we all in agreement."

Harry sighed and even though he knew he was not allowed to contribute to the decisions he needed to say something "Sara isn't Military though, neither is she trained in combat; she is the kindest, caring person I know she couldn't kill a spider let alone shoot someone." "No, but she could be trained. You need to have a purpose and even vengeance to fight the enemy," said Carl and turned to the General. "Was Sara ever told the truth about her mother and the five children's missing bodies? How they were taken by the aliens and that the bus was bombed by the Military to cover it up as a terrorist attack and by what means one of the missing children's organs found its way into the body of the last alien we recovered?" asked Carl. "That's classified!" shouted Grant. "No, that's a fact!" shouted Tom, as he raised himself off the chair and banged his fist down on the desk. "I can't understand why we are even having this conversation; Sara has had to be strong to get through what she has had to face in life and I know you want to protect Sara, Harry but she is tougher than you give her credit for, she should be given the choice at least," remarked Tom. Leah spoke up too. "Yes, I agree. Harry you are too emotionally involved to be able to decide what is in Sara's best interests at the moment and it is understandable that you want to protect her but it is clouding your judgement. To me it is at least worth trying and giving her a suitable choice. The alternatives are by far much worse."

Grant intervened in the discussion. "I think we should take a break there so we can digest what has been discussed. Shall we say meet back here in an hour?" They all agreed and began to depart from the conference room. Harry went back to finish off some work for an hour whilst Leah, Tom and Vlad had a coffee in the rest room. The General went to his car to make a few phone calls, whilst Carl grabbed himself a coffee and followed Harry back to the office. Carl was annoyed with Harry; he had showed no enthusiasm for his suggestion and yet the alternatives were very worrying. He thought he would have been jumping for joy because if all went well, he and Sara could be together again.

Carl pulled on Harry's arm as he walked back to the office. "What's wrong with you Harry? anyone would think you couldn't care less about Sara. We are trying to help here and some positive input from you would be appreciated here." Harry was going through the motions but that was about it. "I'm sorry Carl, I know you are trying hard but I can't say anything, no one will listen to me because I am too "emotionally involved. Anyway, what do I know? I've constantly put Sara in terrible danger, I don't even trust myself anymore. Whatever I do comes out wrong, I'm no good for her, she's better off without me. The best thing for Sara would be to get as far away from me as possible." "Well, she might just do that if the drug doesn't work and they get rid of her. Her choices are very slim Harry and you need to get a grip mate and get the old Harry back and fight for her." Carl walked away from Harry and headed back to the rest room. A few minutes later Harry walked in. "Ok guys I'm sorry I've not been any help. The truth? Harry paused and took a breath ... I'm scared of losing her all over again, Whatever I can do to make this right I will but I need you all to help me, yes, the commander, the boss is not so tough after all and doesn't know what to do for the best so I need you guys to do it for me." Harry went over to Carl. "Did I ever tell you what a great friend you have been to me over the years Carl? You're the best anyone could ask for." Carl was touched and they hugged each other. Leah also hugged Harry, saying. "We are all behind you and Sara, you won't let her down Harry and neither will we."

Harry was not allowed back into the conference room for the next part as they all voted for Sara to be given the chance to go through the strict tests and investigations for SHEALD but first they had to give her the choice. If Sara did accept, she would be taken out of civilian life altogether as she would be too much at risk of another attack.

Her life would not exist as it did before she would be dead to the world. She would lose everything she now had, her home, money, and her career. Her death would be faked but, she would be compensated for her monetary loss by the organization but all ties with her old life would have to be completely cut.

"I don't think that would be too big a problem" said Tom "she has no living family and we were her only close friends and even her neighbours were not close with her living in that rural setting."

"Yes," agreed Carl, "it would be fairly straight forward for her and Sara kept herself to herself at work so there would be little questioning and a funeral would be easy enough to arrange too."

Sara was then asked to join the meeting as she entered with Ivanov, she was nervous as she did not know what to expect. The General relayed everything to her in detail and made sure that she was fully aware of all the scenarios but of course they were all hoping she would pick Carls. The General also chose to tell Sara the truth about her mother's death. It was hard to take in but now it made perfect sense why they had failed to get answers and justice for her mother and the five children.

"The only issue we have here, Sara is could you carry out combat? Do you think you could learn to use a gun and kill if it were necessary?" asked Grant. She didn't hesitate with her reply after what she had been told about her mother's death. "You show me the green faced monster who killed my mother and I will be the best shooter you ever have." Tom whispered to Carl, "Feisty little thing when she wants to be." Carl smiled. "So," Said Grant, "are we all agreed that we meet back day after tomorrow with all the results of the tests and take it from there." There was a unison of agreements from all. Sara would have to stay in the hospital wing for the next two nights and begin the tests tomorrow. She would give it her best, that was all she could do now. However, she did have some concerns over the Psychiatric evaluation after her recent traumas but she knew she could do this if she put her mind to it.

Leah Popped her head around the door of the hospital room as Sara was sat on the bed reading. "Hi Sara, just wanted to wish you luck for tomorrow, not as you need it." Sara was glad to see Leah, she had always warmed to her and she was the reason that she was still there. Sara expressed her gratitude to Leah. "Thank you, Leah, Carl told me it was you who gave him the idea and because of you I have a chance and some hope of a life worth living now." Leah smiled and left blowing her a kiss. As Leah walked down the corridor she had a few tears, she really hoped it would all work out right this time, if anyone deserved a second chance it was Sara.

Sara took a piece of paper and wrote her diary. She had done this everyday of her life since being nine years old and now she would add these writings to her notes at home, though her diary for the previous six months had gone missing which she suspected had been taken by SHEALD after being given the amnesia drug. She realized that they had to make sure there was no evidence of what really happened during those past months and now she remembered, she would have to rewrite them. However, she sensed that she would not really be allowed to take the entry home with her but if she was careful, she may manage to sneak them through security and in any case, it passed the time and was therapy for her. As she hid the papers, she heard a familiar voice at the door.

"Knock, knock," she laughed, "Come in Carl." He gave her a cheeky smile and sat at the side of her on the chair. "How are you doing Sara?" asked Carl. "Scared but ready for the fight," replied Sara. "That's my girl" winked Carl, "You'll be great, I have no doubt." He kissed her on the cheek and got up to leave, "he could be so sweet," thought Sara and as Carl turned to the door to leave, Sara called him back. "Thank you, Carl for all you've done, you are a truly wonderful friend and I am very blessed to know you," "It's my pleasure" said Carl as he gave a bow. Sara chuckled as he left. Tom also called by and had a quick chat and wished her luck for tomorrow but Harry never came. She was saddened that Harry was not around but she understood how he would be feeling.

She knew nothing had changed for her she still loved him just as much as before and would continue to do so for the rest of her life. Harry had yet another sleepless night, He was so close to getting Sara back in his life but would it go to plan? He was afraid to contemplate what would happen if it failed. He had defended and protected the nation and his staff, yet he was unable to protect the woman he loved and that scared the hell out of him.

Strangely enough Sara slept well that night and the dreams had vanished at least for now. She was ready to take on whatever she was given and, in the morning, Doctor Ivanov came to collect her and led her to the test room. A computer evaluated her IQ with shapes, colours, and lots of questions on maths, images, and problem-solving issues. Next, she was put onto a monitor for her brain and heart and asked several questions at speed. Then she was seated at a computer and given scenarios to answer and when she finally finished, she felt exhausted. It was relentless in the questioning and at one stage all the questions blended into one which were difficult and tiring. "You go and have a rest whilst I go through the tests and summarise it for the conference," ordered Doctor Ivanov. A nurse took Sara to a canteen and gave her a coffee and a sandwich, Sara drank the coffee straight away but could not face the food as she was too anxious. It felt as if she was "walking the Green Mile."

It was time to start more tests again and later she had to attend the gym for some physical tests but she would be fine. She had never seen so many monitors in a gym before, but she tried to ignore them and concentrate on what she had to do. At the end of the session, she was allowed to leave, have a shower, and change as someone had kindly brought her some clean clothes from her home. It was all over with for now and there was nothing more she could do.

The following morning, she walked along the empty corridors whilst she waited for Vlad to arrive for the summary of the tests and bumped into Carl. He asked her how it had gone but Sara was unsure, she could only hope for the best. Suddenly, she heard a voice. "Carl, have you" ... It was Harry coming around the corner and Sara came face to face with him. Harry looked awkward "Hi Sara" there was a silence... Carl cut in. "I'll leave you two to have a talk," said Carl moving away. Harry stood staring at her for a moment, she was as beautiful as ever. "How are they treating you?" he asked. "Well, they haven't shot me yet," jeered Sara. Harry smiled at least it broke the ice. "Do whatever is best for you Sara, that's all I have ever wanted for you and for you to be happy." Her heart was aching for him she had missed him so much. "I still love you Harry," but Harry never answered back. "I must go I am not supposed to see you or influence you in any way. Good luck." He moved away slowly as his phone began to ring and answered the call continuing along the corridor away from Sara. "Had he stopped loving her?" He was different with her and she was unsure if he felt the same way about her anymore. It had been a while now and had he moved on? She felt hurt and disappointed with him.

Harry was allowed in the pre-conference meeting to hear the results of the assessments. Sara would be there later, after they had looked at the results and discussed all the findings appropriately. Doctor Ivanov was about to give the synopsis of the tests as they gathered around the desk when Harry noticed Leah had her fingers crossed under the table. He considered how thoughtful she was to Sara but it was not up to fate, this was the real world and a cruel one at that. Ivanov poured himself a glass of water and cleared his throat. "The psychological tests are good, showing compassion, determination, loyalty, independence, and an ability to work well in a team. There was a need to protect those more vulnerable and the ability to make snap decisions. She also showed a good understanding of right and wrong. Her vulnerability was the self-sacrifice that she gave to others, morally she was strong and stayed calm in stressful environments and had excellent critical thinking skills.

On the downside she could be so morally driven that she did not see the danger to herself. That said the data gave her ninety two percent and as our suggestive percentage that clears as a pass for SHEALD is eighty two percent and on average our recruits have achieved eighty five percent it makes her score above most.

On the IQ test she received a score of ninety six percent on average the acceptable score is eighty percent. The recruitment average percent is eighty six percent. There is only one more person who scored a higher score and that is Commander Saunders at ninety seven percent.

Considering her recent injury, her physical examinations were still very good and I would imagine these will improve in the next few months as Sara recovers. Therefore, with all the other tests and data, the overall score was ninety seven percent. Meaning, I can conclude that as the only other person scoring ninety seven percent since the organization began is Commander Saunders, I can say without prejudice that she has passed with flying colours. Of course, like all recruits she will have to go through a rigorous training programme collated by Colonel Peters and Colonel Green as protocol."

Harry was delighted with the outcome for Sara was safe and that was all that mattered. He did not care if she hated him and never wanted to see him again, she would be fine. General Grant continued the meeting reading out the summary. "I hereby agree that the action to be taken is to offer Miss Sara Croft a position within the SHEALD organization with immediate effect. However due to the nature of the risks to herself and those around her she will undergo a complete Re assignment of her identity and will agree to surrender and disown all belongings and contacts in the civilian world. She will receive support to start a new life in SHEALD but all present and past documentation must be destroyed and an organized appropriate termination will be orchestrated. Colonel Peters has a team on standby to appropriate this." He looked over to Carl as he nodded. "Yes Sir." General Grant resumed "Commander can I ask you to leave us now as we need to ask Miss Croft if she will accept these terms. She may still not wish to consent and until she does this the conference is not over."

Harry left the meeting and Sara once again was brought into the room and saw that this time their faces were smiling so she was hopeful that it was good news. The General explained their findings from the tests and then the terms of the conditions she would be bound to and that once a decision was made there would be no going back.

"So, Miss Croft do you accept or do you decline?" asked Grant. Sara looked at the table. These were her friends for now and ever more. "I most certainly do accept," said Sara. "Then I have only one last thing to say to you. "Congratulations and welcome to SHEALD," said Grant. He stood up and reached out to shake Sara's hand but Sara was so thrilled that she leant over and kissed him on the cheek. The General gave a shocked look. "Well now, that's a first." He gave a smile and left the room. The others took it in turn to congratulate Sara. Leah hugged her tight and Sara kissed her on the cheek. Tom picked her up and swirled her round and he too got a big hug. Doctor Ivanov was trying to sneak out and make his departure whilst all the commotion was going on. "Doctor," Sara called. "Thank you," she mouthed and blew him a kiss. The doctor flushed with embarrassment but was feeling quite pleased with himself for having recognition. He grinned and nodded his head to her. They all left one by one; Carl was the last to leave. Sara took Carl's hand. "I hope one day I can repay you for what you have done for me, though it could never be enough." Carl was beaming. "Just remember me every Christmas and Birthday," he jested. "You bet," she remarked. Carl stopped at the door. "Er, I think there's some-one here to see you." Carl winked at Harry as he slowly entered the room and left Sara and Harry alone.

Harry was rather nervous as he spoke quietly. "I believe congratulations are in order." Sara was so happy to see Harry again but he seemed to be holding back. Perhaps he had moved on after all? Sara questioned him. "Harry .... are we ok?" Harry nodded his head. "You don't seem that happy, are we good?" asked Sara. "Are we still ..." She could not find the words to say it but Harry intervened, "You mean, do I still love you?" she felt unsure of his answer. "Why yes, with every beat of my heart, I never stopped loving you, not one second of the day." He grabbed her and pulled her close to him and kissed her like it was the first time and she melted in his arms. "I love you Harry Saunders to the moon and back" He kissed her again and whispered in her ear, "and beyond Sara Croft." Just then the door opened and a very red-faced Carl stood whilst they kissed. "Whoops! bad timing," he muttered and left quickly. Harry was still holding on to Sara and lent over his desk and pressed a button and the door locked with a sign that lit outside saying "Do not enter." "What are you doing?" asked Sara. He smiled. "I have something for you," as he shuffled around in his pocket and pulled out the gold bracelet with the Earth and moon on and slipped it over her wrist. "Oh Harry, you kept it all this time," she was delighted. He put his fingers through her hair, "wait" he said, "there's something else, as he fidgeted in his pocket. He held her hand and stared directly into her eyes.

"There was something I never got to say to you before the accident." He took a deep breath and produced the ring from his pocket "Sara, will you marry me?" Sara's heart missed a beat "Yes!" she shouted, "I will," and threw her arms around his neck. "Don't ever leave me again Sara Croft," remarked Harry. But she had no intention of ever leaving his side, no one would ever part them again.

Harry grabbed Sara excitedly "Come on, we have a wedding to plan" She held his hand as he led her out of the office and through the control room. Carl was talking to Paul and busying himself with the usual tasks. Harry called to Carl: "Hey Carl, could you cover for me for the rest of the day?" Carl nodded, "course, no problem." Then Harry stopped and thought for a minute. Sara wondered what he was going to say. "Oh, and Carl," Carl turned to face them both. "Would you be my best man?" Carl's jaw dropped as did half the staff in the control room. "Wow, yes of course and congratulations, when is the wedding?" asked Carl. Harry casually continued walking out of the office. "a week tomorrow," shouted

Harry as he and Sara left giggling with excitement. "Wow, they don't mess around," said Carl. "I'd better ring Tom."

The wedding was held at HQ in the chapel. It would be easier that way so that everyone could attend. Those on Lunar base, SEASKY and in the field or in another country could still be part via a satellite link. The team in control had dressed the office with balloon and streamers, they had never celebrated or decorated HQ before not even at Christmas. So, they really went to town when given the opportunity. Unfortunately, Fiona was not allowed to attend being a civilian but Tom streamed the event to her mobile phone so she was able to watch the ceremony. Leah and Ali had taken leave from Lunar base to surprise Harry and Sara so they were able to attend the wedding. Even Vlad Ivanov was there with his partner Tim. Though Carl thought he hadn't been invited but knowing Sara she would have suggested it to him. The ceremony went off without any problems. Harry had his fingers crossed behind his back and hoped that SAAM would not announce a "red alert" during the service. If that happened, he would personally be up in a SEASKY fighter jet and blow them from the atmosphere. Thankfully, there were no interruptions and all went as planned.

Of course, Sara stunned the crowd with her wedding dress and looked like the princess that had finally won her prince. Both Harry and Carl wore their Military uniforms as was tradition, looking handsome and very smart for this special occasion. This was the happiest day of Sara's life and as she smiled to Tom whilst he escorted her down the aisle, just for an instant, she imagined her father was the one giving her away. Carl was at Harry's side as his best man while they both waited in anticipation for Sara, and as Carl took the wedding rings from his pocket ready to pass to Harry, Carl's hand began to shake. He wasn't sure why he was shaking after all it wasn't his wedding but luckily no one but Harry noticed. Carl was happy for them both, he would not be losing his mate but gaining another friend in Sara.

Harry had been in charge of buying the wedding rings which were inscribed on the back with Saras reading "to the moon and back" and Harry's with "and beyond." It was Harry's idea to have the inscriptions on the rings and such a sentimental gesture that Sara loved him for, this was the side that very few people got to see.

Once Harry and Sara were declared married, there was a loud cheer from all the onlookers and they were drenched in confetti. Sara laughed when she noticed that the confetti were in the shape of flying saucers that Paul had patiently made and she thought how fortunate she was to have such engaging people around her. These would also be her new work colleagues and friends who would be part of her new life.

Harry had not notice General Grant at the back of the room but he was honoured that he had taken the time to attend. Grant moved forward to congratulate the couple.

"Well, Saunders make sure you take good care of this young lady and I hope she can tame that temper of yours".

Harry and the General had a love, hate relationship between them and Grant always kept his guard accept around Sara. Sara moved closer to the General and kissed his cheek and thanked temper of yours."

Harry and the General had a love, hate relationship between them and Grant always kept his guard accept around Sara. Sara moved closer to the General and kissed his cheek and thanked him for coming. He became flustered and rubbed his face.

"My, twice in two weeks, things are looking up" he joked as he left the chapel to let the celebrations carry on without his interference. Harry was beaming with happiness he could not believe that she was finally his wife.

"To have and to hold, through richer or poorer, in sickness and in health, for better or worse, till death do us part." Harry had Sara for the rest of his life and would live and love this amazing woman every second of it.

After all the celebrations they left SHEALD to head back home and let the staff get on with their day. The car had been adapted with a tin can, an old boot and lots of balloons. Harry knew this would be Carl and Tom but it was all part of the festivities and he appreciated the effort they had gone to for them both. As they arrived at the house it felt strange to think that this was now their matrimonial home where they would both live from now on. As they approached the door Harry stopped.

"Well Mrs Saunders," he pronounced, "here's to our new life together and forever" Harry swooped Sara up into his arms and carried her into the house. They giggled and Sara kissed Harry "I love you Mr Saunders" Harry carried Sara straight to their bedroom as the moon shone through the window, they both felt very contented. There was no honeymoon just a long weekend at the beach house but that was fine by them. They would plan a holiday later in the year at a more convenient time. For now, they had each other and that was sufficient.

Carl and Tom had all the team working on Sara's fake disappearance. There was less than usual due to the fact that there were no close family and friends to consider and her personal life was straight forward. She had given them all the information as possible about any belonging and any documentation that would need to be destroyed. All her other belonging went to a special storage unit so Sara could sort through what she wanted to keep. Bank accounts were closed by a military intelligence solicitor and a false death certificate was made available.

Everyone who needed to know was informed of her passing and the cottage was sold. The story was that an ambulance was called in the early hours and Sara was rushed to hospital with a blood clot on the brain caused by the recent car crash that had gone undetected. She passed on her way to hospital and a fictitious post-mortem concluded the cause of death. This was all staged, as was the ambulance visit by SHEALD and the funeral was a simple affair as she had requested in a will that she wanted a pure cremation with no mourners or fuss.

After the sale of her house and car she was compensated for any financial losses and Money from any bank accounts were returned to Sara. Her marriage certificate had a knew family name of Thomas instead of Croft and the date of birth showed only a difference in the month from December to November. However, Sara kept her birth name of Croft at SHEALD as there was no threat there. Her new title within SHEALD was to be Lieutenant Sara Croft not Saunders to avoid any confusion with Commander Saunders. Now, Sara no longer existed in the world outside of the organization but she had everything she needed in her new life. Sara referred to this occasion as coming out of a cocoon and becoming a butterfly that would embrace the new freedom that she had found.

# New Life, New Wife

Harry and Sara travelled together to headquarters on her first day at SHEALD. She was nervous but Harry would be with her to offer support and advice and she already knew many of her co-workers. Tom and Carl where already waiting for them as they arrived at the office. On their arrival Harry gave out the orders to the two men and scanned through the week-end reports.

Sara was to spend the first week shadowing Harry and meeting with all the departments and staff and try to get an overall picture of how the organization worked. She would be shown all the roles of each employer and have an opportunity to ask any questions as she went along. Later Carl would arrange and mentor her training which would take several months to achieve as there was much to learn but she looked forward to the challenges ahead in particular SEASKY and Lunar base and especially the interceptor training which would be extraordinary.

Harry had mellowed since his marriage with staff finding him more approachable than before but he still had a lot to learn. He had always been well respected by his employees as he was honest and would defend his team to the end but he had little patience with high expectations that were sometime not achievable to everyone, causing others to fear him. He was guarded which created a barrier between him and his personnel and his years in the Military enhanced this hard-set, coldblooded behaviour. Sara understood this behaviour to be related to his fear of getting too close emotionally to other and then being hurt.

On one specific morning Harry had summoned Paul the IT and radio operator to his office. He had inadvertently sent a message under the wrong code which put the message at risk of being exposed to the wrong people which would not do for the Commander. Harry could be heard yelling at the poor man from in the control room. Sara and Carl were heading for the office to meet with Harry shortly after Paul's chastise-ment as Paul wheeled out of the office with his head down Harry could still be heard shouting as he left. "Get out and don't let it ever happen again!" Carl rolled his eyes he did not agree with Harry's approach to staff and Sara was horrified by the way he had been with Paul. "What?" Harry shrugged his shoulders as he looked at the discontentment on both their faces. "Did you really need to talk to him like that Harry?" questioned Carl. "This is the Military and that's the way it is done here, it isn't a nursery," yelled Harry. His face was still red with the rage. "Well may be the Military way is out of date and it is time for change," replied Sara. "Oh, so you think you can do a better job then, do you?" he said sarcasti-cally. Harry pointed to his chair "be my guest."

"There is no need for that Harry," scolded Sara. Carl tried to keep a straight face. He had never seen anyone face up to Harry when he was like this before. He had tried but had given up miserably and now this was beginning to get interest-ing.

"You do not need to dress someone down in that manner. Yes, they would possibly remember to do it right next time af-ter putting the "fear of God" into them but they could also be so intense about getting it right that they messed up even more. You see Harry you know that every member of this team is the best of the best. So, they are neither lazy or stupid and yes, they work to earn a living like anyone else but they are here for the same reason as you are, to defend our world from alien attacks. Every one of them are loyal, dedicated, hardworking and motivated and as humans they make mis-takes."

She continued and Harry listened impatiently. "Harry, mis-takes are made for a reason so we can learn and in order to stop them happening again. For example, I cut an apple in half on the table and slip with the knife and cut my finger. Do I avoid cutting the apple in half again? or even avoid apples al-together? or do I investigate how I managed to slip with the knife and cut myself? Was it the angle I held the knife at that made me lose my grip or was it the knife I used? maybe I have been using the wrong type of knife to complete the job?" Harry sighed. "After deciding what the issue is I can now achieve a safe and better action when cutting an apple. That way it doesn't happen again and I get to eat my apple".

Harry rolled his eyes "OK, OK, point taken," he responded. Sara concluded. "I know you are a much better man than that after all I get to kiss you every night and see the loving, kind, caring man you really are, they don't." She pointed to the control room. Carl couldn't keep his face straight any longer and began to grin "I'm out of here, we can talk later Harry, but please Harry," he began laughing.... "No kissing!" and left. Sara threw a paper clip at Carl that just missed him as he went through the door still laughing. "Oh, you are both unbearable at times" Sara muttered. By this time Harry was beginning to smile and see the funny side of it all. "Now, now my dear, calm down," he mocked, but she just ignored him. Harry walked from the office over to Paul to try and apologise to him. It would be lunch soon and he would offer to pay for Paul's lunch as a pardon for his behaviour. Better that than another lecture off Sara!

Sara and Harry were in the canteen at lunch and a robot was serving them. The robot had given Sara a veal dish instead of a vegan meal. So, she was trying her best to get the robot to understand her. It may have been her northern accent that the robot could not identify with but she was too hungry to wait any longer and lent over the counter to press the vegan choice and her lunch appeared.

"Thank you" she said sarcastically as she carried her meal to the table where Harry was sitting. The robot got even more confused and began to malfunction. "It'll reboot in a moment," Harry told her. "So, not to worry," said Harry, but she wasn't worried, just hungry!

Doctor Ivanov walked over to Sara and tapped her on the shoulder. "Sara do you have that book on ESP that you told me about?" Sara remembered the one. "Yes, I do Vlad, I'll drop it off for you after lunch in your lab," Vlad bowed his head, "Thank you." Harry remained chatting to Sara and finished his lunch before heading back to the office. Carl shouted across the room to Sara as he battled with the robot for a ham sandwich "Sara!" he made a gun motion with his hands, "shooting practice at two o'clock in the firing range." She put her hand up in acknowledgement to him. "I'll be there," she responded.

Before the shooting practice she walked to Vlad's lab with the book. Vlad thanked her for the book and then she noticed the mice in the corner and went over to see them, passing some food into the cage. One of the mice raised itself to recover the treat from her. "I thought you had two mice Vlad, but it seems you have four here, have you been buying more mice?" "No," answered Vlad, shifting from one foot to another. She knew he was hiding something. "I'm breeding them," he replied. "Why?" she asked again. He was nervous, "I can't tell you yet, but maybe soon." She did not pursue it any further but she felt uneasy about it, she knew that Vlad was not a rule breaker and the rules were clear that no animal experiment should cause harm to any animal involved. She also knew that Vlad wasn't a cruel man, but she had no idea what he was up to? Now it was target practice with Carl and so far, she had missed every target so she needed to concentrate harder on the task in hand.

"No, no," shaking his head, Carl grabbed the gun, "you're not holding the gun right, you'll never hit anything like that, hold it like this." She watched what he did and mimicked it, "like this." Carl sighed, "yes that's it." She fired the gun and at last it was a dead hit. She jumped in the air. "Yes, got it!" Carl shook his head. "Now, you have to do that every time you shoot, for goodness' sake hit the blooming target." It was going to be a long session and guns were definitely not her forte. "I think we need more practice" He exhaled, "and again please." Trying to be patient as he pulled his face in despair. After target practice Sara was due in the control room to sit with Paul for a while. At least it gave Carl a chance to rest a while from the stress of training.

"You wanted to see me, Commander?" asked Carl. "Yes, Carl, sit down" Harry had already poured Carl a coffee and placed it down on the desk in front of him.

"I was wondering if you could go through these figures with me for the medical and lab units? I can't seem to get the figures right and you have a much keener eye with these things," said Harry.

"Sure, well let's see." He looked through the sheets.

"There you are, there were several items purchased for the lab on the third of march but they haven't been sanctioned, that's why they didn't show up on your other sheet," said Carl as he read through the list. "There's an incubator, Pump systems, tanks, and several gallons of bio fluid."

"What do we need them for? and whose ordered them?" Enquired Harry. Carl looked up with a puzzled expression.

"It was Doctor Ivanov, what's he up to, I wonder?"

"God knows," said Harry, "he's always got some experiment on the go; you know what he's like." Carl gave a disapproving look he did not care much for the Doc and made no secret of it. "I'll have a word with him and pull the spending back," replied Harry. It was least of his worries what he did in the lab and anyway he was not concerned as when Grant saw his spending, he would soon yell him into line.

At the lab Harry was discussing the lab expenditures with Ivanov. "It stops now!" Said Harry to Vlad. "I can assure you Commander; I will do it with immediate effect but would it be possible for me to continue my work if I fund this myself and did the research in my own time Sir?" Disputed Vlad. "Sure, sure do what you want just as long as it's in your time and your money and it's legal." This side of science was of no interest to Harry and he understood very little of what the Doc did half the time but the fact was that when they needed him to deliver, he always did so Harry tended to leave him to his own devices. Ivanov was by far their best chance of understanding the alien's than anyone else and they needed his expertise. He may not have warmed to the man but it wasn't about him surrounding himself with friends it was about getting the job done to their best ability.

# Floating in Space

The next part of Sara's training was on Lunar base. This was where she would be assessed on flying an Interceptor and being able to fire a missile at an aggressive UFO. She had already completed the simulating training with Tom and now would have to prove her ability on the training interceptor. Although there were three working interceptors, they had a fourth ship that was specifically for training. It was the exact replica of the one's used on Lunar base but had an extra seat for the instructor and the missile had a locked lever so that it was never actually fired during training. She was eager to start the interceptor on the launch station as Tom sat by her side. He did not interfere as he knew that she was more than capable of handling the craft. "So, Sara let's begin," instructed Tom. Sara lifted off from the holding pad perfectly "well done Sara, now keep her steady and follow the Lieutenants orders and keep checking your monitor." Leah Spoke through the transmitter. "Interceptor one move to green area 125.2."

Sara moved in place without any hesitation and a recorded message of SAAM was released by Leah at the appropriate time "red alert, UFO ahead." "In position to fire Interceptor One." instructed Leah. Of course, there was no real UFO only a hologram of a ship emerged. Sara lined up the target. "Target on screen and ready to fire," announced Sara "Permission to fire," asked Sara as Leah quickly agreed her request and Sara fired at the hologram which suddenly disappeared. "It's a direct hit Interceptor one, please return to base," transmitted Leah.

"That was excellent Sara" said Tom "and that was your first attempt so you should be very proud of yourself," complimented Tom. Sara was rather smug with herself, especially as she was having such fun. She could not wait until tomorrow when she would have her final test in the actual Interceptor with an unlocked missile. Although, she would not be firing the missile on this occasion either. "Now, let's get back to base, there's a curry with my name on in the canteen," added Tom. "A Okay," said Sara as they made their way back to base.

On her return there was an announcement over the internal radio. "Lunar shuttle landing in twenty seconds with Commander Saunders on board." Sara was excited that Harry had come to Lunar base as she had missed him like crazy and immediately ran to the docking station to greet him as he departed from the shuttle. He put his arms around her and whispered, "I've missed you too much." "Me too," concurred Sara. Tom ventured over to see Harry after he had eaten his curry. "How's she doing Tom?" asked Harry. Tom turned to Harry. "Best student I have ever trained, she gets it straight away, she's ready Harry and tomorrow she will be flying for real with the Interceptor's." Harry smiled. "Well, what did you expect, only the best for me." Sara smiled at the two men, it was all finally coming together and she was starting to feel part of the team. "So, Harry what brings you here?" questioned Sara. Harry was planning something she could tell, he had that look of mischief on his face. "Well, apart from missing my beautiful wife, I thought it was time we went on a special date and I would show you around the neighbourhood." He motioned his eyes to the window outside. Sara was elated. "You mean we are going on a Moon walk?" queried Sara. "Oh no," replied Harry, "much better than that." Sara was intrigued about the adventure and could not wait to go.

Harry helped Sara to put her space suit on. He was quite used to his but they were tricky to get into if you did not know how. "Are you going to tell me where we are going yet?" asked Sara. "Nope, you'll see," teased Harry as they both got into the spaceship and as the craft took off Harry pointed out to the stars and planets.

"There's no better feeling," reminisced Harry. There was no doubting how stunning the view was and the best date she had ever been on, but somehow, she didn't think it was over yet, she was sure that Harry had something more up his sleeve. The craft came to a halt.

"Here we are, Sir," informed the pilot.

"Thanks Lieutenant," said Harry to the pilot. Then Harry took hold of Sara's hand, leading her to the back of the ship. He put his helmet on and connected a line to him that was secured to the ship, then did the same for Sara. The doors at the back opened and Sara saw the most breath-taking view she had ever seen.

"That's the best view in Town, you ready?" asked Harry. "You mean ...." Stuttered Sara as Harry stepped out of the ship and began to float in space still holding on to Sara's hand as she nervously followed him.

They began to float for several seconds and Sara felt completely weightless, this was an amazing view. There was darkness but space was alight with stars and colour and every now and then a star would flicker and glow. It was a truly magical moment and she felt as if she was flying in heaven and nothing else mattered.

Harry pointed to his left and did a full turn, Sara smiled and followed suit. She looked back at Lunar base it looked tiny from where they were and Earth was a colourful sphere of beauty. In that instance she understood what Harry had been telling her about on his trips into space and it being his piece of heaven. Now, Sara had shared that with him.

When it was time to go back into the spacecraft, they both sat in quietness, there were no words to describe what they had experienced but Sara thought how lucky she was to have had such an opportunity and to be with the man of her dreams floating through space. It did not get better than that.

Morning came around quickly as Sara and Harry stood at the Lunar base guest bedroom door.

"Oh, don't go," begged Sara with her arms wrapped around his neck. He kissed her several times. "You know I have to" explained Harry.

"I know, I know," said Sara, reluctantly letting him go. "You'll be home tomorrow anyway," Harry reminded her. "But it's another night without you," she complained.

"Well," said Harry cheekily, "I'll just have to make it up to you, won't I?" and kissed her again. Carl had just arrived on the Lunar shuttle for the test flight with Sara and Tom and tutted.

"For goodness' sake, you two, you can't keep your hands off each other for one minute, can you?" He joked. "You're only jealous, Carl," taunted Harry.

Harry boarded the flight back to Earth and would be back in the office in less than two hours and there he would be able to monitor Sara's first Interceptor flight into space. Carl put his arm around Sara's shoulders. "So, Let's begin with the computer tests first Sara, then you can have a quick break and we will get going on the real stuff. Tom says you're a natural at this so hopefully we will have you signed off and ready to go after today." Sara was looking forward to this, for her this was the cream of the cream in terms of flying. "I'm ready for this Carl, just tell me when," she remarked.

The computer test was long and boring but it had to be done as it was part of the training. She had done similar before when taking her driving, flying and helicopter license so, would just have to get on with it. The results from the test would be available straight afterwards meaning Sara would know if she had passed or failed. As the computer shuffled out the results Sara stood by waiting. Carl was reading the outcome of the exam. "Come on Carl, how did I do?" she asked impatiently. "Congratulations Lieutenant Croft you have passed with a ninety nine percent success, clever clogs" he jested. "Damn," said Sara, smiling, "I wonder what question I got wrong?" Carl tutted, "come on miss lets go" as he motioned her to the launch pads.

There were three interceptors one for Carl, Tom, and Sara and today Sara was flying solo. Her heart was beating fast with anticipation, but she was ready and seated in her flight chair in no time at all and switching on the controls, radio, and lights. "Interceptor one in position and ready for launch." Informed Sara. Carl was next in interceptor two, and lastly Tom in Interceptor three. Carl was the lead Interceptor on this mission and on Carl's command they were all ready for take-off. "Control to Interceptors 1, 2 and 3 Lift off," relayed Leah.

Harry was now back on Earth and in SHEALD control room, listening and checking the monitors. Positions Interceptors?" said Harry. "Position Green 227.3," replied Sara. Tom and Harry relayed their positioning too. Leah then gave the Interceptors their next positioning and they followed one by one. "Interceptor one A okay," replied Sara.

"Interceptor two A okay," said Carl. "Interceptor three A okay," answered Tom.

They were all verified by Leah as Carl took over to give further positioning to the two interceptors so they could fly side by side. Sara was in the middle of the two colonels and felt an extreme sense of pride that she was not only flying with two friends but the two best pilots that SHEALD had. She smiled across at Carl and he gave her a wink and Tom gave her the thumbs up gesture. This was much better than flying any helicopter, Commercial airline, or light aircraft, this was "real flying" in space thousands of miles above the Earth. Sara was born for this and had finally found her calling.

Suddenly a message interrupted the transmission. It was SAAM (Satellite Alien attack monitor) and it was a "red alert" which meant that a UFO attack was imminent. "Red Alert, UFO sighting and closing in." Harry banged his fist down on Paul's desk "damn," said Harry. Paul jumped at the unexpectedness of the bang on his desk. Harry took charge of the transmission. Sara, back to base, I repeat Interceptor one back to Luna base immediately." "Roger," replied Sara as she headed back to the launch pad. The UFO invaded the two interceptor's space and fired several times. Tom was nearest and was knocked off course. He pulled back but his craft was damaged. "Interceptor three, have taken a hit, some damage to fuel hold but am going back for a shot at UFO." "Roger" replied Carl. Tom aimed at the UFO and fired the missile but his ship tilted due to the damage and he missed the target. Carl appeared at the side of Tom. "Back to base Interceptor three that's an order," said Carl. Carl had the UFO in sight and lined up for target as Tom moved away, Carl fired and The UFO exploded into space. Carl reported a direct hit of the UFO and Tom was nearly back at base safely, he was losing fuel but would just about make it home. Carl was reassured and began his return to Lunar base as SAAM once again announced "Red alert, second UFO sighted in area 250 Green." It was heading straight for Carl and he had no Missiles left to fire. Harry shouted to his friend, "Colonel, get the hell out of there, you have no ammo, you are a sitting duck!" Carl swallowed hard and knew he was in trouble of the worst kind. Tom could not make it back, but even if he could he also had no more missiles. Carl was left with a UFO heading straight for him with nothing for protection or to defend him, he braced himself for a hit, this had to be it for him.

"Interceptor One leaving holding station and on track to UFO positioning 256.6 Green with activated missile. Permission to fire?" said Sara. Carl interrupted. "Permission denied, Interceptor one, return to Lunar base at once, I repeat return to base." The UFO fired at Carl's ship but missed, though it still managed to cause a shudder from the blast making him lose control for a short time. Sara maintained her course to the UFO. "Sorry, Interceptor two I cannot hear you," Lied Sara. Harry grabbed the mike in the control room. "Interceptor One, Lieutenant, this is your Commander and I command that you return to base immediately. Do not breech your superior officer's instructions, I repeat......" Harry was shaking his best friend was in direct line of a UFO attack and his wife who was on her first flight was trying to shoot the UFO down. "Sorry Commander, you're breaking up," replied Sara as she switched the radio off. Paul turned to the Commander, "Sir the radio is dead." "She's switched the darn radio off," cursed Harry. "Override the switch Paul and get me back on transmission." Sara headed for the UFO and quickly lined it up for target and then fired. Leah came back on the radio "Direct hit, UFO destroyed."

Carl breathed a sigh of relief. Harry came back on the radio.

"Do not take my joy for your survival as meaning everything is well, I want you back in my office on your return today and lieutenant Croft you are suspended from flying until further notice." Harry was fuming and shaking at the same time.

Carl made his way back to base and Sara followed. Inside Lunar base Carl saw Sara and touched her hand and mouthed:

"Thank you."

"We are nearly even now," said Sara.

Carl looked concerned for Sara. "Sara, believe me, when I say you are in so much trouble with Harry," warned Carl. "It's fine," said Sara, "and you know what Carl, whatever happens, I'd do it all over again if I had to, I couldn't just stand back and watch them take another person away from me again."

Carl was touched by Sara's comments but more than anything he was glad to be still breathing. "Tom hugged them both, "you two, ok? You had me really worried, someone was watching over you two for sure." "Yep," said Carl "and he is called Commander Saunders and we are about to feel his wrath." They both pulled their faces. Poor sara was in for it now!

Sara and Carl flew back to Earth on the same space shuttle and were back at SHEALD in no time and lined up on Saunders's office floor. Harry was still furious with Sara. "Colonel Peters, how are you?" Enquired Harry. "A little shaken Commander but otherwise fine." Then he turned his attention on Sara. "And You, Lieutenant, you ignored my Command!" Sara, huffed "Oh Come on Harry." Harry stood close up to Sara, he was livid. "I am your Superior Officer and you will refer to me as Commander!" Shouted Harry. "You completely ignored my command and could be on a charge for that." "Yes Sir!" she said sarcastically, "I was saving my colleague from being killed, it is the organization's promise to defend and protect others from alien attack and so I did. I will not stand by like a coward and watch a friend die." Harry walked away. "Colonel Peters you may leave at once, but you stay." He pointed to Sara. He walked up and down the floor as Sara stood to attention. "Your decision making is based on emotions, which is dangerous and you could have been killed!" He shouted again and everyone in the control room could hear the conversation as it was so loud. Carl was cringing as he heard the row. He knew Sara would give as good as she could but there was no reasoning with Harry when he was so angry. "Oh, I see, so I should not be emotionally attached? Yet you are," she argued. "What?" questioned Harry. "It's not OK for me to be emotionally attached to a colleague who is in danger and try to help because I may get hurt but as your wife you are emotionally attached and you would not want me in any danger? you hypocrite!" She shouted and began walking out of the office. "Where do you think you are going Croft?" he bawled. "I'm going home, Sir," she answered. "I've not finished with you yet," roared Harry. "But I've finished with you!" replied Sara and left without further ado. After Sara left the office Carl returned, he could not help but grin, "what are you grinning at?" growled Harry. "You know she's right; I would have done the same as would Tom and you" preached Carl. "Oh, shut up!" Harry knew Carl was right and he also knew he would be sleeping on the sofa tonight.

When Harry arrived home, he hid the roses behind his back and quietly entered the house. Sara was in the kitchen preparing dinner. Harry stood at the kitchen door and pushed the flowers across the work surface towards her. She pretended not to see them and carried on making dinner. "I'm sorry, you were right, ok? He kissed her on the back of the neck and held her. "I was so afraid I was going to lose you; I love you too much." She smiled, "the flowers are lovely." Harry kissed her again. "Does this mean I'm forgiven?" he asked. "Maybe ... Sir!" she laughed. Harry looked into her eyes with an admiration of his brave wife. "So, do you still love me to the moon and back?" "Hmm... possibly, and even beyond, but you are still sleeping on the sofa tonight," she jeered. An argument never lasted long and usually came to an end when Harry admitted defeat and told her she was right. It worked every time!

# ESP

The satellite SAAM had informed Lunar base of a pending UFO arrival. It had been over a fortnight since any sightings. Unfortunately, this was a particularly difficult pursuit for the interceptors as it had managed to weave its way through the Moon restrictions and was on its way to Earth. SEASKY had been alerted soon as the UFO had entered the Earth's atmosphere and the roamers were being transported to the predictive determination which was the Loch Ness area in Scotland. They had all been out searching for the spaceship for days with no success or further sightings. On day six they had a breakthrough with Captain Lee from the SEASKY jet who had a definite sighting of the UFO coming out of Loch ness which was one of the Many Lochs in Scotland. This was a particularly deep loch and the UFO had hidden there under water where it would not be at risk of disintegration from the atmosphere as would normally be the case. It was able to emerge for a fleeting time each day and the aliens could then move around the Loch before re-entering their ship into the water. The SEASKY sub would be too large to get into the loch but it was possible to get some divers to get to the underwater craft and capture the aliens. Unfortunately, the UFO was alerted to the divers and emerged from the Loch at speed but was outrun by Captain Lee who shot at the UFO bringing it to a descent on land. "Well done Captain Lee that was just enough to bring it down without completely destroying it which should mean the alien will be still in there. I want the roamers out in the field now and I want that alien alive," asserted Harry from the control room.

Tom was coordinating the land roamers with their search. He knew the spacecraft would disintegrate soon, now that it was in the atmosphere and the alien would then be on foot in the woodland being easier to capture  but not necessarily

easier to find. Carl and Sara were flying above with helicopters and infra-red lighting. For Sara, she had done this on
so many occasions with the police helicopter and was quick to
detect the alien. Sara gave the land team the Bearings and the
alien was captured but regrettably had been injured in the
crash landing. This time Harry would do his utmost to make
some form of communication with the alien. He needed to
show the committee that SHEALD was moving forward and
had more answers than previously. It was all well and good
stopping the UFOs from visiting and attacking but they still
kept on coming. They were unsure why they visited or where
they came from and more so, were there other alien planets
that where planning similar visits that these aliens knew
about? There were so many unanswered questions that Harry
needed answers to. From the Post-mortems conducted before
they already knew of the alien's physical capabilities and now
Harry needed more by communication.

At two o'clock in the morning Harry received the call that
the alien was on its way to SHEALD for interrogation. His injuries did not appear to be too serious and therefore offered a
greater opportunity. The same morning Harry and Carl were
meeting with Doctor Ivanov and Doctor Tim Walker to discuss the alien's ability to communicate with them. Harry tried
for over an hour with the alien but was unsuccessful. "Either
he cannot or will not communicate with us." Proposed Harry.
The helmet and Bio fluid had already been removed from the
alien earlier and as Ivanov explained before the vocal section
was much feebler than that of a human. This supported the
theory that speech was not their means of usual conversation
and therefore, did not converse with words. It was looking
more likely that they communicated through telepathy which
was a form of ESP (Extra sensory perception) and would be
their only hope.

Ivanov knew that his knowledge about ESP was sparce but
that Sara had a Doctorate in ESP and was much more spe-
cialised in the area, this was her territory. Sara was in the
control room with Tom collating readouts from Lunar base
and putting a report together about the recent capture of the
alien. Harry wanted to find out more about ESP and how they

could possibly incorporate this in their work with the extra - terrestrial. He had asked Ivanov to join him with Carl in his office and to meet with Sara and Tom.

They all convened in Harry's office as Ivanov defined the predicament with which they were faced. "So, do you think they may be able to use ESP and communicate with telepa- thy?" questioned Sara. She had used hundreds of volunteers in her research and found very few had a capacity to use telepathy to a higher level of communication. There were also no subjects in SHEALD who had shown any ability either but there was one person who Sara had discovered with a strong ability in ESP and in particular telepathy and telekinesis which was the movement of objects with the mind. He was only fifteen at the time in 2013 when Sara had met with Marc Taylor who had developed ESP as a child. Marc had been evaluated in every angle of the spectrum including telepathy, telekinesis, clairvoyance which was the ability to see into the future, past and present events, and mediumship, were a per- son is able to converse with the spirit world. Although some candidates had shown some interesting results, they were usu- ally strong in only one area but it was Marc who had left the greatest impression. His capabilities of all areas of ESP were immensely strong but telepathy and telekinesis were by far ex- ceptional to anyone else. Even so, she was unsure how this would be effective against alien life. Marc was now twenty- four years of age and lived in Edinburgh where she had con- ducted her research at the university. He lived mainly as a recluse these days due to the prejudice against his unusual abilities. People were afraid of him and believed that he read their every thought and therefore, avoided him. He had been the subject of many experiments, being treated like a lab rat. Marc was used for their research projects and then discarded once they had what they needed with hardly a thank you for what he gave, during these exhausting tests.

Sara had been different with Marc; she had made the effort to get to know the person and showed him respect for his ability. Marc had been punished for his skills even by his own family who had disowned him, meaning he had been through the care system for most of his younger years. He was described by his teachers as a "disruptive child" and was labelled as being on the "autistic spectrum." Sara was different and had made him feel special, she had told him that "it was not a curse but a gift that others did not understand because they had never experienced it and the unknown was often feared." She also told him "That one day someone, somewhere would benefit greatly from his talent and that he would not have been given this ability if it did not serve a meaningful purpose." Little did Sara know that it would be her who would need his gift to help the world against an evil that had bestowed them from space. Over the years Sara had kept in touch with Marc at Christmas's and Birthdays, but for Sara, he would have had no acknowledgement of his Birthday or Christmas. He was a gentle soul that had little confidence and little self-esteem making him confused about his own identity. None of this was of his own making but of a society that could not put this square peg into a round hole.

"Do you have an address, Sara?" asked Harry. "Yes, although I have not been in touch since my reassignment but I would imagine he will still live in the same place. I need to go with the others and speak to him first to get him to come with us, as I fear he would not co-operate otherwise. He is understandably very wary of people, after all he has been through." "Ok Sara, Carl you go too and pick him up tonight and tell him to bring a bag as he may be here for a while. We can use the amnesia drug on him afterwards so he can go about his normal life when he has finished." Doctor Ivanov could hardly contain his excitement as this was what his work was all about. He had waited   years for a breakthrough like this.

Carl and Sara set off and were taken by helicopter to Edinburgh castle where a helipad was in use. Marc lived only a short distance away from the castle so they would be there in no time. Several security guards who were armed were escorting Carl and Sara to their destination and were trying to be discreet. It was midnight when they arrived at Marc's home. The guards knocked hard on the door but Marc did not answer. After all, they were complete strangers, pounding on his door at midnight. Sara asked them all to back off.

"Please, let me deal with this, you will frighten the poor man," she insisted. "Ok Guys, step aside," commanded Colonel Peters. Sara knocked lighter on the door and spoke through the letter box. "Marc, it's Sara Croft, I'm sorry if we scared you. Please, will you open the door, I know it's late, but I need to talk with you, it is really important and I need your help." She moved away from the door and waited a few seconds. The door slowly opened. "Oh my god, it is you! I thought you were supposed to be dead; I knew you weren't I could feel it!" replied a quiet voice. "It's a long story Marc, please can I come in?" requested Sara.

Carl and Sara entered the flat and stayed for twenty minutes as Sara tried to briefly explain what had happened and who they were. "I will tell you about the rest on the way Marc, you need to pack a bag and we need to leave as soon as we can." At last, they were back up in the air. Marc was still trying to get his head around it all but was enjoying the ride in the helicopter whilst still being in disbelief that he was needed by this secret service that were air lifting him to their Headquarters. It was now early morning and Marc was shown to a guest suite for the night. "Please rest here for a while and we will talk later in the day," requested Carl. Sara Interrupted. "Let him have whatever he needs, he is a very special guest," she demanded to the guards. Marc smiled, he had never been treated so well before and for the first time in his life he felt needed and valued.

Sara went to meet Marc later that morning after he had rested. He was nervous which was hardly surprising but he was glad to see a familiar face. Marc looked untidy and neglected with his slim build. It was unsurprising as he was living on Universal credits to survive and his mental health had been affected by the constant rejection of family and teachers. He was the "class weirdo" that was under continuous bullying from other students and had been ridiculed by the most terrible name calling that made him feel worthless. At five feet six high he was unable to defend himself from the physical bullying and curled up into his shell to protect himself from the harm of the outside world that had decided to hate him so much. Lack of regular nutritional food left him pale and against his red hair that was ungroomed he hid his face with a bushy beard, but this unkemptness was mainly through lack of motivation and self-worth. "I Hope they have been treating you well? asked Sara. "Oh yes, they have been great," replied Marc. "You see Marc, you are our only hope and your ability could save many lives. This is your calling," said Sara. Marc was pleased that he could at last do something important and something no one else could do, but he hesitated. "What if I can't do it, you know, him being an alien and that?" "Marc you are not on your own here and if we don't succeed then at least we tried, but I know you can do this. You have waited your whole life for this," said Sara. He smiled and thanked her. Then Sara turned to him and joked, "though, we may have to shoot you and hide your body with the others, if you don't deliver." He laughed, it helped with his nerves and lightened the air. "Are you ready Marc?" asked Sara. "As I will ever be," he replied. Marc took a gulp of air and hoped it would all work out as he followed Sara into Harry's office where he was greeted by several people.

Harry introduced himself, "Sara of course you know and Carl you met yesterday. So, that only needs me to introduce you to Colonel Tom Green and Doctor Vlad Ivanov." Ivanov was delighted to meet Marc; he had never been so friendly before and from his reactions it was obvious that Vlad was looking forward to collaborating with him. Tom shook Marc's hand. "Please call me Tom, we don't stand on ceremony here; any friend of Sara's is ok with me." Marc liked the fact that Tom had referred to Sara as his friend and was astounded at how they had made him feel so welcome, he had never experienced such friendliness before. "Right said Harry Let's get on with it, Coffee anyone?"

It was a lot for Marc to take in but he managed and every now and then when they got carried away with the terminology Sara would stop them to explain in layman terms what they meant. "Any questions Marc, feel free to ask" commented Harry. "You are an essential role to this undertaking." Harry also wanted to offer a financial incentive in return for his skills they had employed. He could see that Marc was not fortunate in monetary matters from what Carl had relayed about him and his impoverished appearance. "Marc is there anything we can offer to help you with as a payment for your expertise afterwards and although you will be given the amnesia drug to forget the whole event, for security reasons, we can still arrange something without any suspicion. Marc had never been offered any payment in the past and had never felt confident to put a value on himself or what he did.

"No, thank you I cannot think of anything." He was only glad to be of service to something so momentous.

Sara intervened: "We could start with a new apartment and some modern furniture, if that is alright with you Marc?" Marc agreed obligingly. His present flat was dark, cold, and damp with many repairs that needed attending to that had been overlooked by the landlord. He had little furniture and what he did have was worn and second hand. So, this would be a significant improvement to his life. "Ok," said Harry "I'll get someone to organize that straight away." Marc thought what an impressive place it was and the people who worked there too. He would have loved to have been a regular part of an organization like this. Sara was lucky to have all of this.

Eventually it was time to meet the alien. They all retired to the Lab that had been purposely set up for the event and in the room awaiting them was Doctor Tim Walker with a nurse and the alien. There were security guards everywhere with guns at the ready. It was intimidating to say the least as the alien was sat on a large chair with his arms and feet tied down. He looked similar to the human form but his face had a green tinge to it that Harry had mentioned was due to a fluid they used to help them travel the huge journey. He was also a smaller build of Five feet four with reddened eyes that he had received from wearing special lenses to protect his eyes from the bio fluid but his hair seemed a normal brown in colour. Even with his small demeanour he still manged to look menacing and Harry had warned Marc of his capabilities to kill and mutilate bodies of innocent people and that he should be aware of the danger he could cause at any time. Marc should not let his guard down for one second.

The alien looked weak and did not struggle as Doctor Ivanov asked everyone to leave though, Marc requested that Sara stay with him, he needed her to help him make contact. Harry, Tom, Carl, Tim, and the nurse went into the next room. Doctor Walker set up a monitor which would assess the aliens brain pattern, blood pressure and heart rate in an adjacent room to the lab. There was a large connecting window visibly, making it possible to observe the experiment from. A speaker transmitted their voices and a microphone on the wall of the observation room allowed them to talk to those in the laboratory. There was a table in front of the alien and Marc sat down on a chair on the opposite side. Sara stood at the back of Marc while Vlad was situated behind the alien with several monitors and recording equipment which included a camera to catch all movements to give sound evidence of the event. Marc beckoned Sara to sit on a chair at the side of him as the chair shuffled forward on its own. Harry became alert and checked Sara was ok. Sara put her hand on Marc's shoulder to reassure him, "it's ok Marc, just take your time." "I'm sorry Sara, I didn't mean that to happen it does that sometimes when I'm nervous." Sara smiled and seemed unnerved by the incident.

Tom and Carl watched intently as they had never experienced this before, this was ground-breaking even for SHEALD. Harry felt his stomach tighten, at the end of the day as Commander he was ultimately responsible for this and he had three lives at risk in there and one of them happened to be his wife. He was hoping they would be safe and that it was not a step too far. Doctor Ivanov slipped some wires onto Marc and the alien and switched on the computers and monitors.

"We are ready when you are," said Vlad to Marc and Sara. Sara took a long breath to prepare herself and began to speak quietly and gently to Marc. "Relax Marc and I want you to breath in deeply and then exhale gently, Marc followed Sara 's instructions. "I want you to imagine you are floating happily and comfortably around the room. Take a look at the room Marc, there is nothing to fear. It is not threatening to you in any way as you feel your eyes getting heavier and tired." She could hear the gentle pips of the monitor and looked up at the window seeing Harry, Tom, and Carl all watching in anticipation.

"Close your eyes and relax Marc you are as light as a feather as you float. I want you to now see through your mind's eye, your third eye Marc," she reiterated. Marc closed his eyes. Harry was impatient.

"Does she have to do that; can she not just get on with it?" "shush" said Carl, "she knows what she's doing." Carl knew that Harry was getting uptight and concerned for their safety, this was uncommon ground to them all and anything could happen. Vlad nodded to Sara and turned the recording on. "Ok, Marc Look at the light, can you see the ball of light?" Asked Sara. "Yes, yes I see it," replied Marc. "Good, now keep following the light, now it's moving Marc, moving over to the alien and hovering over his brow.... Follow the light Marc, follow it into the alien's head and into his mind."

Suddenly, the alien began to shake and his chair rocked from side to side. "Slowly Marc, not too fast, you don't want to hurt him," said Sara. The chair stopped rocking. "Why don't you ask him what planet he is from Marc?" asked Sara. Marc spoke and described the images he saw. He was moving extremely fast through space. "I can see the sun but I'm going past it and I'm passing many solar systems far away."

Doctor Ivanov spoke "How long have you been travelling to get to Earth?" "Many Moons ... many months ... of our Earth years," answered Marc.

"Why do you come to Earth?" Said Vlad.

Marc looked sad. "I can see them; it is dark here; the planet is dying and they are sick. They need to replace the sick organs they have and take the minerals from the soil and rocks so; they can replenish them in their World. They are taking specimens of insects too. I... I feel sick, I don't feel well!," said Marc.

Something was wrong.

Sara spoke faster now: "Marc, I want you to follow the light back out of the alien at once, now you must leave Marc you must do this at once." Panic hit the room. The room began to

111

shake as if an earthquake had begun, there was a rumbling noise that began to intensify and a swishing as if a strong wind were present. The chairs and table flew across the room at great speed and then lifted into the air whirling around above their heads. Harry pressed the mike button at the side of the window and shouted to Ivanov.

"Stop the experiment Ivanov and get out of the room, all of you now!" Ivanov was pushed off his feet and struggle to get up, he tried to drag himself along the side of the wall to the door but the force was heavy like a hurricane. Tom ran to the door and dragged him from the room but Sara and Marc were still trapped in the room with the alien.

The alien screamed in a piercing voice as if in great distress and began to slowly levitate. Harry ran to the room he had to get to Sara but as he got to the door it slammed shut. Harry rattled the door to try and open it but it was shut tight. Sara was unexpectedly hit by one the chairs and fell to the floor but fought her way back up. Harry was still behind the door shouting to her to get out and kicking as hard as he could at the door but it was firmly closed. Sarah was grabbing at anything she could to keep herself on her feet when the door flung open and Harry held out his hand to Sara.

"Take my hand." Sara tried and stretch and Harry pulled with all his force to get nearer to her but was again pushed back out of the room. Carl tried next but was also pushed back "It's hopeless," said Harry "I can't reach her no matter how hard I try it's too strong." They could hardly hear each other talk with all the noise of the furniture banging around and the harrowing wind and without warning Sara and Marc where elevated into the air, spinning uncontrollably. Sara stretched out her arm and shouted over to Marc.

"Marc, grab my hand." Marc pushed and tried several times before he eventually gripped hold of her hand and Sara caught hold of the window holding on as hard as she could. Harry was back in the other room trying to think what he could do as Sara shouted to Harry.

"Harry, break the window," he scanned the room quickly and picked up the nearest table, throwing it with all his force at the window and the glass shattered, releasing the pressure as both Sara and Marc fell to the ground, it was over. The alien dropped to the floor with blood oozing from his eyes, nose, and mouth. The monitors were still working, then abruptly they flatlined and the alien was dead.

Two of the computers exploded and caught fire as Carl and Tom ran into the lab and rescued Sara and Marc. They had some cuts from the broken window but were otherwise un-hurt. "What the hell happened there?" asked Carl. "It was the build-up of energy from the auric field which was too strong," said Sara, "Yes," said Ivanov with a smile, "but apart from that I would say that was a success."

"Really!" said Carl "well if that was a success, I would have hated to see a failure." Harry quickly took charge of the situa-tion.

"I want guards in here now and the room sealed, are you two, ok?" he asked Sara and Marc. They both nodded but they were exhausted.

"Get them both checked over and out of here," ordered Harry to Ivanov.

"Yes sir," beamed Ivanov. This was the best experiment ever and he was exceptionally pleased with himself. Everyone else was in shock and horror and it would take time to digest what had happened and what could be learned for the next time.

The debriefing in Harry's office took place two hours later but was still very fresh in all their minds. Marc was resting af-ter the event and was not present at the debriefing. "We have a long way to go but it is a good start," said Ivanov. "Marc is a useful tool and we need him further; he would be an asset to our work, especially if we intend to move forward in this area. He must join the cause," insisted Vlad. Harry, Tom, Carl, and Sara all agreed with the doctor for once. There was some-thing and someone to work with and bring communication with the aliens forward to another level and break down bar-riers. Albeit primitive at the moment but with time and guid-ance this could be the vital instrument they needed to guide them in their understanding of the aliens. If they knew why and how they came then maybe they could work an amiable agreement between them to bring it to a peaceful ending. It was agreed unanimously that Marc would join SHEALD.

After a short rest Marc was asked to join the meeting and Marc was overjoyed at the prospects of his new post. He would work hard and prove his worth to them all. Doctor Ivanov would supervise Marc and they would work together.

"And no more animals Vlad" warned Harry.

Marc looked up and spurted out: "He's doing it for the baby, Sara" Sara looked confused.

"What?" Ivanov took Marc's arm and pushed him out of the room. "I think I need to check him over now for any injuries and he needs to rest, he seems a little bewildered," getting Marc out of the room as quickly as he could. Marc's comment was quickly overtaken by the day's events and nothing more was said about it.

"Well, I don't know about you but I think I need a stiff drink after that before I go home to the wife and kids," Muttered Tom. He mimicked Fiona's voice, "hello darling did you have a good day at work today? What do I say? Oh yes dear, Just the usual, captured an alien, collaborated with a guy who was telepathic, and we all spun around a room for a bit," he shrugged his shoulders. Harry pulled out the bottle of whisky he had in his desk and poured some into two glasses, one for Carl and the other for Tom and then he filled the other two for him and Sara with Juice.

"Where else would you get so much diversity in a day? The excitement and no two days are alike." Harry lifted his glass "Cheers and here is to SHEALD and the Fab four Harry, Tom, Carl, and Sara"! and they all clicked there glasses together. Harry could not wait to draft his latest report about the alien. General Grant would be tearing his hair out at the costs of the refurbishment of the lab and observation room, extra security and now another mouth to feed with a new recruit who was a Psychic. The fact was that they had delivered the goods the committee wanted and they would be overjoyed with the results whilst Grant would be counting the cost and having to balance the books again.

Marc worked really hard with his training and his confidence soared. He had shaved off his beard and had his hair cut and he had also put on a few pounds looking much healthier these days. He decided to take one of the apartments in Carl's block with some of the other staff and Ivanov was like the doting father often asking Marc around for dinner with his partner Tim. Carl liked Marc and thought he was a fine young man with great promise but Tom was a little wary after the levitating stuff but he was one of them now and so he would soon be out with the gang for drinks.

Sara was taking some of her old work from her PHD on ESP for Vlad to read and as she was chatting to him in his lab, she picked up some treats for the mice.

"I thought Harry said no more mice Vlad?"

This time there were six mice. The numbers were going up.

"Oh no," he replied. "They have been breeding."

"What one at a time, I thought mice gave birth to multiples," questioned Sara.

"The others sadly died," he replied.

"I had better not find three monkeys in that cage next time I visit," she jested. There was definitely something going on but he was not for telling. Anyway, she thought to herself, "he is funding this himself and spending his own time on it so, really it was not anything to do with her or SHEALD." In truth the animals were well looked after and he even had toys for them and a heat pad. She knew that Vlad had a good heart that the others did not see, so whatever it was, it was most likely positive.

Sara took the opportunity whilst at the lab to speak with Marc and found he was settling in well at SHEALD and his new life. Marc had no formal qualification but was highly intelligent and had thrived throughout his training. He was also a good support to Ivanov in the medical centre and laboratory with its everyday running and embraced his work with enthusiasm and dedication. This included his continuous work with Ivanov on telepathy and ESP. Recently he had become much stronger, supporting the theory that because Marc's mental and physical health was improving and he was practicing his skills, it had given him a clearer and more responsive connection to his Psyche. During their conversation Sara had tried to cunningly wean out of Marc what Ivanov was doing with the animals in the lab, but to her frustration he was not giving anything away.

Harry appeared from behind the door. "Oh, hi Sara you're here, I was looking for you and wanted to check if you fancied lunch out as it's such a lovely day." "That sound great Harry, I can meet you in half an hour at your office?" replied Sara.

"Yes, that'll be fine." He blew her a kiss and made his way back to the office. Marc stared at Harry with a glazed look on his face.

"What is it, Marc?" asked Sara. He jerked back as if coming out of a sleep. "You really love him, don't you Sara?"

Sara smiled. "Yes, I do."

"Then enjoy every moment together and make the best memories ever, life is much too short." Sara was puzzled and saw a tear roll down Marc's face as he quickly wiped it away. "He is a good man your Harry" he said affectionately. Marc was so sweet and emotional at times.

That night Sara went into a deep sleep and her dreams were disturbing. She saw Harry flying in space and then there was a large bright flash and he was gone. She jolted and woke from the nightmare "Sara, Sara are you ok?" She was sat up in bed shouting, causing Harry to be concerned about her. "I'm fine Harry just a bad dream that's all." Harry pulled her closer to him and wrapped his arms around her and she felt safe again. Maybe she needed a break and some time off work. It could get intense in her job and events would pray on the mind atight resulting in nightmares. She would mention it to Harry in the morning and plan a short trip away with him.

It was Harry and Sara's first Wedding anniversary and Sara was wakened with a tray of coffee and toast with a red rose and a card on. "Happy Anniversary to my beautiful wife." Said Harry kissing her long on the lips. "I never thought that a year on from our wedding I could possibly love you more, but I do."

116

"You are such a romantic Harry and don't ever change," she replied. They had booked a few days leave to enjoy some time together and celebrate their special day. "We never got that Honeymoon, did we?" said Harry. "So, this afternoon we are off to Paris to stay in the best Hotel in town and I am going to show you the wonderful sights of Paris." Sara was thrilled. Harry had already packed their suitcases and had hired a helicopter for the weekend which was parked on the helipad at the beach house to take them both away.

"You spoil me," said Sara "I am so lucky to have you." Well said Harry, let's make some great memories, life is too short not to." She had heard that somewhere before that "life was too short." In SHEALD They all knew what that meant, as each day they all risked their lives and often found the body parts of those taken from their loved ones by the aliens. Sara always enjoyed every moment with Harry and thought how precious those memories were. The year had been eventful but had gone amazingly fast.

Every Friday afternoon Harry, Tom, Carl, and Sara congregated in the office to go through the monthly expenditures and reports for that week and this Friday was no exception. Harry's mobile was flashing as he had put it on silence and when Sara glanced down at the phone, she noticed the display illuminated the caller as "Mom." Sara stopped the conversation. "Harry, I think you need to get that call it must be important for your Mum to ring at this time." Harry agreed and answered the call whilst they all took a coffee break. Sara could tell by Harry's facial expression that it was not good news. Sara gave Carl a worrying look. "Can you give us a moment guys?" asked Sara. Carl knew something was amiss and did not question it. He signalled to Tom. "We'll continue this in the control room," proposed Carl and they both left sharply.

Harry was quiet after the call and sat with his head lowered. Sara locked the office door with the desk switch and walked slowly over to Harry. "What is it, Harry?" She asked. "It's my dad, he's been killed in a train crash in New York." They had heard about the train crash in New York on the TV news this morning but paid little attention to it, not realizing that Harry's father was involved. "It's not connected to any alien attack just a terrible accident," Harry recalled. Fifty people had been killed and this tragedy now had forty-nine other families getting the horrific news that a loved one was dead, but right now Harry could only consider his father and his grieving mother.

"I am so very sorry Harry, you must go to your mother, she needs you," Sara insisted and sat at his side holding him tightly. "I can't Sara," replied Harry, but Sara would not take this for an answer. "Harry you are going and I'm coming too, there is no excuse, this is your Mum. Carl and Tom can run things until you get back, right now the priority has to be your mother." Eventually Harry agreed. "I'm glad I have you with me Sara but it breaks my heart to think that the first time you will meet my mom will be at a time like this." "I know Harry, but it's not me you have to worry about now," said Sara.

Harry had not been back home since his brother's funeral as he had found it difficult to face his parents, feeling guilty that John had died and he had survived. It was unbearable seeing his parents so hurt over their youngest son's death and typical of Harry, when he hurt, he shut down and stayed away but Sara was not letting this happen this time. She would support her grieving husband and mother-in-law Jan, just as any other family would do. They could take a couple of days off to attend the funeral at least. Carl had arranged for the SEASKY Jet to take them to New York which meant they would be there in less than two hours.

As they arrived at the house it seemed dark and empty. Harry's Aunt Ali opened the door to greet them and took them through to the lounge were Harry's mother sat grieving her husband's loss. Harry's Mother threw her arms around her son, it had been a long time since she had seen him.

"Mom this is Sara, my wife." Harry's mum looked up and hugged her tightly. "You are as lovely as he said you were," she replied. Sara smiled and noticed the wedding picture of her and Harry hanging proudly on the wall. Harry sat by his mother's side and Sara left them to spend some time together and followed Aunt Ali into the kitchen. Aunt Ali and Sara sat talking for some time drinking coffee. Sara found her easy to talk to and felt she had known her for much longer. Harry's father Steven Saunders was sixty-three years old and was on his daily commute to his job in the city as a Banker when the train crashed. He had retired early at forty years old from the RAF after an injury that prevented him from flying and taken on a career in Banking in the City. According to Aunt Ali, they were still investigating the reason for the train crash but they believed it was to do with the driver having a heart attack at the controls.

"You know, Jan has been fighting breast cancer for the last ten years?" said Aunt Ali. "Oh, no, that's dreadful," replied Sara. Sara was stunned by the news but Jan had decided to keep it from Harry as she was mindful that he had suffered enough with his brother's loss. She had told her sister that she considered that the shock of her youngest son's death had contributed to the onset of the cancer. Sara thought how awful it was to lose her son and then be given the devastating diagnosis of cancer shortly after and whatever the reason for the cancer it was still a horrible disease to be burdened with. "I just thought it may be time you knew about it," reasoned Aunt Ali. Sara thanked her for her honesty and knew it could not have been easy for the sister to have to keep this secret for so long. She would wait until later to tell Harry, as it was enough to suffer the loss of his father at this moment and he needed to first grieve for him.

Aunt Ali had made some soup and baked cakes but was not having much luck getting her sister to eat anything yet. She showed Sara to the room where they would be staying for the night and left the bags in there before heading back to the kitchen to make coffee for everyone. Sara took the coffee and cakes into Harry and Jan but she doubted either of them would eat anything. After coffee Aunt Ali said her goodbyes and left for the day, she was glad that Harry and Sara had visited and knew this would help her sister at this troubled time. Jan lent over to Sara and held her hand, "I am glad that Harry

119

has you, he was so lost when John died. I only wish you could have met Steven, Harry's father, they were so alike. It was Dad's proudest day when Harry and John became astronauts and were working together in space. We could never have imagined how it would end so tragically. Harry has achieved so much and being a Commander gave his father such hope and pride, it was just a shame that he was so far away in England." Jan smiled at Sara, "then he wouldn't have met you, Sara. You know, fate has a strange way of bringing people together."

Harry and Sara sat with Jan until the early hours of the morning talking.

"Harry why don't you get the photo's out of the loft to show Sara."

Harry didn't argue with his mother and carried a huge old box down and placed it on the table in front of them. Harry did have a stunning resemblance to his father.

"Oh, here are some photos of Harry and John as kids," said Jan. They were young and seemed so close. Sara did not have any siblings but the photos told the story of how difficult it must have been to lose someone so close and young. Jan reminisced on the boy's childhoods and how wonderful they were.

"You'll know one day when you start a family, just don't leave it too long, it would be nice to be able to meet my grandchildren." Harry was lost for words but Sara lent over to kiss Jan.

"Well, we will have to see what we can do then," Sara was tired and it was very late, so she made her excuses and made her way up to bed, "night Jan."

Harry got up and whispered to Sara, "Thank you", It may have been a lie but on this occasion it was acceptable. Tomorrow was the funeral and would be a hard enough day for both Harry and Jan.

After the funeral Harry and Sara headed back to England. Jan held on tight to them both in the taxi to the airport.

"Take care of Harry for me," asked Jan. Her eyes looked desperate and lonely and Sara knew this would be the last time she would see Jan in the flesh. Sara hugged her and kissed her cheek.

"Bye Mom, we love you."

Sara gave Harry some extra time with his mother until it was time for the jet to leave and with a tearful sadness they journeyed back to England.

It was a further six months when Harry's Mother passed away from cancer. Despite this, they had been in regular touch with Jan through video links weekly and near the end, daily and Harry was finally able to build a bridge that had been missing for so long. He felt comforted to know that it had been rectified before she left. Furthermore, he was able to see his mother at the hospice the night before she died where she had told him that she felt ready for the next part of her journey and was grateful that her life with her two wonderful sons and loving husband had been everything she had ever hoped for. It would be the first and last time that Sara ever saw her husband cry.

# K9

Paul was discussing a therapy dog with Sara to help him around the home and office. She was telling him about a recent dog rescue service that had brought stray dogs from abroad and trained them to be working, therapy dogs. Paul was extremely interested and contacted the rescue centre within days of their conversation and after some training he was the lucky owner of a little scruffy brown cross Yorkshire terrier that he had named K9 after his favourite childhood TV show "Doctor who". The dog on TV was robotic but he thought it was appropriate with the alien theme in the story for SHEALD. He brought K9 to work every day not because he needed him but mainly because he did not want to leave him alone at home in his apartment all day. K9 loved it in the control room as everyone made a fuss of him and he had free run of the place.

He particularly liked Sara as she brought him nice treats when she came to the office and he would follow her around all day, even sitting in the office with her at her desk. Paul did not mind as he was happy to have him at work and found K9 a great companion at home. It also got all the young ladies to stop and stroke him when they saw him which gave Paul the chance to chat with them. Paul referred to K9 as having "the pulling power for the girls" and Carl had suggested that "maybe he should get a K9 too or perhaps he could borrow K9 to take for walks when he spotted a good-looking woman," but Sara made it clear, that it did not work quite like that to Carl's great disappointment.

Sara was always buying K9 jumpers, coats, and fancy collars but Harry never concerned himself with this as he put it down to the fact that she did not have a dog herself to fuss. He also felt K9 reminded her of her three- legged black rescue dog Jack who died, so he tolerated it and if it made Sara happy then he was happy. Paul was soon to have a stay in hospital for an operation on his foot. He wasn't worried about it as he had spent many years in and out of hospital with surgery as a child. It was only a routine operation so he would be home and back to normal in no time at all, but he was worried about K9. Sara had volunteered to take the dog for the week during his hospital stay which K9 was more than happy with. Though, Harry knew he would probably be sharing his bed with the mutt for the next week and he also knew that he would have no say in the matter.

Carl and Sara could be silly when they got together, they both had a similar sense of humour and were always playing practical jokes, usually on Harry. The positive side to this was that the office was a much happier place and had a lighter atmosphere since Sara's arrival and she had found her partner in crime with Carl and even though Harry showed his disapproval they often caught him having a snigger when he thought no one was watching.

"That dog is not coming with us to Lunar base," Shouted Harry. "He'll be no trouble, I can't leave him he'll fret, he's already missing Paul."

Sara held onto Harry's arm. "Please!" and fluttered her eyes at him.

"Oh, but I don't want him running around Lunar base when we're out in the interceptors. The staff there have enough to do without taking a dog for walkies or him barking while they are on the transmitters."

"I promise they will not know he's there Harry." Sara blew Harry a kiss and Harry shrugged his shoulders. Sometimes it was just easier to give in.

Carl lent over and whispered to Sara, "You're such a creep with the boss," Sara laughed, "yes but you don't know what I've got planned?" She had that look of mischief on her face that Carl knew meant trouble. Tom stayed out of it, he could tell Sara was up to something and wandered what she had planned for poor Harry. One thing he knew for sure is it would involve a scruffy dog. Tom, Carl, Harry, and Sara were at Lunar base for a catch-up session on the interceptors. Anyone who piloted an interceptor even on a rare occasion had to do ongoing  practice tests every few Months. Tom, Harry, Carl, and Sara always did theirs together. There were only three working interceptors usually but there was a fourth ship that was used for training purposes. It had the same functions apart from having two seats, one for the trainee and another seat for the mentor, so this would be sufficient for a practice test.

Leah was organising the practice run for them in the control room. "This is a test practice red alert," she transmitted. Tom, Carl, and Harry were ready in the interceptors but were waiting for Sara who was using the training ship at the other side of the building. "Interceptor One in place and ready for practice test," said Harry. "Interceptor two ready for launch" said Carl and then Tom in interceptor three was ready. Finally, Sara transmitted that she too was ready for launch and they all set off together and formed a perfect line. Tom was the first to notice something and then Carl. Sara had brought K9 and had him sat on the spare seat with a small helmet that had previously hung on the wall normally in the rest room, it fit K9 perfectly. Sara waved at them and pointed to the dog who looked as if he was enjoying the ride sat at the side of Sara. Both men fell about laughing, Harry had not noticed yet until he saw the two guys in hysterics. As he looked over to Sara, she picked the dogs paw up as if the dog were saluting him. Carl was laughing so much he could hardly see where he was going, but Harry was fuming.

"What the hell is that dog doing here?" he yelled. "I thought it would be better than having him wondering around Lunar base unattended and he has his seat belt on and helmet so he is quite safe," Sara said mockingly. "You are in so much trouble when we get back," threatened Harry. "Whoops," said Sara. Leah burst in. "Interceptors, is everything alright?" "Everything is fine Leah, over," replied Sara.

The practice flight went well without any hitches and they all returned to the landing stations intact. As they all entered Lunar base Carl and Tom made themselves scarce quickly before the shouting began. Harry grabbed Sara's arm, "just remind me why I married you, will you?" He had a red face and a stern look but Sara was not perturbed by him. Sara lent close to him and kissed him on the lips, "because you love me, for better or worse," she replied and walked on with the dog. "God woman! You'll drive me to insanity," Harry muttered. Sara smiled "I know, I know, now let's get you some treats K9!" and the dog followed happily wagging his tail. Harry headed for the canteen and entered to lots of laughter as Carl and Tom were relating the story to everyone in the room. Carl called over to Harry. "Hey, Harry that wife of yours is barking mad"! They all fell about laughing again including Harry. He never could stay mad with her for too long.

Paul's operation was a success and K9 went back to his apartment the following week but the little dog still followed Sara around at work. Sara was always taking photos as well as keeping her diary of all the events that happened at SHEALD and had a great picture of K9 in the interceptor with his helmet on that Paul kept on his desk in a frame to Harry's great displeasure.

Life ticked by happily for Harry and Sara whilst SHEALD was as busy as ever. They often had their friends around at the beach house for dinner and dined out at their friend's homes too. Carl was the habitual great cook and always made the effort to cook a vegan meal for Sara and Harry which they both found thoughtful and Fiona and Tom would have barbeques so the kids could be part of the fun. The twins loved to see Uncle Carl, Uncle Harry, and Aunty Sara as they would spoil them and give them lots of attention. The three were also God parents to the twins and Luna and Leo never wanted for anything. Marc, Paul, Vlad, and Tim had also joined the group with Ali, Leah, Jo and Saphy, this was something that everyone looked forward to, it was a chance to unwind and enjoy good company. Leah and Ali had also moved in together and recently married but there were still singletons in the friends. Carl would date but never with the same woman for more than once and Marc was "still looking." Paul on the other hand was trying to persuade a new recruit to go out on a date with him but she was "playing hard to get" at the moment, or so he said.

There had been many UFO attacks but the interceptors were getting much better at stopping them from getting to

Earth. Harry had requested the purchase of some new interceptors that would fire several smaller missiles that would be
more suitable. Instead of just one missile each and was still arguing the cost with Grant for now, but he would get them
eventually once he had worn Grant down.

They had not had any more live aliens since the earlier capture so Harry was planning to let a UFO through to Earth
then he could apprehend another extra-terrestrial to further
their knowledge. Marc was eager for another challenge and
would be better prepared at this Instance. Nevertheless,
Harry would need to put a fail-safe plan that was tight and organized to guarantee a success. Harry had already begun
preparations by organizing teams. It would require all of
SHEALD to play their part and there could be no errors. It
would be costly and Grant would be breathing down his neck
at the costs so it had to be worthy of the cause. If it were too
obvious the aliens would suspect a trap and so it would need
plenty of thought. In recent times there had been a pattern to
the UFOs Visits to Earth showing that they were more active
during certain weather conditions. The clearer the skies the
better visibility such as during the summer months and they
also had an awareness of seasonal celebrations and used these
times such as Christmas with the hope that people would be
preoccupied. Though, SHEALD was always prepared whatever the season or weather conditions.

They would need to make the crafts entrance realistic and
look as if they were defending as usual, but somehow have an
unfortunate miss, after all this did and could happen. The only
difference this time would be a planned failure to stop the
UFO getting to our world. Harry and his team were ac-
quainted with the fact that the aliens had gained knowledge
regarding SHEALD and managed to utilize some of the messages and transmissions even though they were coded. They
were familiar with Commander Saunders and General Grant
as the founders of the organization and had in past events
made attempts on both their lives endeavouring to abduct
them and of course the attempted kidnap of Sara. Hence the
high security measures that were taken to protect them.

Harry arranged with Carl and Tom to alert all stations for the conference of every member of SHEALD who would be involved. Most would be through electronic links and computerised communications but it would happen concurrently so that everyone could contribute to the discussions. Harry began "SHEALD associates I need your ears, thoughts, and expertise to bring this operation to a successful outcome. It must be seamless and precise as there will be no room for error with only one opportunity. We must be prepared and organized which will mean extra training and even more sacrifices." The presentation was mapped out for all to see as Colonel Peters delivered the proposal.

Carl took over, "As usual Lunar base will receive their alert from SAAM when the threat of a UFO comes into Luna sighting. "Red alert" will have the usual three interceptors launched for defence where each Interceptor will give chase and then fire at the UFO once on target. However, the targets will be purposely missed but interceptor two will have a small tracker device that needs to be fired directly at the craft whilst interceptor's one and three are distracting the UFO in a chase. They will then allow the UFO through the earth's atmosphere where each will report a failed hit. All SEASKY Jet fighters will be in the air ready for the signal and depending on the termination of the UFO, the SEASKY Jet fighter nearest to the predicted location will be waiting to assume the chase with the tracking device guiding them to the UFO. SEASKY will fire but will only damage the spacecraft to bring it down, it must not be destroyed therefore, a meticulous shot has to be created in order to cause just enough damage to bring the UFO to a subdued crash landing. Transporters will already be in place from the predictive determination with the land roamers. We will have a brief window of opportunity to have the UFO on land before it destructs and need to be swift with the land action. Every available vehicle and aircraft will be needed worldwide but it is hoped that the interceptor's chase will be forcing a predetermined termination of the UFOs landing. We will instigate a termination in the north of England for ease of transportation of the alien back to the SHEALD medical centre but if this is not possible it would still be viable to bring this operation to a success as far as Australia. Fingers crossed, if we keep this simple then we have less chance of failure." Harry spoke again. "Thank you, Colonel Peters, this will require skills beyond your usual requirements, but I have faith that your accomplishments are achievable. This is a huge operation and our most important endeavour yet, but I have confidence in you all and I am certain we can pull this off. Any questions?" But there was none as everyone was too focussed on the huge task ahead. Harry drew a breath. "We begin training tomorrow, don't let me down."

Everyone began their training and a week later they were prepared and equipped for the mission. When SAAM gave the "Red alert" the plan kicked into place. The adrenalin was running high as no one wanted to be the downfall of this event. It was a heavy burden on all their shoulders but this was what SHEALD did best in a crisis, they all pulled together for the greater. Tom was on duty on Lunar base with Leah and Ali so there were no mishaps. The tracker was released and fixed itself onto the UFO as the other interceptors fired as planned and veered the Craft into the chosen area for the determination on land. Captain Lee chased the craft through the clouds and for a while the spaceship escaped his chase but a burst of sunshine cleared his view and he was back on track. Jo was able to give the predictive termination in the Yorkshire Dales from Lunar base in a rural spot making it easy for the transporters to land and release the land roamers and their crew. It was slightly off the course they wanted but still achievable. Carl Commanded the land team as they closed in on the capture of the ship. The alien was now surrounded by a huge array of weaponry and aircrafts and there was no escape.

Harry listened with pride in the control room as the operation delivered the result they had needed. When the message came through from the helicopter team that they were landing at SHEALD with the alien unscathed there was a round of applause and cheering from everywhere. The sound was uplifting but deafening as excitement filled the air Harry was elated that his plan had worked and they now had the alien safely in their grip. Doctor Ivanov, Sara, and Marc were anxiously awaiting and were in post ready for the humanoid. Security was vast as at this stage no one was taking any chances. Sara headed up to the office to meet Harry who would be joining them in the lab later on for the interrogation.

The spaceship was still in one piece too being found within two hours of landing. As the land team quickly took what they could in order to gain knowledge of the materials that made the craft and the fuel content. Some of the smaller parts of the spaceship could be dismantled and saved before it destructed. These UFO specimens were to be their find of the decade and was a huge leap forward in understanding how alien life travelled millions of miles through solar systems to our world. However, it would take many years for scientists to fully unravel the significant mechanics and materials used from an alien planet as our science needed to catch up with these new technologies and chemicals not of our World. These would eventually be scientific breakthroughs of great advancement.

Harry and Sara waited for Carl and Tom to return before they headed to the laboratory. As Carl and Tom entered the office Harry got to his feet, "are Marc and Doctor Ivanov ready Sara." "I think they've been ready for the last year Commander," remarked Sara as they made their way to the lab and observation room. SEASKY and Lunar base were still on yellow alert and all staff leave had been cancelled for now. The possibility of a UFO attack was of a substantial risk if they knew that the alien had been captured and so the whole of SHEALD would need to be vigilant and ready for anything. The Alien was already in the lab and as before was strapped to the chair by his ankles and wrists for security and the safety of everyone involved. Furthermore, he was a good deal younger making him a stronger humanoid than previously. Dr Ivanov entered the room and took his place behind the alien and switched on the monitors and recording machines.

A guard stood poised with his gun in the doorway as Marc walked into the lab. Harry, Carl, Tom, and Sara where in the observation room next door, watching through the large observatory window where Doctor Tim Walker was also present with two nurses and even more monitors. It was calm at first but Marc remembered that it could change quickly as it had done last time. Sara stayed in the observation room this time as Harry refused to take any more chances with her after the previous event. Sara put the mike around her neck and began with a short meditation. Sara and Marc had been practicing and Marc was getting better at entering a state of relaxation. Soon he would not require Sara's help but she was there to support Marc emotionally until he managed alone, after all this was only his second time. Marc went into a silence as he heard Sara's voice and saw the ball of light enter the alien's brow and followed it into the being's mind, "tell us about your people?" said Ivanov. Marc took his time and felt a sharp pain in his head but this soon subsided and he began to talk.

Ivanov had developed a machine that could transfer the images from Marc's mind into pictures that would be reflected onto a screen. This was being recorded by transferring them into the observation room for Tim to a machine that was collating the images. It was still in the prototype stage and the impressions would fade in and out but it gave an innovative idea of what was being projected into Marc's mind. Marc spoke in a trance like state.

"We were once a successful race and began our space travel early on but the inward fighting and wars took over. Our land was rich with nutrients and minerals but bit by bit we destroyed the land with poisons and vicious chemicals that we made to destroy our enemies, instead we destroyed ourselves. We had no respect for the land or for life that we stole and we took it all for granted that it would always be there, how wrong we were. Bombs of great destruction ate away at the planet until we could no longer repair it and our food sources became scarce until these habitats were gone forever. The very essence of our world was slowly dying as we grew sick and sterile and less people led to less productivity. We saw trees fall and plants wither into dust never to grow again and the skies grew dark. We were arrogant and selfish and took until there was no more so now, we come to take from you. You have plenty so we do not understand why we cannot come and take what we need. We do not need your permission and if you continue to stop us, we will use force as we have in the past. If we take from you, we may survive and we will do what we have to in order to stay alive. We are much more intelligent than your race and could wipe you out in an instant if we choose to and our technology is far more advanced than any of yours. We only take a few bodies and rocks samples from your planet as we have no long-term use for you and little interest in your planet. We need a few pieces to bring us back to strength as with your insects that can help to cultivate our land again."

Harry spoke. "Can we not help each other and offer another, alternatives to killing our innocent people if we worked together? Would your leaders not consider collaborating with us instead of fighting us? You said yourself your past attitudes led to your destruction, surely peace is the best solution here?" "No, we have no interest in others. we do not need your help we can take what we want, we have no personal need for an inferior race like yours, you cannot defeat us!" Harry did not like were this was going and so changed his questioning. "Are there other alien planets? "Yes, but they did not stay as we had no need of them either so we fired at them and they left," related Marc from the alien. Images appeared on the screen of ships visiting and being attacked and then leaving. Marc was becoming more aware and in a less state of trance. "If only they had been peaceful and cooperative then they would survive. They have learned nothing from their destructiveness and continue in the same way. They are a cruel race." said Marc.

Marc was becoming distressed and his heart rate was rising as the monitor showed signs of exhaustion from his brain waves. Ivanov put up his hand. "I think that is enough for now." Sara led Marc back slowly from the light. As Marc came back and opened his eyes he got up from his chair and moved towards the alien. The alien starred chillingly into Marc's soul. "He wants me to remove the restraints. He says they are hurting him." Carl moved towards the other room; he had a feeling something was not right. "No!" said Harry, "they stay put." Marc was acting as if he was in a hypnotic trance and began removing the restraints. Next the alien had his hands around Marc's neck and was choking him. Doctor

Ivanov tried to sedate the alien with an injection but he threw him to the other side of the room and knocked him out. He held Marc by the throat, up in the air and Marc's body became limp whilst his legs wriggled as he fought for breath. Sara screamed.

"Let him go you monster!" But he was not going to until he had squeezed every ounce of life from his body. "Bang!" Carl had shot the alien through the head and he was killed instantly as Marc's body fell to the floor. Sara and the guard ran into the lab whilst Tim was seeing to Vlad and the two nurses conducted CPR on Marc's body. They had got what they wanted but paid the price or rather Marc had.

Sara, refused to leave Marc in the hospital as he was so seriously ill. There were wires and tubes everywhere and he had been put into an induced coma. As Sara sat quietly by Marc's bedside she was hoping and willing him well. Harry went home alone that night but he understood why Sara was still at the hospital. It was the kind of person she was and that was one of the reasons Harry loved her. Harry had a report to write and an investigation to bring together for Grant and the committee. Although, at the back of his mind, he felt a terrible responsibility for a young man he had brought into SHEALD whose life was holding on by a thread. Besides, he was aware that Sara would be blaming herself too. They would do everything possible to help Marc through this horrendous ordeal, but for now he just hoped that he would live.

Carl entered the medical room to a solemn sound of beeps from a hospital monitor. He whispered, "How is he doing?" Sara looked tired and teary. "He has a crushed larynx and it's still touch and go." "I'll stay for a bit with you if you like?" said Carl. Sara thanked him. "I hope that alien race die soon they have learned nothing and are self-destructive, evil, war mongers," said Sara. It wasn't like Sara to be bitter but Carl was with her on this. "The trouble is there are some people like that on Earth and if we don't learn from this it could well be us in a few centuries." He was of course right but Earth had some very caring, kind people too, so to Sara the good outweighed the bad in her eyes as these aliens were just pure evil.

Vlad was back in work two weeks later with a broken arm and foot and hobbling around. He found it difficult to be at home doing nothing and needed to be working. Tim and Vlad visited Marc every day as did Sara and slowly Marc became well again. It took a three month stay in hospital before he was allowed to go home. During which he had sustained damage to his vocal cords and could only whisper when he spoke but Marc remarked that he would do it all again for SHEALD. He still believed this was his home and he was amongst the best of people. The work he had achieved was innovative and had the world been aware of what he had achieved he would have been a Hero, Knighted, a TV Personality and all-over social media, but he was just another member of SHEALD that quietly risked tooth and nail every day.

"This would be a great time to push the new base project on Mars" said Harry, "we have the proof that there is other alien life out there." "Yes, but they don't sound aggressive at all and these lot are on their way out so, once they are gone, we will be redundant," replied Carl. "Nonsense," said Harry, "we can never be sure as long as there are other beings out there, we are always going to be at risk, anyway we can diversify. Mars could hold a base for those on long journeys to stop off and exchange communication between planets. The other aliens visited our aliens but left when they saw all the destruction and wars, they obviously didn't want that and would be more suited to us. They may need to advance their technology and so to get here could take time, but you'll see Carl, they will come and when they do we need to be ready for them. If they landed on Earth people would be afraid and think we were under attack and could attack them." He walked up and down the office in deep thought. "No, Carl, they need  somewhere safe away from fear and attack, somewhere to make decisions and deals, Mars would be perfect for that."

Carl tutted, "you could sell beer to a brewery, what a salesman you could have been."

"I'm selling Earth to the aliens, that's what I am doing and right now I'm going to be selling Mars to the committee," lectured Harry. "You'll never get it," said Carl. "Oh, but I will

Carl," replied Harry confidently. "Mars is ours." Said Harry as he left for the committee meeting. "I don't know why you bother Carl; he'll get it, he always does," said Sara. "Oh, I know he will." said Carl, "I just like winding him up before the meeting once he gets his fighting hat on there's no stop-ping him." "Honestly," said Sara, "You two are as bad as each other."

Harry came back from the meeting with a smug look on his face. Tom had arrived on duty and Sara and Carl had been explaining to him about Harry's project for a base on Mars. "So, Harry did they buy it?" asked Tom. "Had them eating out of my hands" boasted Harry. "It'll take time to convince them to raise the funds, but it will happen." "Now," said Sara, "You need to work on a shuttle that will get people to Mars in hours." Harry pondered. "Yes, I had better get on to that." He messaged Paul. "Paul, will you get me the engineers?" asked Harry. Sara looked over to Tom and Carl and mouthed, "poor General Grant."

# Tragedy

"It's two years on Thursday since we were married and it's gone so fast," said Sara to Carl.

"So, what have you got planned this year?" asked Carl.

"Oh, I don't know, Harry will come up with something he's an old romantic," said Sara.

"You know Sara, you are so lucky to have found each other, some people go a lifetime looking for the right person and never find them and most settle for much less," said Carl. Sara nodded.

"I know Carl, how lucky I am, every day I'm grateful for the time I have with Harry." Carl turned around to Harry's desk that was empty.

"So, where is the man in question?" asked Carl. "Oh, he went to Lunar base this morning" replied Sara.

"There was something needed replacing on SAAM so, he went to show Ali how to do it for next time. You know what he's like with satellites, especially SAAM you would think he had given birth to that thing the way he nurtures it," said Sara. "I hope he doesn't bring that bug back," commented Carl. "What?" asked Sara. "They have all been coming down with a sickness bug up there" replied Carl. Sara rolled her eyes. "I hope that's not what I am getting for my anniversary?" They both pulled their faces.

"I'm sorry Sara I have to stay another day as Ali has the bug and there are not enough Interceptors if needed. So, I will have to stick around until he feels better," declared Harry.

"It's ok," responded Sara, "tell Ali to get well soon and you be careful, I'll miss you Mr handsome." "Hey, look through the telescope at ten tonight and I will wave at you and shout I love you." Sara laughed, "you're crazy!" "Too much Moon atmosphere," retorted Harry and blew her a kiss down the phone, but she couldn't stop giggling at him.

Tom, Carl, and Sara were all at Headquarters whilst Harry was covering for Ali at Lunar base. Tom was finishing for the weekend today and was catching up on some reports for Harry. Sara was working with Paul on the new radar as she wanted to make sure she knew how the new system worked in case she had to show any other staff. Carl was standing in for Harry as second in Command in Harry's office which they all referred to as the "hot seat." None of them were particular to holding the fort for the Commander as it was such a great responsibility and it never stopped.

SAAM put Lunar base on "Green alert" with a possible sighting. Carl and Tom made their way to the control room to Sara and Paul. Within a minute the code changed to "Red alert." Harry had not been on a real call out on an interceptor in a while but he was proficient enough to handle the challenge. "Interceptor one A okay," reported Harry. Then Came two and three interceptors. As they flew into the area a sudden flash caught Harry's eyes, it was interceptor two with Lieutenant Pete Davis who was a recent recruit. He had been hit and fell through space, exploding into nothing. When Harry looked again, he could see a second UFO SAAM sounded another "red alert." The UFO fired at interceptor three. "This is Interceptor three, I've been hit" reported AJ. Carl took charge of the radio. "Interceptor three how bad is the hit?" "I'm losing power sir, looks like the engine is damage." replied AJ. "Back to base Interceptor three, immediately," ordered Carl, as AJ returned, he fired at the second UFO but the damage he made was minimum and the UFO was still in flight. "Interceptor one return to base. I repeat interceptor One return to base now" called Carl. Interceptor three was almost back at base and thankfully safe.

"Don't worry Harry, we'll get them once they are through the atmosphere, just get back, there is nothing you can do, you only have one missile and there's two of them," said Carl. "Roger," replied Harry, "on my return now." SAMM interrupted. "Red alert, third UFO sighted and heading in the same direction". Sara felt her heart miss a beat. "Harry, please, get out of there now!" she said nervously. "I can't" replied Harry, "they've surrounded me," Harry sounded de-

feated. "This is a set up; they know who's in this ship other-wise, I would have
been blown away by now. I can't go anywhere; they want me alive for now I'm sure of it." Carl was horrified. "Don't worry Harry, we'll get you out of there." "No, Carl you won't, It's over, there's only one way out of this." Harry's tone of voice was lower. "No," said Sara. "You've got to find a way-out Harry." "They want me Sara and if they think they are going to get me alive and force everything about SHEALD out of me and threaten our world then they are very mistaken," said Harry.

"It's set, Code black," said Harry. Carl dropped his head down. "What does that mean Carl?" Sara was in panic now. "I'm sorry Sara I've detonated the missile; it will go up and take all of them out. "No!" Screamed Sara. "Harry, get out of there, you can't leave me, please!" Harry spoke calmly. "It's done and there's no going back now." Tears streamed down Sara's face; she was in deep shock. Harry asked Carl to turn on the SHEALD speakers, this would allow everyone includ-ing Lunar base, The medical centre, SEASKY and General Grants office to receive his voice. "Are you sure?" said Carl. "Please Carl" asked Harry. Carl nodded to Paul and the mes-sage from Harry went worldwide throughout the whole orga-nization. Vlad, Marc, and Tim rushed into the control room. Everyone was listening intently as Harry spoke Calmly. "I only have three minutes before this bomb blows. I can't let them take me with what I know, it's much too dangerous. I've always known it could happen. Sara don't grieve for me too long. I don't want you wasting your life like that. Life's too short, I want you to live your life for both of us. You've made me the happiest man ever for the last two years, I really have never been happier." Sara sobbed.

"Carl My friend, it all falls on your shoulders now I'm afraid, but I wouldn't have made you my second in command if I didn't think you could do it. You will do it your way and that's how it will be. Live your life well my friend and take care of Sara for me, will you?" Carl teared up, "I promise mate." Then Harry turned to Tom "Tom, you'll be the sec-ond in command and one day you'll take the reins and I know you'll do me proud. "You can count on me Sir," said Tom as he saluted him through the airwaves. "Look after those gorgeous twins and tell Fiona you love her every day." Tom nodded his head, as he was too distressed to speak. Harry addressed General Grant. "General, I know we didn't always see eye to eye all the time but we shared a mission and we did it. We started it together and it looks like you will finish it. You always did have the last word," joked Harry. "There's so much I want to say to you all but I am afraid my time is running out. To all of you who risk your lives every day I thank you from the bottom of my heart and if I shouted at you I did it because I cared, but I am so proud of each and every one of you. Remember me and keep up the magnificent work and don't let it all be for nothing. There's not much time now." Sara rushed in "Harry, I love you so much.... to the moon and back." Harry gulp, "and beyond my beautiful wife." There was a large explosion and Leah reported with a tremble in her voice, "all UFOs destroyed." Harry was gone forever.

Sara fell back screaming "No, no!" as Carl grabbed her and held her tight to him with a tearful look, holding back his emotions. Vlad slipped a jab into Sara's arm and she fell into unconsciousness. Carl picked her up in his arms and took her down to the medical wing, Vlad, Tim, and Marc followed him down. There was a terrible silence and sobbing everywhere. Tom tried to get a hold of the situation the best way he could and shouted to the team. "Ok everyone, I need you to get back to work, we can deal with anything else later. Paul, put us into code C (Critical) for now, until we get things on track." Paul shook himself and wiped his face of tears. He transmitted "Code C, Repeat Code C" and then he switched off the transmitter. It was all over.

Carl rushed Sara into the medical centre and Vlad showed him to a hospital bed. "Put her there." He patted Carl on the shoulder, "you go, I will take care of her from here, you have much to do." It was all still hazy for Carl and he hadn't got his head around anything, it was so surreal and he didn't know where to start. He walked slowly back to the office. He had just lost his best friend, his boss, and his mentor. "How was he supposed to walk in the shoes of a great man like

Harry? Harry was SHEALD." Carl recalled their first day to-gether, SHEALD had not even been built then and was just a plan on Grant's desk. "Poor Sara, how would she ever get over Harry? truthfully, she wouldn't but he would look after her as he had promised Harry and try not to let either of them down."

Tom and Carl stayed at the office all night and messaged all staff to ask if anyone wanted to take time out after the tragedy, but not one staff member accepted there offer and all turned up for work the following day. Naturally, there was no banter or laughter for days after but they got the job done to their best. Carl had visited the Davis family that night to tell them that their twenty-five years old son had been killed in action. He could still hear the screams and wails of his mother in his ears as he drove back to the office. Pete Davis was the baby of his family and Carl remembered Pete's first day at SHEALD and thought at the time how young he seemed; his life had just begun but now he was dead. There would be no wedding day or grandchildren for them, just a funeral without a body. He pulled the car over to the side of the road as he vomited. "Get a grip Peters," he said to him-self, "the whole world depends on you from now on." That was a terrifying thought, he had no idea how Harry had done it and made it look so easy but Harry was special and he was just a guy from London.

Grant arrived the following morning, he had come to offer support especially to Carl and Tom. Sara was going to be let home that day but was in no fit state to be left on her own. She had been sedated so was not fully alert. Grant suggested Carl stayed with Sara for the first night and he would cover the office to let Tom take the weekend off so he could be with his family. Then the two men would take over on Mon-day morning. This would give them time to digest what had happened and what needed to be done.

Later that day Carl went to collect Sara from the hospital, she was still in terrible shock and heavily drugged. Carl helped her to the car and took her back to the beach house. She leaned on Carl as she had no strength or will to do any-thing and had completely shut down on herself. Carl guided her to the sofa and sat her down and made her a coffee, but when he gave her the cup, she shook so much she was unable to hold it. Carl held the cup for her so she could drink. It was sad for Carl to see the usually bubbly strong woman unable to even hold a cup to drink but Sara was too distraught, "I can't go on Carl, not without Harry," she cried. "You will, your strong and you have to for Harry, it can't all be for nothing Sara." He put his arms around her shoulders and she sobbed uncontrollably into his chest. He did not know what to do or how to make this right as she finally, fell asleep. She needed to rest, so he decided to pick Sara up into his arms and carry her to the bedroom where he lay her on the bed. There he removed her shoes and threw the duvet over her and sat quietly on the chair at the side of her bed. He was exhausted as he put his hands into his head and felt the burden of the world on his shoulders and wept. "How was he ever going to do this? But he would have to, somehow, everyone depended on him now."

Throughout the night Carl could hear Sara crying in her sleep and calling out Harry's name, but there was little he could do and when morning came Leah and Ali arrived to relieve Carl so he could go home. They would stay both day and night with Sara. There was little said as Carl left, he was drained emotionally and physically and there was a terrible emptiness.

# Life After Harry

The following months were difficult for SHEALD and Carl and Tom fought their way through the days until finally it all started to come together again. Harry's funeral was a Military affair and those who were working watched on the screens. Sara was still coming to terms with Harry's death and the fact that there was no body to cremate hurt even more. For many nights she felt Harry close to her and sometimes even felt his arms around her whilst she slept.

In her dreams he would be there smiling at her with his radiant blue eyes, tall and as handsome as ever and usually in his Military uniform that he wore when they were married. She would hear the strong American accent saying. "I love you to the Moon and back and beyond," but when she woke, she would find him gone and she was alone. She rambled around the large house and walked on the beach every night looking at the stars and to the Moon, talking to Harry but he never answered back.

Everyone from work sent their kind thoughts to Sara and there were many visitors. Especially Carl, Tom, Fiona, Leah, Ali, and Marc. Carl became Sara's rock, always there for her just as he had been for Harry. She had noticed that he joked less these days, then again, he did not have a great deal to joke about anymore and after two months at home Sara decided it was time to return to SHEALD. She knew she had to at some point and that time had now arrived. It was now or never.

It was sad to see Sara looking so pale and thin, she had lost her light and her face said it all. She was nervous at the thought of going back to SHEALD as the last time she was there she was witnessing the death of her husband. Everyone turned as she entered and there was an awkward silence. They all knew that even though they were glad to see her this wasn't a particularly happy day; they too were all still grieving for their Commander. Carl strolled up to Sara.

"Ah, Sara, come, we have a lot to catch up on." K9 broke the ice and ran up to her wagging his tail and Sara bent down to stroke him "I'm sorry K9 I forgot to bring you some treats" she said softly. She had lost all her confidence and joviality but K9 did not seem to bother and still followed her into the office. "Good to see you," said Paul. Sara smiled and tapped his arm in approval.

Now it was up to Carl to try and bring some normality back to the place as he had been doing for some time since Harry had gone. Tom had been a good support as had General Grant. Sara looked around the office, nothing had changed but Carl sat on another desk in the office close to Harry's desk but not at his. Sara thought that was a thoughtful gesture as seeing Carl sitting at Harry's desk would have been hard.

The first week back was the most difficult as around every corner there were memories of Harry and people were wary of saying something that would upset Sara, which was thoughtful but tedious. By the second week she noticed a group surrounding a box which they were trying to hide when she entered the room. Paul quickly put the box under his desk but Sara was tired of secrecy around her and the way that they all tip toed about, it made her feel isolated. That was not how Sara was, she needed to be part of SHEALD and for others to be open with her again. Sara walked over to Paul's desk and took the box from under his desk. Paul said nothing and awaited her response in anticipation.

On the box was written "The Commander's Statue." Sara opened the box and found many notes. There were bids of money from all the staff some bids were of a hundred pounds. Carl and Tom came close up to her when they noticed her with the box and Tom took the box away. "Sorry, Sara, we didn't want you to see it yet, we were not sure you were ready," said Carl. "I'm ready," said Sara. "Please, I need you all to be as you were with me before, I've lost enough and I can't lose you guys too." Paul turned to Sara, "you know how we all respected the Commander and it was him who put SHEALD together yet to the world out there he isn't known.

We thought that we would have a statue as a monument to him with a Garden and a remembrance plaque were those who died in service could be inscribed to remember them forever. Staff could sit on a bench and look at the great man who inspired us all and the commander could continue to influence new staff even though they had never met him. Lieutenant Pete Davis will be inscribed on the plaque for his bravery too and we can celebrate all their lives and one day, when the world is less fearful maybe they will get to know what they did." Sara's eyes were moist but she was so proud of Harry and those she worked with. "I think it's a marvellous idea and thank you everyone and I too would love to contribute if you would allow me." Tom Spoke. "We are a family here Sara, one of us hurts, we all hurt." Sara smiled, this was her family and she was grateful to them all for their support and love.

Carl was on his way to see General Grant about the plans for the base on Mars and asked Sara if she would like to accompany him to the meeting. He knew that the General was less likely to shout at him if she was there. "Good morning, General," said Carl. "Commander Peters, ah, good to see you back Sara and how are you?" He asked. "Fine, thank you sir, I have been surrounded by good people who have been supportive and given me strength," responded Sara. He smiled. "Good, well let's get down to business and keep the costs down for god's sake," he begged. There was still a lot to do and an engineer and architect were also present at the meeting to advise were possible. There were parts that needed changing and although they had some previous experience when they built on the moon this was a new project and they wanted to improve on this as it was much bigger and further away. So, it would be complicated and take longer to build. They had the expertise, now all they needed was definite funding. "Ok I can't see how we can improve on it anymore at this stage so, I will take the rough draft to the committee tomorrow." This would be a multibillion-dollar project and even though it would be split up into each country contributing separately, it was still a big ask.

There were other ways by incorporating NASA somewhere into this with a separate training facility and a docking station for them to use and even stay over if they had to whilst working on their programmes and certain projects in the vicinity. Sara had been discussing with Doctor Ivanov the potential of a Terra Forma project on Mars but this would take many years to come into actualization. They were both aware that scientists were keen to do this and had already begun research papers on this subject. Recently, Mars had shown signs of water from the past and by releasing certain gases from the planet it was possible to allow some formation of plant life eventually to exist. Once this was possible it would create the start of oxygen and water coming back to the planet just as Earth had been formed. Seeds from out of space had made their way to Earth and planted in the ground forming Microbes, plant life, insects, oxygen, water, animals and eventually Man.

This had taken millions of years to develop but it was possible and if this began now it would be a start of a promising future many years later. This was beyond SHEALD but there were Governments and scientists willing and able and if they could get them on board it would help with the costing. The only difficulty was to keep SHEALD classified and out of the picture though, it could be done if the will was there. The NASA station would be an easier task as they would just have a separate base. There was enough room on Mars for them all Including aliens. The possibilities were endless. It would be called the Saunders project after Harry; Sara knew that he would have been thrilled to have the base named after him, especially as it was originally his idea.

Back at the office Sara was searching through the drawers for a spare computer cable when she noticed that one of the drawers was locked and there was no key available. This was Harry's personal drawer and no one had the heart to break it open so it had remained closed. The office was empty and Sara wanted to see inside her late husband's drawer, as there may be precious memories in it. Sara thought for a moment, "where would Harry keep the key? "Yes! he always kept it under the desk with some blue tac and sure enough there it was.

At first, she hesitated, "was it too soon for her?" it would be upsetting but her curiosity was getting the better of her. There was an old photograph of Harry's younger brother John, they looked alike. "Now they would be together," she thought.

This was pitiful that they had both been killed by the aliens. Though, Harry had given them a good run and had more than avenged his brother's death, several times over. As she rummaged further in the drawer, she came across another small picture of her and Harry on their wedding day that Tom took and just behind it was a larger photo of Tom, Carl, Harry, and herself standing just outside the entrance to SHEALD. They were all so happy and stood close to each other. Sara was in the middle with Harry on one side and Carl and Tom on the other. On the back Harry had written "The Fab four," she liked that, yet she felt her heart break a little more, as she longed for those days when they were all together and happy. She heard a jangle as she pushed her hand around the drawer and there it was. The silver keyring with the moon and earth hanging from it with the inscription, "Love you to the moon and back and beyond," that Sara had given to Harry all that time ago. The one that he took everywhere with him and meant so much to him. He did not take it to the Lunar base as it housed his keys for his car and he had no use for it up there so had locked it away safely. She had something of Harry's that he treasured and was not destroyed by the aliens, they could never destroy their love and the proof was right in front of her. She squeezed the keyring tight in her hand and then placed it back into the drawer. Her wedding and engagement ring where staring back at her and she did not know why she did it but she felt compelled to remove them and put them with the keyring. She also removed her bracelet that Harry had given her and put that with the other mementos. It felt right that they should all be together as she locked the drawer and returned the key to the blue tac under the desk.

The artist who would sculpture Harry had contacted Sara for her approval and wanted to know more about the Commander. Zoe Rosenburg came highly recommended and When Zoe removed the clay sculpture that would eventually be put into a bronze cast, Sara was overwhelmed, as Harry was standing there in front of her. Whilst the two women chatted Sara felt It was an emotional journey for her, but at the same time it was comforting to talk about him again. It felt therapeutic to talk about him to a complete stranger who listened without any judgement and of course, Sara did not disclose too much regarding his work. Instead, Sara talked more about the man he was. Harry had a degree in astrophysics, was an astronaut and a pilot and the commander of a large organization. He was a brave, highly intelligent person, a searcher of truth and extremely loyal to others, but most of all he was a loving, caring and compassionate man. He fought for justice but he fought just as much for those he loved and eventually his need to protect others led to his death. Sara mentioned Harry's great love for space and Sara showed the keyring that she had made for Harry and its significance to them both as she described how it had become a symbol of their love. Zoe was stirred by the story of the keyring and asked Sara if she could incorporate it into the statue which Sara agreed to happily. That way Harry would be holding the keyring just as he always did in life and now it would be for eternity. Before Sara left, she thought about the wedding and engagement rings she had and asked Zoe if there was some way of adding them into the statue too. They were wasted hidden in a drawer as Sara could not wear them so close to her skin, it was too painful to be reminded of his loss and tore at her heart. Zoe gave a moment's thought. "Leave it with me Sara, I am sure I can do something."

When the statue arrived at SHEALD it was erected in the remembrance garden with the commemoration plaque. Sara and all the staff at Headquarters came along to the unveiling. As General Grant unveiled the statue there was a gasp from everyone, he looked handsome, important, kind, and powerful, just as he really was. Zoe had captured the very essence of him and in his hand was the keyring with the moon and earth on it with its inscription and on his left hand lay a golden wedding ring made from the rings Sara had given her. He may not have had his blue eyes but, the artist had placed a diamond in each of the pupils from Sara's engagement ring. Everyone clapped and some shed a tear but they all felt the pride from seeing their commander back where he belonged. On the small inscription at the base of the statue read: *"Comman-*

*der Harry Saunders aged 37 years. Died 20th November 2024 fighting to defend the world from its evils. "To the Moon and back and beyond."*

It was the first anniversary of Harry's death when Carl received the phone call. NASA were doing their yearly clear up of space junk for safety reason's when they had come across some of the pieces of Harry's interceptor and some remains of a body. The remains were small but they felt it only right that they should be returned to their loved ones. After DNA identification they were cremated and were being returned today in a sealed container to headquarters for Sara. Carl wasn't sure how Sara would take this news and was not looking forward to telling her.

As soon as Sara walked into the office and saw Carl's face, she knew something was not right. He sat Sara down and gently unravelled the story of Harry's ashes. Although she was glad that she had something of Harry back she felt hurt. "They've brought parts of him back to Earth he would never have wanted that, he wanted to be up in the stars in space, which was his heaven. He said that when he died, he wanted his ashes to be released into space. Explained Sara. Carl held Sara's hand and spoke softly to her. "Then that is what we shall do Sara, we will scatter his ashes in space, me and you, together." It would be a way for Sara to say her final goodbye to Harry with his best friend at her side. Carl began making plans with Lunar base straight away.

Both Carl and Sara travelled to lunar base on the Lunar shuttle with few words said from both of them. This was a solemn occasion but it was the right thing to do. As they proceeded their journey, they were both in thought of Harry. Sometimes it did not feel real that he was gone and that he would come charging through the office with all his demands. Sara thought of the time that Harry had taken her out into space for a date and how they had floated together in peace. At that time, she could never have imagined that three years on she would be doing the same with his best friend and letting go of his ashes, "How could life be so brutal?"

149

They were greeted by all the friendly faces at Lunar base though they were not as cheery as usual. Leah helped Sara into her spacesuit and hugged her. "Good luck." Sara turned to Carl and mouthed, "ready?" Carl nodded and they entered the craft that would take them further into space. Carl checked the camera on his suit so that all at Lunar base would be able to watch on screen. Ali and AJ were flying the craft and had come to the planned destination. Ali tapped on Carl's Helmet to let them know they were ready and AJ opened the door after testing that their attachment lines were secure and then signalled for them to go. Carl took the lead and held onto Sara's hand as he went through the door followed by Sara.

Their eyes met and Carl nodded and smiled as if to say it would be OK. The microphones in their helmets were switched on. As they floated around, she remembered how beautiful it was with Harry as the tears ran freely down her cheeks. Carl stretched out to the box that he was holding and passed it to Sara. She opened the container and let the ashes slowly float out into space. "Goodbye my old friend," said Carl. For a brief moment, Sara did not want to let him go but she knew she had to. It was like losing Harry all over again for them both and as the ashes drifted deeper into space the dust seemed to glow against the darkened space and just at that moment Sara felt Harry was with them. She imagined Harry would at last be at peace as he floated in his own paradise.

On their return Sara said nothing and as Carl held her, she let her tears go. When they arrived back at Lunar base Leah, Jo and Saphy were waiting for them with a tearful greeting. "It was so beautiful Sara," said Leah. "Now he will always be with us when we look outside of here. Sara and Carl did not stay at Lunar base that night as they were both ready to return to Earth. They had achieved the duty for Harry and that was enough and though it would be nearly two more hours before they arrived back it was good to be home. Carl stayed over at Sara's that night as she was in a fragile state and he did not want to leave her. "Thank you, Carl for being there for me, you are a truly wonderful friend," acknowledged Sara. "I'll always be there for you Sara, I promise," he responded and she knew he would be.

Tom and Fiona's twins were 3 years old now and were running around the office being chased by "The Sweety Monster" alias Uncle Carl, he would act all silly with the kids when he saw them and Luna and Leo loved it.

"Aunty Sara, where's the doggie?" asked Luna but K9 had made a swift exit and was hiding under Paul's desk until the coast was clear. He liked finding their sweets but he found the twins rather noisy and Leo was always pulling on his tail, no matter how many times Tom told him to stop.

"Oh, Luna I think K9 has gone for a sleep, he's tired," replied Sara. Fiona had gone to see her mother in hospital and Tom had been left in charge. Tom had once said he would rather look after a fleet of alien UFOs as they were less trouble that the little monsters he had, but he did not really mean it or at least they thought he didn't. Sara and Carl loved seeing them and loved their energy. So, Tom thought he would amuse them at SHEALD. After all they were much too young to understand what they were really doing at SHEALD, meaning there was no security risk.

Sara had hidden sweets all around the office for Luna and Leo to find but between K9 and Carl most had already been eaten so she had to go around and put more sweets out again.

"Aunty Sara, I found one," said Leo. Carl was still pretending to be the "sweety monster" and pinch all the toffees and was lurching behind Leo who was now screaming and hiding behind Sara giggling away.

Tom raised his voice in authority. "Right, you two, get your coats on, it's time to say goodbye to Aunty Sara and Uncle Carl." Both the twins were unhappy about leaving as they were having such fun. Tom turned to Sara and Carl, "they will be on the ceiling with all that sugar and excitement, pity I can't work tonight, Fiona will go mad." Sara whispered "sorry," but Tom just laughed, he didn't mind he loved seeing their faces light up when they saw Sara and Carl. They gave the kids a kiss and said goodbye but they could still hear them all the way along the corridors, until they had left the building, giggling loudly. Now K9 was back in the room clearing up the left-over sweeties before Carl got to them first! Sara was still laughing when they had gone, they were such a delight. "You see Sara why being aunty and uncle is better as we get the best bits. Sara tutted. "You are more of a big kid than the twins Mr Carl Peters." He smirked as he found another sweet and popped it into his mouth. There was laughter again in the office and it felt good.

It had been two years since Harry died and SHEALD was back on its feet. They were still waiting for the go ahead on Mars to be built as the funding had still not been fully approved. The group of friends had begun meeting again as before and dinner was always a pleasant distraction from the stresses of work. Marc had recovered from the alien attack but still had problems with his voice and was told this would continue in the same manner for the rest of his life, but he had learned to live with it and everyone was able to understand what he was saying albeit, quietly. He had learnt some simple signing that helped those who knew him, such as "ok, cuppa, car, hungry, yes and no." They were easy signs that anyone could easily work out, meaning that Marc did not have to keep repeating himself.

Marc had recently been collaborating with Doctor Ivanov and Sara on "Remote viewing" which could be especially useful against the aliens, but for now they were practicing more locally. The signs were looking very promising but it was still hard to prove if it was getting the right results. Remote viewing is a way in which a person uses their mind and psychic ability to journey from the body to a specific place and view what is happening somewhere else. This had been used in the past for spying on enemy weaponry and a way of getting through secu rity as there was no person just a thought looking in. They had recently attempted some remote viewing on a near Military base who were designing a new aircraft of great speed that was top secret. Carl had shown their Commander a drawing of what Marc had seen and although he denied this, the look on his face was enough to tell Carl that

Marc had mastered it. Twelve months later Carl witness the launch of this very craft at the same Military base.

Sara was about to drop off the report to Vlad's office when she heard a screech coming from one of the research labs which Sounded like a monkey. She entered to find a baby monkey with the two other male monkeys. Vlad had seen Sara enter the lab and followed her in quickly.

Sara confronted Vlad, "have you been buying monkeys again Vlad?" Vlad wriggled nervously, "No, I am trying to breed them," said Vlad.

"I'm not stupid Vlad, the other two monkeys are male so there is no way you are breeding them," challenged Sara.

Vlad held his hand up "Ok, I will tell you, but you had better sit down first, it may take some time to explain. Vlad began, "I have been working hard for years on something incredibly special. It was your unfortunate attack from the aliens that gave me the idea. Without your womb you cannot hold a baby even though you still have ovaries it is impossible to carry a baby through gestation. Yes, there are some choices such as adoptions but of someone else's child or surrogate motherhood, which may have its own risks and these are not for everyone and I think they are not for you. What if you could have your own child by your egg and your partners sperm to be fertilised and the embryo put into a womb that did not have any connection to anyone else? Where you could watch your baby grow and develop and witness the baby being born similar to if that womb was in your own body not in someone else's?" Sara listened though she was not sure where this was going. There are so many women like yourself who have been robbed of the opportunity of motherhood because they have no womb due to illness, disease, accident or that they have been born that way. I saw the agony of loss on your face when we had to tell you, you could no longer bear a child and it stayed with me and I knew I had to do something. If only I could replicate the womb in a simulated way. All I would need would be a fertilized egg and the right nutrients that are given via the umbilical cord at the right temperature and so. The cycle of gestation for animals varies in each species as you are aware and my early experiments were with mice. They were never harmed or dissected; I promise you."

Sara was baffled but listened to try and understand. "The embryo's that did not make it were disposed accordingly but once they began to grow, they went full term, some were less than their natural gestation period but they still survived with an incubator."

It was all beginning to make sense to Sara now.

"So," asked Sara, "the mice were not born naturally?"

"Only two were, the rest I used the simulated womb system, as I call it, I haven't got a name yet."

"But that is only on mice?" suggested Sara.

"Yes, but I have recently tried successfully on primates," said Vlad.

"The monkeys?" guessed Sara.

"Yes, it is still early days and I have quite a way to go before it can be redesigned for humans, but it can be done." He put his hands together as in prayer.

"Sara, I beg of you, please do not speak of this to anyone. Think of the good and happiness it can bring to so many?"

It was a lot to take in but she supposed a lot of scientists started out this way and she could not stand in the way of progress.

"I may not be jumping for joy about this but you have my word Vlad, your secret is safe with me." He held her hand "thank you, thank you Sara." She left stunned by what she had heard and unsure about the ethics of this, but he did have a point. The chance of having a child when you were unable to, was nothing short of a miracle.

# Moving On

Sara looked around the house. It was such a beautiful home and Harry and her had been incredibly happy there but she did not feel it was home anymore.

Harry once said to her when they first met that "it was just somewhere to sleep." Because he was alone at the house in those days and now, she felt exactly the same. It had lost its warmth and love and she was isolated. "Was it time to move on?"

Carl was on his way to meet the committee with General Grant and was trying his best to look smart with a tie but it was not going well.

Sara laughed at him, "Come here I'll do it!" offered Sara.

"Oh, thanks Sara it just won't sit right when I do it." said Carl gratefully.

She leaned in to neaten up the knot and as she checked on her efforts she glanced up at Carl. He was looking down into her eyes and their eyes met and something stirred in Sara. He had such kind; emotional eyes and she felt her soul connecting with his. She wanted to lean in even more and kiss him. She shook the thought from her mind.

"What am I doing?" She thought to herself. Just then Tom walked in.

"Ooh, what you two up to, you should have locked the door first?" He taunted. They both looked awkward. "I was making sure he was presentable for the meeting; he couldn't do his tie," clarified Sara.

"So, that was all you were doing?" smirked Tom, "listen you don't need to make excuses to me, your both single and old enough to do whatever you want." Sara left the office looking rather embarrassed.

"What did you say that for Tom?" asserted Carl. "What's up with you two, I was only joking," replied Tom. Carl did not

understand what Tom was going on about Sara, was just being her usual "mother hen" as always.

Sara had never felt like that around Carl before, he had
been her rock and always there for her and he had been her
husband's best friend. Its wasn't right to have feelings like that
about him. They had always been close and had joked around
all the time but that was different. Sara had begun to notice
Carl in a different way lately, his aftershave smelt good and
she had thought he was much more handsome these days. He
had always been just Carl before but now she saw him in a
different light. He was a wonderful friend to her and she
would never ruin that, if she lost Carl now, she would never
forgive herself. Anyway, it was probably part of the healing
process and was most likely a sign that she was ready to move
forward and put Harry in the background. Though she would
never stop loving or forget Harry and he had told her to live
her life which she hadn't done for a long time, but it could
never be with Carl."

Sara's phone rang in the office at the other side of the room
on her desk from where she was standing. "Carl, could you
answer my phone for me and take a message please." She was
on the other phone to the General's secretary. Carl picked up
the phone and took the message. When she had finished her
call, she looked over to Carl to find out what the message was
but Carl looked serious and locked the office door by press-
ing the button. The "do not enter" sign appeared outside.

"That was the estate agent Sara, are you thinking of moving
away?" Sara sighed, "Yes, I'm going to sell the house." She
put her head down. "It's time to move on Carl, I can't rattle
around that big empty house on my own anymore." "I see,"
said Carl, "maybe your right Sara, perhaps it is time for
change." Contemplated Carl. "I need to Carl; it's been over
two years now and I want to start living again." Carl nodded,
"yes, I get it Sara. Actually, I think I need to do the same."
"You do?" quizzed Sara. "It could be time I left the old bachelor pad too." "Oh, so are you're thinking of starting to date
again? I mean, you haven't done that in ages," teased Sara.
"No!" answered Carl "I mean, grow up a bit and get a home
instead of a singles pad." "Right," responded Sara. Carl turned

the tables on Sara and teased her back. "Perhaps, its time you started dating again, it would do you good to meet someone and be happy again?" Sara pulled her face. "It was never for me the dating game, I couldn't do all that dating stuff, getting to know someone all over again and then the disappointment when they don't turn out to be who you thought they were. At my age they all come with baggage and I don't think I have the patience for all that now. Anyway, I'm all right as I am, I have friends and a decent social life, so I want to keep moving forward, you know what I mean?" Clarified Sara. Carl changed the mood. "You know Sara, we will probably be eighty years old and still single, flying planes and teaching combat!" "Most probably and what's wrong with that?" laughed Sara.

"So," said Sara, "what did the estate agent say?" "They have a viewing for you tonight and it looks promising," relayed Carl. "That was quick," said Sara. "Well, it is a lovely home for the right person or people. Have you looked at any houses for you yet?" asked Carl. "Funny enough, I am going to look at three possible places tomorrow," she replied. "Do you want a second opinion; I could come with you if you like?" said Carl. "That would be great Carl, it's good to have another pair of eyes and you know me well enough to know what I like, you can be my voice of reason," said Sara. Sara was happy to have Carl with her to support her through this important part in her life.

The estate agent called Sara back shortly after the viewing to tell her that the young couple were, moving back to England from New Zealand after a success in business. They loved the house and had made a good offer that Sara accepted without question. They also wanted all the furniture which would be better for Sara as she wanted a fresh start and it would save time removing it all. Money wasn't an issue so she could easily afford to buy new. The buyers would be returning permanently to England in two months and as cash buyers they wanted the sale to be through to move into by then and Sara was happy to oblige. She would rent somewhere until she found her new home.

Carl picked Sara up the following day to view the houses and suggested that he drove so that Sara could take in the surrounding area properly. The first two places were not suitable and she did not feel she could make them her home. It wasn't something to be rushed into and if it didn't feel right then she would keep looking until it did. Carl pulled up to the third house and Sara looked around, it certainly looked inviting from the outside. The detached cottage was set in a pretty garden with a long and spacious drive. It was closer to SHEALD too so the commute would be less which appealed to Sara especially on dark winter nights. It was in a rural area but was spaciously scattered with other properties around but at a distance so they would not intervene on her privacy. "Didn't you used to live in a cottage before you met Harry?" asked Carl. "Yes, and I also lived in a farmhouse as a child, said Sara. "This really is a lovely place, Sara; I think I could go for this myself. It's homely, warm, and inviting, this is you Sara, I can see you here," encouraged Carl.

As Sara walked around it felt right and each room was just as Sara would have liked it to be. It had a large stone fireplace in the lounge that was a good central point with large windows that let the light in and a lovely view of the gardens. A kitchen veered off with a utility room and at the end was a large dining room and hidden away at the back was a study. An orangery led off from the dining room revealing a pretty back garden with a pond and a dove cote. She could see herself sitting in the garden in the evenings through the summer, feeding the birds and visiting squirrels. Upstairs were two large bedrooms and a smaller third bedroom. The master had an ensuite and dressing room which would take all of Saras clothing. "This is the one Carl, I love it!" informed Sara excitedly. Carl agreed and hoped that Sara would find contentment hear and be at peace with her past.

Sara's offer on the house was accepted and Carl and Sara went for dinner to celebrate her good news. The solicitor had informed Sara that it would take a further two months from the sale of her home before the cottage could be finalized, but Sara was not deterred. "I'll rent an apartment for a few months" said Sara to Carl. "Or you could stay with me for the time. I have a spare bedroom that isn't being used so you could stay there if you don't mind sharing a bachelor pad with me?" suggested Carl. It was a touching thought but would be a lot to ask for two months.

"Thank you, Carl, but I couldn't accept," said Sara.

"Why not?" asked Carl, "I said I would always look out for you and it would be company for me having a house guest. We get along ok, don't we? what do you say?" said Carl. "Only if you are sure and if you get fed up with me you must tell me and I will go and not take offence." "So, are we agreed then?" asked Carl. Sara smiled and kissed him on the cheek. "Thank you, I would love to." It would be a couple more months before Sara sold the house so there was still time for Carl to change his mind and if he did, she would be fine with it. She knew Carl had a big heart and would always help her out but she did not want to take advantage of his good nature and she was hoping he would help her to move!

Carl was cleaning up his desk when Sara walked into the office the following morning "General Grants on his way in. God knows why? must be serious if he's coming," said Carl. Tom had just informed the team and they were making the place look busy ready for his arrival and Sara made herself scarce in the control room. General Grant arrived on time as always. Sara had recently been promoted to Colonel and Grant had been the one to inform her of this so, Sara was not perturbed that she was the issue and, in any case, the General had a soft spot for Sara so, she was never at the end of his criticism. Tom was also in the control room with Sara as he passed by on his way to the office. "Colonel Green and Colonel Croft, would you please join me," he ordered. They both followed obediently.

"Oh, dear," said Tom, "someone must be in for a roasting." Sara and Tom took their seats, Carl was already sitting at his desk looking jittery and had the coffee ready and poured everyone a cup.

"Right down to business" he said. "The Mars project – You have the funding and it will be through next week. It wasn't easy, but I've got it and the new interceptors with better firing capability will be delivered in a month's time. Anything else you need sorting you must tell me now." He persevered. "There will be a change in command of General for the committee and SHEALD soon so you will have a different General. They may not be as willing, especially if they are new to SHEALD and its undertakings. So, considering I have been here since the start I feel it my duty to honour what is needed at this moment in time. They were all stunned with the announcement. "I can't think of anything at the moment but I will let you know in the next day if that is possible," said Carl. "Good, but it must be soon," said Grant.

"When do you leave Sir? We shall all be sad to see you go, you have looked after us well Sir," said Tom.

"Thank you, Colonel," replied Grant. He appeared tired, to Sara. "I don't have a date as such, but it will be soon, within a month." The general dropped his head. Something did not seem right and Tom wanted to know more. "So, will you be retiring Sir?"

"No, I am afraid I am dying, I have aggressive terminal cancer." Sara Gasped, "oh, I am so sorry!" He was close to her seat and she put her hand in his. "Well then," He chirped, "that's sorted, better get on, lots to do and little time to do it in." "I'll walk you to your car Sir," said Sara. He did not argue with her and they walked out of the building together.

"Do you have any family Sir," asked Sara. He turned to Sara, "Please call me Sam, we've known each other a long time now and no there's no family, married to the job, never had time and now it's too late," he replied.

"Though I saw you lot as family. I know Harry and me were always at loggerheads but he was like a son, he made my dream a reality and you ...... always so kind, like a daughter I never had." Sara put her arm through his.

"You know at the end we all need someone, I would like to be there for you, if you would let me, Sir... Sam," she asked.

He smiled and she noticed how sad his eyes were. "I'd like that," said Grant. He opened the door to his car "I'll be in touch soon," he said and started up the engine of his car. That was so sad, yet another brave hero soon to be leaving without any recognition for what he had done. If she could find a way to tell everyone about all the bravery and sacrifices made by wonderful selfless human beings then she would shout it from the roof tops.

It was three and a half weeks later that Carl received the call. As Sara danced into the office, she sensed something was afoot.

"It's the hospice Sara you need to go now," said Carl. She grabbed her car keys and ran out to her car at speed.

Within twenty minutes she was at the hospice and was shown to the room were General Samuel Grant's lay dying.

"I'm here Sam" she said, "It's OK I'm here now."

He looked up with his pale fading face.

"I'm glad you made it Sara," He whispered, "and I'm glad Harry found you, even if it was only for a short time, you made him happy."

Her eyes filled with tears. He tried to speak, but it was getting more difficult. The door creaked open and Carl entered. "I thought you might want some moral support." he whispered and stood at the back of the room out of the way.

"Is that you Peters?" asked the General.

"Yes Sir," replied Carl. Sam smiled at Sara, "He's a good man" he said.

"Yes, I know," said Sara and you are the bravest, strongest man I have ever known," she said holding Sam's hand.

"He was right you know ... Harry, you should live your lives as much as possible, don't be a lonely old devil like me on your death bed," he jested.

"Damn near broke my heart when that man died so suddenly."

He was referring to Harry of course. "Still, he's done a grand job, great guy."

Grant pointed to Carl. Carl stood up and saluted the General and the machine bleeped a long loud tone that told them he was gone. Sara sat by his bed and cried with her head on his chest, just as she had done when her father past way.

Carl once again, brought the flag to half-mast in respect for the General at Headquarters and everyone shared a minute silence for the great General.

Naturally, he would have a Military send off with the full works, which was just how he would have wanted it.

161

The biggest surprise was that he had left a Will leaving all his estate to SHEALD. They decided that the base on Mars would have a meeting conference room and a training room which would be named the Grant conference and training room and would one day hold alien visitors to allow them to communicate with others and find peaceful solutions to their situations. But for the present time it would facilitate the most advanced training centre for SHEALD staff from all over the world in the Generals memory. The base on Mars was named "The Saunders base project," after Harry, here they both would never be forgotten.

It was time for Sara to leave the house. She had packed all her belongings and sifted through all her memories with Harry. They were boxed away for now and held in storage with everything else. It was a sad day when she finally closed the door and as she looked over at the beach for the last time she looked up at the Moon and said her goodbyes. Carl carried out the rest of her belongings in the suitcases that she would be taking to his apartment and placed them in the boot of his car. "Are you ready Sara," asked Carl in a gentle voice. Sara looked at the house for one last time and then took a deep breath and blew a kiss towards the house, "Farewell, she whispered as she got into the car.

Although it was a day of endings, it was also a start to her new life. Carl was happy to have her at his apartment and she immediately felt comfortable and at home. She was also gratified that Carl was such a good cook and would be making dinner for them both most evenings. Once settled Carl showed Sara to her room and left her to unpack her belongings. It was comfortable and inviting but she was too exhausted emotionally and physically from the day's upheavals to take much notice.

However, she was content that she had achieved a large step forward as she fell asleep instantaneously and slept soundly for the rest of the night. She was thankful for what she had, good friends, a great career, and a promising future ahead of her. Life had not always been good, but Sara would make it right, she was in charge of her own destiny and it was up to her how that would play out.


Sara had lived at Carl's for the past few days and everything was going well. Carl was always first up in the morning and usually had the coffee on when Sara got up. On occasions they would travel to work together if they were going to be in the office all day and on days off, they would go shopping, Carl had noticed an increase in his wardrobe with new clothing and was looking extra smart at work with the help of Sara's touch. He had always been smartly dressed, but now he wore clothing that suited him more and complemented his figure and colouring and showed the character of man he was.

Tonight, Sara was out with the girls, Fiona, Leah, Jo and Saphy. They had reserved a table at the new restaurant that everyone was raving about. The guy's Ali, Tom, Paul, Marc, Vlad, and Tim were meeting at Carls place for Lasagne and a drink with a pack of cards. They had plenty of beer and spirits to get through and none of them were great drinkers yet, there was enough to keep a public house going for a week. So, it was likely that they would end up having a little more alcohol than planned.

Fiona had managed to get a babysitter for the twins and was looking forward to some adult chatter rather than baby talk. Fiona was a sweet person and pretty with her dark curly long hair and brown eyes. She had been modelling when Tom met her and was travelling around the world on a photo shoot in Israel when she met him. Tom had been on some business for the Military at the time and a terrorist bomb had been activated near the Dead Sea, where the shoot was taking place.

When Fiona spotted the strong Military man coming towards her, she said she had felt weak at the knees at this hunk of a guy who swept her out of harm's way. He had left his hotel number in her pocket so that she would call him later. She was surprised to learn that he lived close by in England where they began dating.

Since having the twins she had not pursued her modelling career but was studying a Bachelor of Science degree in Sociology. No one knew how she managed to study with the lively twins to take care of and still manged to keep a perfect figure and looked so good but nothing was any trouble for Fiona.

The girls were giggly and happy to catch up and the wine was flowing freely. Apart from Sara who stuck to her usual water. It did not make any difference as she still knew how to have fun with or without alcohol and was bubbly enough without a drink.

"So, it's been a month since you moved in with Carl," asked Leah, "how is it going at the Bachelor pad?" Sara smiled, "it's actually lovely, Carl's good company and I think it helps that we were such good friends before." "Only Friends?" Joked Jo.

"So, have you seen him naked yet?" giggled Saphy.
"Saphy!" said Sara in a disapproving tone.

"Well, you know what I mean, you must have seen him coming out of the shower at some time?" Sara felt a bit awkward at first but then she was amongst friends and they were just having a bit of fun.

"Actually, (they all moved in closer to hear the gossip) he was getting out of the shower the other day and the switch in my room wouldn't work, so I called Carl."

"And and...!" asked Leah impatiently. "Well, he came in my room and he was all wet with this towel wrapped around his waist," "Ooh, should we be listening to this." jested Fiona. "Has he a good body then?" asked Jo.

"Hmm," said Sara.

"He has a nice bottom too."

The giggles were getting much louder. "Anyone would think you fancied him, Sara?" said Leah. Sara quickly defended herself, "just saying, you know, female observations and all that." They were having a brilliant night of laughter from start to finish. "Well," said Jo to Saphy we had better be off, early shift tomorrow. They all frowned. Leah and Fiona came back with Sara as their partners were still finishing a game of cards at Carl's.

The guys had, also had a good night and as the drinks were plentiful, they were all a little worse for wear. Paul asked Carl how it was going with a female guest in his bachelor pad? "She's not cramping your style then?" "No, it's been good, she mothers me a lot, does all my washing, and there is always food in the fridge, so what more can a man ask for?" said Carl. "A lot more," said Paul drunkenly.

"So," said Tom, "is she as perfect as she seems or has, she any annoying habits?" "Only one, she gets up on her day off and walks around the place in her so-called "nighty" with nothing else on," protested Carl "and your complaining? Chance would be a fine thing," said Paul. The men laughed. "No, I mean it's not good for a bloke to keep looking at those lovely legs and that short nighty," said Carl. "You should marry her," said Tom, slurring his words. Carl got serious for a moment, "it's not like that with me and Sara and anyway why would she fancy me?" Ivanov butted in "Yes, you do have a point," as he fell off the chair arm on which he was sitting. "I think it is time we left Vlad," said Tim helping Vlad up off the floor.

Sara entered with Leah and Fiona. "Oh, dear," said Leah, "looks like you guys had a good night." There were bottles, cans and glasses cluttering the table in front of them and one by one they struggled to their feet and left. "Coffee?" asked Sara. He certainly looked like he needed it, but when she returned with the coffee Carl was fast asleep and snoring on the sofa. Sara smiled and brought his duvet and pillow from his bedroom. "Looks like you're sleeping on the sofa tonight, Sir," She taunted. "Aren't you going to get in with me?" he muttered patting the side of the sofa. Sara ignored him and put the pillow under his head. She then began to take his shoes off. "What about the rest of my clothes?" he slurred Cheekily. Sara laughed and threw the duvet over him. "Spoil sport," he taunted. She kissed him on the forehead. "Is that it? Go on, on the lips," he pleaded. Sara leant over, "goodnight," and kissed him again quickly on the lips and laughed. She did love this guy, always there for her and he made her smile and yes, he did have a good body and nice lips too. "So, what!" She thought to herself.

Sara was up and dressed and, in the kitchen, putting on the coffee and had cleaned up the mess from the night before when she heard Carl waking. "Oh, my head!" complained Carl as he struggled to his feet, "never again!" Sara put the cup of coffee in front of him and two paracetamols. "I've left the shower running for you so, don't let it run too long." "You're an angel Sara," commended Carl. "I'd better go Carl, I'll see you later," she grabbed her bag and left for work. "Yes, thanks Sara," said Carl, rubbing his head. He hadn't felt this rough in a long time and hoped the pills would kick in soon, preferably before he got into work.

At the office Sara had brought supplies for the guys from last night. Coffee and two pain killers were welcomed by them all. K9 was hiding under Paul's desk and made a quick run for the office after Paul had refused him a treat for barking at him. Tom was incredibly grateful for the painkillers and coffee as he had just dropped the noisy twins off at the nursery and his head was about to explode. K9 sensed he had to be quiet and trotted over to Sara's desk and lay down quietly until he got his treat. Carl finally walked into the office. "She's worth her weight in gold," said Tom, sipping his coffee and swallowing the pills. "Morning!" said Sara brightly and on purpose. "Oh please! quieter if you must" said Tom holding his head. "I hope we don't get a red alert now, with you lot or we're doomed," joked Sara. Although Carl could have gladly thrown Sara out of the office this morning, he was pleased to see the old Sara returning to herself.

Before Sara left the office with K9 behind her, she had received an email that should have been for Carl. It was from a Miss Stacy Gombos informing him that she would be visiting tomorrow morning and dropping off the final papers for the Mars project. She was one of the main architects and needed Carl to sign them off before work begun. "Thanks Sara, I'll put it in my diary," he replied and was grateful it wasn't today as he didn't think he was capable of signing anything for now.

At ten in the morning on the dot, Miss Stacy Gombos waltzed into SHEALD. Tom had been sent to greet her and showed her into the office. As soon as she entered the office her perfume hit the back of Sara's throat, making Sara cough. Her nails were sharpened and manufactured and she had definitely had work done on her face. Long fluttery false eye lashes fanned her face and Sara felt that if they were any bigger, she would have felt a draft from them when she blinked. She was Sassy and made a bee line for Carl. "Ah, so you are the hand-some new Commander I have been hearing all about," said Stacy as she shook Carl's hand. It had been a long time since any woman had flirted so obviously with Carl and he was flat-tered.

"Carl was taken in by this old fox," thought Sara and with those nails she was certainly clawing at him. After the presen-tation of the plans and a discussion they all agreed and Carl signed the papers. "Work will start next week," said Stacy.

"That soon," said Carl? "Oh yes, I'm a fast worker," flirted Stacy and Sara nearly choked on her coffee. "I bet you are," replied Carl flirting back. Sara looked at Tom and rolled her eyes. "I'm booked in at a nearby hotel for the week to make sure it goes ahead and on time; it is a long week when you are in a strange area and you don't know anyone." She fluttered her lashes.

"Well," said Carl, "we need to change that then, don't we?" Sara was getting annoyed with the toying and hoping he was not expecting her to show her the sights. She was too flirty for Sara and she was even a little older than Carl by the looks of her, but it didn't seem to bother him. As Miss Stacy Gombos left the office she put her card into Carl's hand. Carl smiled and put the card in his pocket.

"I will be in touch Miss Gombos." She tried to smile, but Sara supposed the Botox was preventing her from doing so as she waddled out of the room with her fluttering lashes and claw like nails. "You are not seriously thinking of dating that?" Barked Sara.

"Ooh," said Tom put your claws away girl."

"Why not?" asked Carl. "You said, I should start dating again, so I am." He left the office to see Paul in the control room. "He could do better than her," snapped Sara. "I think you should put the green-eyed monster away Sara," said Tom. Sara tutted and left in disgust.

A few days later Carl appeared in the lounge while Sara was writing in her diary. "What do you think?" He asked. "Don't you look handsome!" remarked Sara and he smelt good too. "Don't wait up for me Sara, I may be back later, then again!" Sara was not happy that he was about to date with Miss Gombos but she could not say anything to him. "Have a good night, Carl and hope it goes well," She hated being two faced, but what else could she say.

When Carl arrived at the restaurant in the hotel Stacy was waiting for him. She had a tightly fitted dress with a low-cut front. Her makeup was immaculate and her hair was in perfect place due to the amount of hair spray she had used on it and would probably never move again. She was an attractive older woman with a very teasing manner and Carl liked this. It was a change from having to chase after a woman, this time she was the one doing all the chasing and it flattered his ego.

They tucked into the starter as she peered across the table at Carl but as they chatted for a while, he found the conversation a little strained. She was quite shallow and self-obsessed but at least it was company. He wasn't asking her to Marry him he just wanted to have dinner with an attractive woman and have some friendly conversation.

Halfway through the meal the flirting became more pronounced "I hope you will join me later for drinks in my room." Toyed Stacy. Carl was slightly taken aback; he wasn't sure if she was what he wanted anymore. "We'll see" he remarked. However, Miss Gombos was not taking no for an answer, she usually got what she wanted from a man and a "we'll see," was not good enough for her. She already had three failed marriages behind her so, she did not take likely to his attitude. She had heard through the grapevine that Carl was sharing a place with the past Commanders wife and wanted to know more to see if she was any threat to her chances.

"I believe you have Sara Saunders living with you at the moment," she questioned. Carl realized she was prying about their relationship and probably thought there was something more than there was between them.

"No, no, it's not like that between us," he explained. But Stacy wasn't convinced, there was something in his eyes when her name was mentioned and she knew men better than they knew themselves. She had more than enough experience of the opposite sex to know how they operated.

"Sara's just a friend, she's waiting for her new house to come through and I said she could stay with me until it was completed." Carl felt as if he were about to get the third degree and didn't know if he wanted that.

"Aren't you the gallant one, maybe she has a thing about Commanders," she jested. Carl was uncomfortable with talking about Sara in this way. She did not know her or should not be making aspersions on her character. "Sara's not like that," Carl had realized that she saw Sara as some kind of threat and wanted to put her straight. "There really is no threat to you from Sara, I can reassure you of that." But Carl was making the matter worse by saying that she was a threat, and that Sara was better than her. Stacy had little tolerance if she was not centre of attention and was hurt by this as she fired back without thinking "What has she got that I haven't? at least I have the capabilities of giving a man a family. I believe Colonel Saunders to be barren!" She hissed. Carl was stunned and disgusted by this comment. He slammed down the napkin, "How dare you talk about Sara like that? You are a vicious, nasty woman and I have no intention of staying a moment longer." He stood up, opened his wallet, paid the bill, and strode out of the restaurant at pace. "What a horrible woman! how could he have imagined that they could have shared a few moments together?"

Sara could not go to bed early as she had planned due to her thinking about Carl on his date with Miss Gombos. If the date went well then, she could lose Carl for good. Then that was selfish of herself to think that way, if she really cared for Carl, she should be happy for him. He looked so handsome and had made a significant effort for his date, he deserved someone to love him. She felt sad and alone but that was her problem not Carl's. Her thoughts were intervened by the key turning in the door and it was only nine o'clock in the evening and Carl was back home. "Hi, only me, I'm back," he said cheerily. "Your early," said Sara. "Oh, she wasn't my type so I made my excuses and escaped." lied Carl. He could not tell

Sara what that vile woman had said about her, she would be heartbroken. "Coffee Carl?" said Sara (it always tended to help). "I am sorry it didn't work out Carl" she said. "It's no loss," he replied but Sara felt guilty as there was a part of her that was relieved that it did not work out but perhaps, she had sensed that she wasn't right for him. She wanted only the best for Carl, he was a good catch for the right woman. "Hey, guess what?" said Sara. "What!" asked Carl. "I'm going to the Ball this year." Carl was delighted to hear this as she had not been since Harry's death so this was another positive step forward for her. "Will you be my plus one?" She asked. "Yeh, all these women fighting to date me, I am doing well." mocked Carl. "It's your aftershave" joked Sara.

The dress that she had chosen for the ball was a strong, vibrant red coloured material with a sequin finish and against her pale skin and blonde hair it complemented her fittingly. As usual Sara brought glamour to life as the gown covered all the right parts of her body. Whilst hugging her hourglass figure to perfection with a "V" back that draped to her hips adding even more elegance. It was a lengthy robe that stopped at her ankles showing what could only be described as ruby slippers. Sara never failed to impress and with her mother's ruby necklace and drop earrings to match the 'lady in red' was ready.

When Sara walked down the stairs of Carl's penthouse it brought back memories of the first Ball that she attended with Harry.

"You were stunning then and are stunning now," declared Carl. "You looked like a princess that night and I could not believe my luck when I had the chance to dance with you. I was so proud to be dancing with you on that floor and tonight I am lucky to be able to get to do it all over again." Sara was beaming:

"Thank you Carl and you look dashing too," she replied. In fact, he looked more handsome than ever before and she was glad that her knight in shining armour was accompanying her. The usual gang were waiting for them and beckoned them both to the table. Everyone was thrilled to see that Sara felt able to attend the ball again and join in the celebrations. As she sat down the waiter hovered over her with a tray of drinks and smiled offering a choice of cocktails.

"Which are the non-alcoholic?" asked Sara. The waiter looked confused but the room was full of music and chatter, so she repeated the question. He smiled and handed her a flute which she sipped slowly at first, but after finding it pleasant drank the rest in no time. A short while later the waiter returned with another drink. It was his job to make sure that everyone always had a drink of their choice on their table.

Carl did his duty and went around the room welcoming and chatting with everyone. Sara was happy to be chatting with Leah and Fiona and was later joined by Jo and Saphy. It was good to catch up with them all and have a dance with the girls as they continued to chat and laugh. The waiter had appeared at the table again and was leaving the drinks. He nodded to Sara so she could see what he had done and she waved to acknowledge him. They had been dancing a good while when a familiar face walked in. "oh no," groaned Sara, "it's the maneater." She was referring to Stacy Gombos who was heading straight towards Carl. "She had better not be trying anything on with Carl tonight." Threatened Sara. "Oh Sara, I do believe you are jealous," said Leah. Sara ignored this remark but kept a close eye on the cougar.

"Hello Carl," said Stacy much more subdued this time. Carl coldly greeted her back. "I'm not here to argue with you," putting her hands in the air as if in submission. "I just want to apologise for what I said and you were right it was vicious. I guess I was jealous of the young pretty woman that Sara is and I believe she is a lovely person too. It's hard when you are getting older, your looks start to fade, and you are still single looking for that special someone. Don't let her get away Carl, she is a keeper," Carl smiled "Thank you Stacy." "Don't leave it too long Carl or someone will come along and steal her from you," she warned. "It's already been done" replied Carl. "Then it is up to you, life's too short," Stacy said. "Yes, you're right, Stacy" Carl lent over and kissed her on the cheek and she quietly left.

The waiter was back at the table again giving Sara another drink. Carl had made his way back just as she finished the flute. "What on earth are you drinking Sara?" asked Carl. "Oh, its OK, its non alco...ho....lic," said Sara. "I don't think so," said Carl as he sipped the new drink in front of her.

"That's strong stuff, he replied.

"No, no, it isn't he told me, that waiter there," insisted Sara. "That waiter couldn't tell you anything because he can't speak English," informed Carl. "Whoops," said Sara but it was too late as she took another sip of her drink. Carl laughed, "I've never seen you, drunk before, you're bad enough sobber," he teased.

The band made the announcement "Please take your partners for the Waltz." The music began and Carl looked over to Sara and held out his hand to her, "May I?" he asked. Sara jumped to her feet and they danced happily around the floor as before. Carl loved this moment with her and Sara held him tight to her, "I love you Mister Peters," she said. "I know you do," he laughed, "and everyone loves you madame," he replied. By the end of the evening Sara was stumbling and was obviously intoxicated by the flutes of drinks she had been consuming all night. She was singing and laughing as she left, after hugging and saying goodnight to everyone including the waiter.

Carl had been the one on orange juice tonight so drove them both home. As Carl drove, Sara began to run her hand up and down his leg, singing to him. "Sara!" shouted Carl, "I am trying to drive, do you mind!" However, he was laughing at her cheeky behaviour. He had never seen her like this before and knew when he told her what she was like in the morning she would be cringing, but it was funny seeing her in this way. She was still singing when they got back to his apartment.

"I think plenty of coffee for you madame," said Carl.

"Oh, I love it when you're masterful" said Sara, as she began to giggle.

"Come on Carl let's have a dance," as she grabbed Carl around the waist.

"You are Crazy," said Carl.

"It has been said before" remarked Sara.

"But you love me," she replied and they both laughed again.

"Drink your Coffee Sara."

Carl passed her the cup, again, Sara grabbed Carl by the waist "come on Carl dance with me, please!" He, put his arms around her waist and looked down at her. "It's late," he said. Sara starred into Carl's eyes. "I do love you Carl," she said to him much more sincerely. Carl stood still and appeared more serious. Sara held onto his neck and pulled him close to her and gently kissed him. There was a silent pause. Then Carl re turned the kiss, this time it was much more passionate as he held her tightly to his body. He then pushed her dress strap over her shoulder and caressed her neck, it felt wonderful. She felt alive again and in love. Carl kissed her lips again; he was warm and gentle and she did not want it to end. Carl could not believe he finally had Sara in his arms, he had waited what seemed a lifetime. Her lips were soft and her skin was like silk it was everything he had imagined it to be. He wanted so much to sweep her up in his arms and take her to his room and make love to her, but something shuddered in- side of him.

Carl broke away and sighed.

"What am I doing, you're drunk." Sara tried to kiss him again but Carl pushed her away. He was angry.

"Go to bed Sara," he shouted. Sara was too drunk to argue or make sense of what had happened and clambered the stairs to her bedroom, falling across the bed with her feet dangling over.

Carl was so angry with himself "what the hell was I doing? I've ruined everything now! he cursed.

"I can't believe I did that." He sat in the kitchen drinking his coffee until much later still angry about what had hap- pened. Eventually he went to bed and as he passed Sara's room her door was ajar as she lay hanging off the bed. Carl entered her room, took off her shoes and placed her comfort- ably on the bed before covering her with the duvet. She was sound asleep as he looked down at her for what would proba- bly be his last time and kissed her forehead with affection.

"I'm so sorry Sara," he whispered. Carl did not sleep all night, tossing and turning with the events of the night running through his mind. It had started perfectly and now was in ruins, Sara could never be part of his life anymore now.

When Sara woke the following morning, she was experiencing an unwelcomed hang over of which she had never had before. She shouted to Carl but there was no answer so she ventured to the kitchen where she usually found him on workdays but he was nowhere to be seen. He must have had a call from control and had to leave in a rush. She was sad she had missed him but knew they would catch up later at Headquarters.

Carl arrived at the office incredibly early and when Tom appeared he was surprised to see Carl so soon. Tom was usually the first in during the morning as he would be dropping the twins off at the school. "You're early" said Tom to Carl. "Yes, I have a lot to do so I thought I had better get an early start. I am going up to Lunar base for the week as I have a lot of sorting out to do that I have been putting off. It needs to be done so I thought I had better bite the bullet, so to speak." Tom was taken aback by this news as normally Carl hated staying over at Lunar base and would do anything to avoid staying the night there. "Must be important for you to spend the whole week up there?" questioned Tom. Carl did not answer but continued to give his orders for the week.

"You and Sara will have to run things down here whilst I'm away, I'll be in touch if you need anything, but your more than capable so there's nothing to worry about," said Carl. "What time does the shuttle leave?" asked Tom. "It's not for another hour so if you have any queries, I have got time to run through anything with you before I go." "No, I think I'm fine for now?" replied Tom.

Sara walked into the office holding a coffee and some pain killers. "Boy, do I feel rough," she complained. "I bet you do, next time read the label," joked Tom. Carl kept his head down all the time that Sara spoke and made his excuses. "Well, I had better go," said Carl. "I thought you said the shuttle wasn't leaving for another hour?" queried Tom. "Yes, but I need to call elsewhere before I go." He quickly picked up his bag and scurried out. Sara was surprised, "where's he going in such a rush?" "Lunar base for the week," replied Tom. "For the week?" quizzed Sara. She was moving house in two days and thought Carl would be around to help her, but obviously not. He had always been there for her yet now it seemed as if he could not bear to be in the same room as her. Tom was also puzzled by Carl's behaviour and found it odd the way he was with Sara.

"Have you two been arguing?" asked Tom. Sara shook her head, but they both knew something wasn't right with him. Later that day Tom spoke with Carl on the screen at Lunar base regarding work.

"Ok I will get on to it now Carl. Do you need to speak with Sara about anything, she's here at the side of me if you do?" suggested Tom.

Sara moved over to the screen, but Carl brought the conversation to a halt swiftly, "no, that's all for now," and the screen went blank. Sara was upset but kept a brave face on the matter. It was obvious that he did not want to talk. She could only think that it must have been about her kissing him. Surely, they could work something like that out as they had a good strong bond normally and had been friends too long for a stupid kiss to spoil their relationship.

Leah was also surprised to see the Commander at Lunar base and especially that he intended to be there for a week. Even though he was busying himself she could not imagine it would take more than a couple of days to do what he needed to do. He was different too, more melancholy. He did joke less these days as Commander it was less appropriate to be the jester but he was always engaging and pleasant. He was approachable and staff felt comfortable that they could talk to him if they needed to but now, he appeared guarded. Something was definitely bothering him. Leah had known Carl for many years and this was so unlike him. She began the conversation "I have to admit Commander, I am surprised at you being here for a week, you normally can't wait to get away from us." "Needs must," he replied. Leah persisted. After all last night he was beaming and laughing the night away with everyone. Leah tried again. "I know it's none of my business, but it is as if you are trying to avoid something back home, is everything alright?"

175

"Yes, you're right, it isn't any of your business!" snapped Carl. Leah moved away she had never experienced Carl like this and knew when it was time to say nothing. Carl tutted, "Leah, I'm sorry, I didn't mean to have a go at you, I just can't talk about it." Leah smiled and said softly, "it's ok, I understand but if you need to talk, you know where I am." Carl thanked Leah and continued his work.

The screen monitors bleeped and Sara's face appeared. "Hi Leah, I wondered if I could have a word with Carl, please." Carl, moved to the door, "I am really busy, just ask Sara to pass the message on to you and I will sort it later." Carl hurriedly exited the room. She related the message but could tell by the look on Sara's face that there was something wrong between the two. Sara later, tried several times on Carl's mobile phone to speak with him, even leaving him messages to ask him to call her back, but he never did, this was so unlike Carl.

Sara moved into the beautiful cottage and the move was surprisingly easy. There was little to do as the house was perfect and to Sara's taste so she only had to unpack the boxes and have the furniture delivered. The sofa had already arrived, fitting perfectly into the lounge and all the other furniture arrived shortly after, it was a smooth operation. Tom, Fiona, and Marc had come along to help too so it was good to have some company, but it felt strange without Carl there. This was her new start but it would have to be without Carl and she would have to get over him. She had endured her mother, father, and Harry's death so, she could deal with this.

That evening Leah telephoned her friend. "Hi Sara, how did the move go?" she asked. "It went well, everything's here and it's all in place, thank goodness," replied Sara. "Great, I'm glad it went OK for you, but what about Carl?" she asked. "That is more complicated. I really don't know any more Leah; he's refusing to even take my calls," said Sara. "Well, he is going to have to speak to you at some point, he can't hide away on Lunar base forever," replied Leah. "I really don't know anymore, Leah, I kissed him and told him I loved him after the Ball which has upset him," explained Sara. "And do you?" asked Leah "What?" said Sara "Love him?" replied

Leah. "Yes, I really do, but he obviously does not feel the same way," sighed Sara. There was a quiver in her voice.

"I can't believe he doesn't love you, Sara, we all believed he did and even Harry said it too," replied Leah. "Well, maybe he has changed his mind now it's real," suggested Sara. "I just want the hurt to go away." "I know, I know, I'm so sorry Sara," comforted Leah. Leah wished she could do something for her friend but she could not. Carl's behaviour was so odd but then she did not know what was going on inside his head. After all, they said that "women were from Venus and men were form Mars, and Carl, well, he was on the Moon hiding away from something!" thought Leah.

Sara sat in front of the fire and the flames glowed. The only sound she could hear was the crackle of the logs as they were devoured by the fire. It was Friday tomorrow and Sara would be finished for the weekend. Carl would be due back from Lunar base and the thought of Monday morning with Carl ignoring her was unbearable. She had already begun the changes in her life, maybe she needed a few more. She had lived for SHEALD and worked hard, but now it would never be the same. "I'm sorry Harry, I can't do this anymore, Please Harry, help me," she begged as she looked up above her.

Tom was busy in and out of the office all day but Sara didn't seem to have the energy to do much. Tom had been aware that Carl was avoiding Sara but he did not know why so left it alone for now. It was late and she had been informed that Carl was on his way back from Lunar base and wanted to make herself scarce. As she left, she placed the letter of resignation on his desk. He would know immediately what it was as it was in a special envelope that SHEALD had for such notices and he would probably work out it was her handwriting on the envelope too. It wasn't a game to Sara but she could not carry on like this anymore, seeing him at work, knowing the way she felt about him and worse that he was so angry with her.

The lunar shuttle arrived at SHEALD HQ at Eight in the evening and it had been a tiring week for Carl but he needed to get on. He always had to get on with it. That's what he did but inside he was aching and hurt. He would have to ride this storm through as he had done many times before. Carl called into the office before his weekend leave to check for messages that may have needed an urgent reply. Tom would be working this weekend and covering the office and had realized that he had left his car keys there so needed to pick them up before he left. "You still here Tom?" remarked Carl. He jangled his keys in front of him to show Carl why he had returned. Carl opened the letter on his desk and sighed. "So, whose resigned then?" asked Tom noticing, the type of envelope. Carl put his head down and spoke quietly "Its Sara," Carl took a moment "Maybe it's for the best." Tom was outraged, "for the best!"

Tom shouted, "That woman has given everything up for SHEALD, her former life, her husband, the chance of having a family, and you say it's for the best! Look Carl I don't know what has gone on with you two but you need to sort it and fast!" said Tom as he stormed out of the office. Carl placed his hands in his head "I'll sort it, I will, I will...." he muttered, shaking his head. Tom had never raised his voice to him before but he was right and Carl needed to hear it from someone.

He picked up the telephone to call Sara but she did not answer as she had switched her phone off so not to be disturbed. She had fallen asleep on the sofa after hours of crying. Carl left a message on her phone to ring him but in truth he had not answered any of her messages, "so why should she reply to him?" He grabbed his jacket and headed over to Sara's new home. It was ten in the evening when Carl arrived at Sara's cottage. He knocked on the door but there was no answer, then, he realized the time. She would not want to open the door to strangers at that time of night and so he lifted up the letter box and called. "Sara it's Carl, please, I need to talk with you." When Sara heard Carl's voice she woke from her sleep. She had not slept all week and her eyes were red and swollen from weeping. She quickly rubbed away any tears and tried to hide the fact that she was upset. As she opened the door Carl looked straight at her. "Can I come in?" he asked. Sara nodded and held the door open as Carl entered into the cottage.

He looked around as he entered the cottage. "It's looking really nice, you have made it very homely," he remarked nervously. "What a stupid thing to say?" she thought, she didn't care what he thought anymore. She continued to the kitchen, "Coffee?" she asked. Carl nodded.

She made them both coffee and Carl stood in the lounge waiting for her return with her resignation in his hand. "I can't accept this" as he waved the letter in front of him. "Oh, you can't?" she said sarcastically. "I'm not asking for your approval; I am telling you I am resigning," raising her voice at him. "No Sara, you've worked too hard and SHEALD needs you." "look" he paused, "you can work somewhere else, SEASKY, Lunar base or even in the new base on Mars in the Saunders project. You could be Commander and run things on the new base, you would be good at that." But he was digging a bigger hole. "Oh, that's nice," replied Sara. "Do you think I would be far enough away from you, then again, you would still have to see me on occasions and that would not do, would it?" she growled. "Ok I'll go, it may be better that way," offered Carl. Sara looked up in dismay. "Don't be so ridiculous, you're the Commander of SHEALD you just can't leave like that. It's not that long since they lost one Commander, losing another would be fatal to the organization. You know commanders are hard to come by, they just don't grow on trees!" said Sara. She still had her wit even when she was angry, something Carl found endearing about her, amongst other things. "I think you had better leave Carl while you still can," she threatened.

There was a silence for a while as neither of them knew what more to say. "Ok, so I'm sorry, I'm sorry I kissed you. I can't help the way I feel about you. Obviously, you can't put this behind you and move on and I am not sure I want to be at SHEALD with you anymore when you make me feel so awkward. I thought we were both better than that and our friendship would have stood up to this better, but it appears not." blurted Sara.

"No, it isn't your fault Sara, it was me," said Carl. Sara was not impressed. "Oh, please Carl, not that one. It's not you, it's me rubbish." ranted Sara. "No!" said Carl, "I had no idea you

179

felt like that about me, you had too much to drink and the person you had always trusted took advantage of the situation. What kind of man does that make me Sara? I'm disgusted in myself that I could do that to you." His voice became much gentler as he spoke now. "I have loved you from the very first time I set eyes on you. You were and still are the most beautiful woman I have ever known inside and outside. When you fell for Harry my best friend, I was glad for you both. You were so happy and you both deserved that. I couldn't and wouldn't compete with Harry, though it never stopped me loving you any less. When Harry died, I like most people was gutted and I was grieving for my best mate. Then I was shoved into taking Command, filling the shoes of a great man. Which was no easy task and on top of all that I had to watch you fall apart and know there was nothing I could do about it. I made a promise that I would look after you and I failed by putting my own feelings first. That's unforgivable Sara." He held her hand and spoke even softer "I never wanted to hurt you, never, but I did and I am sorry I let my feelings run away with me when you were so vulnerable. All I wanted to do was sweep you up and make love to you when you were incapable of making that decision and that was wrong of me."

Sara spoke in a much lighter tone now. "You could have taken advantage of me and God knows I wanted you to, but you didn't. You stopped, not many men would have done that Carl. You have always been there for me, you're my rock", said Sara. "You were the one who brought me to SHEALD, you saved my life twice and you stood by me when I cried at the loss of my husband, you've always been part of my life at SHEALD." She continued, "when I met Harry, I saw no one else, I was smitten, but you were always making me smile and close by my side. When Harry died you held me and showed me compassion though, you had your own grief to contend with and the shoulders of SHEALD to carry. For a long time after Harry, I was in a dark place and my feelings were on hold. Then it happened slowly, I started to feel again and I noticed your kind eyes, your smile, how handsome you were, the way you smelt when I was near you and I knew then that the man I loved was standing right in front of me". Tears flowed fast down her pretty face. Carl wiped her face with his hand and kissed her long and devotedly whilst carrying her in his strong arms to the bedroom where they made love for the first time. He was gentle and caring and most of all it felt right. They were two pieces of a jigsaw puzzle put finally together. "Marry me, Sara? I can't live without you." said Carl and Sara accepted without any hesitation.

They married the next day as they had already waited too long. Carl had a friend who was a Military clergyman happy to wed them in matrimony without waiting. Carl moved into the cottage with Sara straight away as he equally liked the cottage as much as Sara so it made sense to stay.

There was no reason to move anywhere else. On the Monday after the wedding, they both arrived at SHEALD to an applause from all the staff and they had even managed to rustle up a wedding cake for them. Tom and Leah could not keep this secret to themselves for long and word quickly spread. Sara felt sad that General Grant had not been able to see them marry but she was sure he would have approved and she knew that Harry would have been looking down on them both too with his blessings. Harry would never be forgotten by either of them.

General Paul Jackson was different to General Grant, he was younger and his approach was to stay in the background and leave the running of SHEALD to those who knew it best. In the office Sara had the photo of the 'fab four' enlarged and framed on the office wall for all to see. It reminded everyone of the trust, loyalty, passion, and friendships made in SHEALD when fighting for the good of mankind. They had also made a gallery in the entrance too which included General Grant and Harry and all those who had given their life to SHEALD so that from now on their lives would be celebrated and never forgotten.

Leah gave birth to a baby girl in the following year that Carl and Sara married. Alaina would be their only daughter but Ali was a doting daddy, reminding Sara of herself and her father's relationship. Leah decided to reduce her working hours so that she could spend more time with her daughter but she saw

Carl and Sara and the others regular and their friendships remained strong.

In the year of 2028 the twins were seven years in age and as they grew Sara and Carl's love for them continued. It had been their birthday on the Friday and Mother's Day that Sunday. So, Tom and Fiona had organized a birthday party for Luna and Leo on the Sunday whilst they were all on a weekend off. Leah would be bringing baby Alaina to meet everyone and was showered with lots of attention as she was passed from knee to knee without complaint. The grown-ups were all gathered together as the children were chased around by Uncle Carl until he and the kids were at exhaustion point. Luna came to sit on Sara's knee. "Aunty Sara, Leo and I made Mummy breakfast in bed this morning for Mother's Day. We made toast and a cup of tea but Daddy ate most of Mummy's toast" giggled Luna. "Did he Luna? well that is very cheeky of daddy," replied Sara. Tom mouthed, "the toast was burnt to a cinder." "It was ok because Daddy helped us to buy Mummy some flowers," continued Luna. "Oh, that is a lovely thought, I bet Mummy really liked them," said Sara." "Yes, she did. Did you get any flowers for Mother's Day aunty Sara?" asked Luna. There was an awkward moment but Sara covered it well, "no darling, I am not a Mummy," said Sara, Carl was a bit unsure how Sara was feeling and Fiona quickly altered the conversation. "Luna and Leo are you going to blow the candles out on your cake and we can all sing Happy Birthday?" Luna jumped from Sara's knee and ran towards the table. As they all sang Happy birthday and had a slice of the cake. There was only one cake for the twins but it was extra-large in size to compensate. Alaina was getting restless and tired by now, so Leah and Ali said their farewells. Sara and Carl decided that it was a suitable time for them to leave too and made their excuses as it was getting late. Leo stood next to Carl and gave him and Sara a hug and said thank you for their presents but Luna was nowhere to be seen. Tom shouted Luna, and she appeared, running excitedly in from the garden and looking incredibly pleased with herself with a handful of freshly picked flowers for Sara. "There you are aunty Sara, I got you some flowers for Mother's Day" as she passed the flowers over to Sara. "Oh, Luna that is so kind of you and very thoughtful, thank you," Sara picked her up, kissed her and gave her a big hug. Luna was a kind and thoughtful child and as the children waved goodbye they ran back into the house and Sara and Carl drove away.

On their return home Sara went to the kitchen to make tea as Carl sat on the sofa relaxing. He was getting too old to be the "sweety monster" these days and he was hoping that the twins would grow out of it soon as he wasn't sure how much longer he could go on for. Sara seemed to be taking a while at making the tea so Carl went into the kitchen to join her where Sara was arranging the flowers in a vase. She had been crying. Carl put his arms around her waist and hugged her "Sara darling whatever is the matter?" She carried on dressing the flowers. "Oh, ignore me Carl, I'm just being silly." She wiped her face quickly and started on making the tea for them both and was trying hard to play it down, but Carl knew there was more.

"Hey, you," he teased "it's not like you to keep things from me." Sara still seemed upset and put her head down and with a quiver in her voice she remarked "I love you so, very much Carl." Carl looked her in the eyes and kissed her. "Well thank goodness for that, so you are not divorcing me then?" He joked. Sara smiled, "never, I just wish I could have your baby and I can't and you are so good with the twins and when I see you with them, I think how it would be if we had children." Carl comforted her caringly, "You are everything I have ever wanted. It really doesn't matter to me, yes kids would have been good but if I had to choose between them or you then I would choose you every time." But Sara felt it shouldn't be an option.

# The Embryo Experiments

Doctor Ivanov was looking very pleased with himself and had asked Sara to visit. Another baby monkey was sitting in the cage in the lab. "I have done it Sara," said Vlad. I know how to grow a human embryo. "Congratulations Vlad," said Sara. She knew how much time, money, and effort he had invested in this. He had successfully grown and delivered two primates and had considered the human possibilities. He had vast reports on every angle of his papers. He just needed to now conduct the procedure on a human. "Is this all legal and ethical?" asked Sara. "Oh Yes, I have gone through every medical board and authority needed to move forward and have received some funding too," replied Vlad.

"Do you realize what this could mean to so many people?" He was glowing with pride at the thought. All I need is an egg and a sperm donation, fertilize the egg and then I can begin." "You make it sound so easy," said Sara.

"Well not quite, it is long hours lots of observing and perfect timing. I have the rest of my equipment here and if the baby comes early, there is an incubator which, incidentally, has been used on both primates as they tend to have a less gestation time in the tanks and just like a premature baby may need more time, but I am sure I will eventually perfect it."

"Someone has to be the first to try it though. There always has to be someone brave enough to give it a go, a guinea pig, without them science would never move forward." What do you say Sara?" asked Vlad.

Sara was taken by surprise at Vlad's offer and being part of a trial experiment was not something she would have considered.

"Oh no, I'm sorry Vlad, I don't think I could and Carl would never agree." This was all a bit too vague and risky for Sara, she had faced too many disappointments already. She wanted to help Vlad because she knew he had something for the good of others, but it was too extreme for her. Vlad understood and did not push the issue.

"Could I please ask that you keep it a secret as before? I don't think others are ready for this yet, just like with UFOs," asked Vlad. "Of course, Vlad and I really hope you find a volunteer and have the success you deserve," he smiled at Sara and thanked her. If Sara had mentioned it to Carl, he would definitely not have been willing to partake in such an experiment. He already believed that Vlad was a "crazy, mad, professor!"

Sara woke on the Tuesday morning and was getting ready for work whilst Carl made the usual breakfast. As she leaned over to get her jacket, she felt the sharp pain in her side again. She had been training in the gym all last week doing combat and thought she had pulled a muscle, but this did not seem to be going away. Carl sat at the table with breakfast, Sara only had toast and a cup of coffee but it was always made for her lovingly by Carl. She sat at the table and looked at the toast and as the smell hit her it made her feel nauseous. She ran from the table to the bathroom where she began to vomit. Carl followed her with concern and waited outside the bathroom door asking if she was ok. "I'll be alright, it must have been something that I ate, that didn't agree with me." When she came out of the bathroom Carl looked at her worryingly.

"You look grey darling, why don't you take the day off." She didn't argue with Carl and went back to bed but within a few hours the sickness had disappeared. So, Sara returned to the office later that day, but unfortunately for the next two mornings the same symptoms appeared repeatedly.

"If I didn't know Sara's predicament, I would swear she was pregnant. Fiona was like that for weeks when she was having the twins," said Tom to Carl.

"Well, I think we can safely rule that one out mate," replied Carl.

"I keep trying to get her to see the medics but she's not having any of it, keeps saying she will be fine, but she's not," said Carl sounding concerned.

By the fourth day the pain was much stronger in her side and she was now having dizzy spells too. She decided that she would pop into the medical centre at lunch time and see Tim and get checked out. Tom and Carl were going through the monthly rosters in the office and Sara had been with Paul in the control room when Paul buzzed Carl. "Sir, I think you need to come now, its Sara," He did not need to say anything more, as Carl dropped the files and rushed through to control. Sara was doubled up in pain and holding on to the desk as she passed out. Carl was just in time to catch her fall. "I've called the medics Sir, they're on their way," informed Paul.

The medics arrived and placed Sara onto the stretcher and raced her to the medical centre with Carl by her side. Doctor Walker was waiting for them and quickly took charge immediately giving her a shot for the pain and eventually the pain subsided. Tim took bloods and began a scan. As he checked the scan, he could see a swelling in her left side and decided he would need to do further investigations. Carl waited patiently until they had Sara comfortable and stable and Tim had gone through all the tests. At the back of Carl's mind was the thought that it may have something to do with the car crash with the aliens all those years ago. It was a profoundly serious accident and she had been given life changing surgery.

After what felt like an eternity, Doctor Walker came out to see Carl.

"How is she Doc?" asked Carl bracing himself for the worst.

"She is comfortable now, but we will be taking her for surgery in a while so you can go in and see her before we take her to theatre. This is extremely rare and took some time to diagnose, but your wife is around four to five weeks pregnant."

"What?" said Carl in complete dismay. "You obviously weren't around the last time Sara was rushed into theatre. Pregnant! Well frankly that is impossible. I want another Doctor in here now!" Carl raised his tone to the Doctor.

"Possible? Yes, but as I said before seldom, please I know you must be upset and worried for Sara but I can assure you my diagnosis is right." Carl listened to what he had to say.

"Let me explain, Sara had her womb removed, we are all agreed on that, but her ovaries were left as they were intact, yes?" Carl nodded. "Have you ever heard of an ectopic pregnancy? asked Tim. "Isn't that when a baby grows outside the womb?" asked Carl.

"Yes, that's right, and in Sara's case the embryo has become embedded in the tube in her ovary which we refer to as an ovarian ectopic pregnancy. The egg must have got lodged in the ovary tube and was fertilized and then began to grow. Sadly, it cannot survive more than a few weeks, but as it grows it stretches the tube and causes terrible pain and can rupture which can lead to other problems. So, I will need to remove the ovary and Sara will be fine. The surgery isn't too invasive and I will most likely be able to do this through key-hole surgery so don't worry she will be back to normal in no time at all." It was a lot to take in but Sara would be well and safe so that was all that mattered to Carl. "Thank you, Doctor, can I see her now?" asked Carl. The doctor nodded to the nurse to leave and allow Sara and Carl some privacy.

It was quiet when Carl entered the hospital room and he sat at Sara's bedside. "Gosh, you gave me a real fright there, my head was racing with all kinds of thoughts. Thankfully, the doc says you will be well after the operation. Don't ever frighten me like that again, I love you so much Sara." Carl, kissed Sara on the cheek but her face was wet with tears.

"Please don't cry Sara you'll be fine," assured Carl. "It's our only chance of a baby Carl and it will be taken away from us, how cruel can life be?" cried Sara. "Don't Sara, please, I love you, we can get through this," said Carl. "I don't think I can Carl, I really don't, I'm tired of fighting one disappointment after the other, I just want something normal for once," she sobbed. Carl held her and he too was saddened that for a second there was just a glimmer of hope that they may have a child, but the reality was there was never any hope of a family. It was a cruel trick and a terrible torment but this was out of their hands. He just wanted Sara to be happy again, he would give anything for that.

Doctor Ivanov, stood at the door and knocked, Carl beckoned him in. He walked towards Sara and Carl. "I am so very sorry to hear what has happened. If I can help in any way you know Sara you only have to ask." Carl knew that Ivanov was fond of Sara and was very loyal to her. After all, he was the one who had to take away her womb and baby in order for her to survive. He saved her life yet, he still felt responsible in some way. Sara, looked towards Vlad. "Can you still help us Vlad? is it still possible?" she asked. Vlad paused a minute, "yes, it is possible and I will do everything in my power to help this become a reality but of course, there are no guarantees and you must be prepared for the worst outcome," said Vlad. "The worst outcome is here Vlad; the baby is about to be terminated," said Sara. Carl was confused to what they were talking about.

"Hello, can someone please tell me what the heck you two are going on about?" This was going to be a lengthy conversation. Vlad and Sara explained everything about the trial and how this would be the first time it had been tried on a human embryo.

"No, no, you are not experimenting on any embryo of ours, its sick, it's not natural. Sara is very vulnerable at this moment and you are talking about experimenting on a baby that she is grieving for, she has been through too much already and I will not let you fill her head with this crazy idea, never!" he shouted.

Vlad stood up: "I am sorry Commander, I never meant to make you angry and I do understand how you feel, please forgive me, I will leave you two alone." Vlad gave a nod and left the room.

"He's mad," said Carl, "growing babies! you stay away from him in future Sara," he warned. Sara spoke. "When I go into that theatre, they will remove the ovary with the embryo in it and it will not survive, that will be the end of a life. Ok some people will say it isn't a life or developed into a baby yet but from the day it was conceived it's a living being in my eyes. So, we let it go and that is the end of it and our last and only chance we could ever have of a family. Vlad is not crazy he is a genius who believes he may be able to bring joy to someone's sadness.

Everyone thought similar to you about the first heart transplant, the first test tube baby, kidney transplants and the fertility drug, that these were crazy and unnatural. Some even said they were playing God, but without them there would be no progress. I won't say anymore Carl, I love you and I respect you too much and I am not angry with you, just sad that it won't be us".

The nurse came in. "I'm sorry to disturb you but we need to do a few observation tests before you go for surgery." Carl did not know what more he could say. "I'll be back before you go in Sara," he promised. "Will you be, ok?" he asked. Sara put on a brave face. "You know me, tell Tom to keep my seat warm and I'll be back to work sooner than you think and I will see you later," as she blew him a kiss.

Carl made his way back to the office and sat at his desk. Tom was telling him about a possible new recruit but Carl was struggling to listen and his mind was drifting as he thought about Sara.

"Have you heard anything I said?" asked Tom.

"No, I'm sorry Tom," said Carl in a haze. Tom pressed the lock button on the office door.

"Right," said Tom, "now talk to me." Carl tried to relay the story and how he had felt about Vlad's experiment.

"Wow that really is a tall order," said Tom.

"Let's turn it around, it's me and Fiona in exactly the same situation. What would you say to me?" asked Tom. Carl thought for a while, "I'd ask you what Fiona wanted," said Carl.

"But what if I didn't want what she wanted?" said Tom.

"Normally, I would say you compromise and meet halfway, but there isn't a halfway with this," said Carl. "Sadly, no," replied Tom.

"So, we go with my decision then, after all I know best?" remarked Tom. "I don't Tom, but I need to protect Sara this is huge," said Carl. "Then you are doing it for the right reason's you're looking out for your wife not because you are scared or that you don't understand it but because Sara will be protected and won't be hurt." said Tom. "I think so," pondered Carl.

"Do what you believe is right Carl, that's all you can do." He was trying to protect Sara but he was making the decision for them both because he thought he was right. She had, to compromise with him by doing what he believed was right for her, because she was in a vulnerable state at present and so he had to step in.

His desk transmitter buzzed. "Sir it's the medical centre informing you Sara is due to go into theatre in five minutes." "Thanks Paul," said Carl. "Lunar base to SHEALD control this is red alert, Interceptors have failed to hit the target. UFO on way to Earth. Predictive termination Malaga, Spain." Carl went with Tom to the control room. "SEASKY follow and fire when the UFO is sighted," commanded Carl. "UFO sighted sir will trace and be in position to fire in ten seconds,10, 9,8,7,6,5,4,3,2,1 UFO destroyed sir," said Captain Phillips of SEASKY. "Well done, Captain Phillips!" Praised Carl. He was late to accompany Sara to surgery now. "I'm going Tom," said Carl as he ran down the corridors to the medical centre and to the theatre catching a glimpse of Sara entering through the theatre door. She was so upset and the nurse was trying to comfort her. He was scared, scared of the unknown, trying his best to protect Sara, but it was because he was scared and was unsure of what it was all about. He ran into Vlad's lab.

"Come with me now" Carl demanded to Ivanov. Ivanov followed loyally to the door of the theatre. "Do what you have to do," said Carl, "Sara knows better than me and I trust her judgement," said Carl pushing Vlad in through the door.

"I won't let you down," pledged Vlad. "You'd better not," warned Carl.

When Sara came round from the anaesthetic, she was unaware of what had actually happened. Carl was at her side smiling and holding her hand and Sara was so pleased to see him.

"You made it," she smiled. "Only just, but I'm here now," said Carl. Vlad entered the room "Commander, Sara," he nodded to them both, smiling. "Everything has gone to plan and the embryo is now in the first tank Med1 where it will stay for three months, this is the crucial stage where the em-

191

bryo is at its weakest". Sara could not believe what she was hearing.

"You mean ...," she could not say anymore.

"They had put you under by the time I had gone for Vlad," said Carl. "Just in time," replied Vlad.

"The first tank is connected to the Synthetic umbilical cord and is now attached to the embryo. The replicated amniotic sac with fluid is surrounding the embryo and I am now feeding the correct nutrients through the umbilical cord which will change daily. The computer works out the correct quantity and quality with the monitor giving me data on other functions such as heart, blood pressure, and so on. So, I will soon know if there is any distress felt and can deal with it as and when. The temperature is also checked and kept steady. I would highly suggest that you wait until after the three months stage before visiting and the embryo moves to the second tank Med 2 for the next three to five months. Then, should the worst happen there would not be too much attachment. After that we go to Med 3 from Five to Seven and the last tank Med 4 seven to nine months. Though, the primates never went full term, but I cannot be sure if this will be the same for humans. However, we have an incubator on standby with the ability to keep baby going from seven and a half months onwards if needed. Therefore, it would not be a problem. Each tank along means we have an even better chance of full term. So, let's hope for the best. Nevertheless, I must stress that we are still in early days and an uncertain time so go about your lives and I will keep you informed and when we reach the correct point which will be around the three-to-four-month stage you can come and meet your baby".

Sara was delighted and thanked Vlad over and over.

"I must go now and leave you both as I have a new patient to attend to, but I will be in touch" said Vlad with pride. Soon after Vlad's departure Marc popped in to see Sara and Carl.

"Hi Sara don't worry I will be helping and give your little one my greatest attention," said Marc.

"So, you knew about this too? seems like there was only me who didn't know. I thought I was supposed to be Commander of this operation?" joked Carl. More than anything Sara was overwhelmed with the love for her wonderful husband and whatever happened he had stood by her. Even when he was scared and unsure, he had shown faith in her that this was the right decision.

"Did I tell you how much I love you?" declared Sara.

"Yes, but you can remind me again if you like," said Carl.

Vlad was back in his lab with the four large tanks with only one was full at a time. He named them Med1, Med 2, Med 3, and Med 4. The fourth tank was the last and largest before the baby would be born between the age of seven to nine months. This was not only bigger but had a birth canal that would release baby from the sac and through the canal lead- ing out into the world. The computer offered a perfect labour timing for the release of the baby but this had a manual over- ride if needed. Each tank had a clear see-through window so parents could visit and see the baby but also to help with ob- servations. Music was also piped into the womb and stories read to the baby for extra stimulation. This had been studied and evidence showed that babies read to and hearing soft mu- sic whilst still in the womb were more likely to develop edu- cationally. He had also provided a microphone so that baby could hear the parent's voices and would offer recognition and bonding before birth. There were screens that were mainly shut as in the womb a baby would not see light until after birth and this could consequently affect the sight. The screens only came back at observation times. There was also a tilting mechanism for night-time as mothers would be lying down normally for sleep, so this would be replicated in a tilt- ing action.

At four months Vlad informed Sara that the embryo was through the worst part and now had a ninety five percent chance of survival. Vlad invited both Carl and Sara to meet their baby and although Sara was excited, she also felt scared of what she would see and how she would react because at some stage she would still need to bond with the baby. She tried to calm herself and think how wonderful this was going to be as she did not want the embryo to pick up the stress from her in case this had a detriment on its development. Carl held on to Sara's hand and squeezed it with anticipation of what they were about to see as they entered the laboratory. Would this be like seeing a Frankenstein monster in a tank? They hoped not, but their imaginations were running wild with them.

There was a large wall with what could only be described as water tanks filled with liquid. The four tanks laid in line. Baby was in the second Med 2 tank but the shutters were closed at this phase. Vlad pushed a button on Med 2 and the shutters slid back slowly. Carl and Sara braced themselves, but they had nothing to fear as they witnessed their four months old baby floating in front of them.

"Say hello to your son," said Ivanov."

Sara gasped, "oh, he is beautiful, we have a son Carl!" said Sara and she felt an instant connection with the baby. Carl was in awe of the greatness of what was before him, it was a wonderful sight to see their child growing naturally and it felt normal. Sara touched the window of the tank and placed her hand on the glass. The embryo moved and it was almost as if it had reacted to the touch of Sara's hand. I find that the foetus can sense a mother and mother's do make a psychic connection to them early on, even in the womb." Informed Vlad. "Yes, said Sara, I have read studies on that subject. A mother can sense a child's danger from great distances, they call it a mother's instinct but it is much more." said Sara.

Carl and Sara visited the lab regular and each time the love and bond for their unborn child grew. Vlad had suggested that they visited often and speak with the foetus to help with the bonding process. Sara would sit in her lunch break and read a story to the baby and sometimes she would sing to him just as her mother had done to her. The foetus had now developed into the last stage in Med4 and at eight months all the signs were positive. Vlad was hoping that the foetus went full term, but it would be close either way.

Soon Sara and Carl were preparing for their son. Carl had worked hard on decorating the nursery with Sara and it was furnished accordingly. As the weeks got closer the anxiety be came more prominent as they had now bonded with their baby. To lose the child at this phase would be exceedingly difficult as would it be for any parents at this stage, though they need not have worried. Vlad had slept in the lab several nights and even Marc and Tim had done the occasional night shift. It was now just a matter of waiting.

The base on Mars had been finished nearly two years ago and it was now up and running. The NASA training centre was also coming together well on the East side of Mars and was now functional.

The Grant conference and training room in the SHEALD operation centre was on the west side of Mars and looked very impressive with all the latest technology and other spe-cialised equipment that was of the highest quality. The SHEALD base was named the "Saunders project" and housed a large portrait of Harry with a biography of his achievements and how as Commander of the organization he was involved in bringing the Earths defenders together, whilst protecting our world from alien attack. There was also another portrait of General Grant with his Biography and the two founders of SHEALD stood side by side as they did in life. New mem-bers would learn about these brave men as the history of SHEALD had begun to write itself.

The Saunders project on Mars was not as busy as Lunar base when it was first set up but that was understandable, due to the success of the interception in the past. Occasionally a UFO would still get through into the Earth's atmosphere and as usual the Earths defenders, SEASKY and the land roamers would be waiting for them.

On the last communication Marc had with the aliens he had gained more information about other planets around the solar system that also had life. The aliens of these planets were not as humanoid as the others had been but were highly advanced and peaceful. Soon they would develop crafts and travel to Earth and communicate with Earthlings. On Mars it was hoped that new alien travellers would come peacefully and be offered a more pleasurable welcome when intercepted. Nev-ertheless, there were many more solar systems that probably had other forms of alien life who may be less peaceful meaning, that there would always be the threat of an attack. This signified that the risk would always prevail and whilst it did SHEALD would exist.

NASA still had a separate base to train on Mars to avoid any intelligence leaks but talks had begun suggesting that soon SHEALD would be more open to the world. This would not be complete transparency but an acknowledgement that they existed and defended their planet from alien attacks. If the threat of an alien invasion were minimised then the fear would also be lessened from the public and more likely to be accepted. General Jackson had been involved in several meetings with Carl, Sara, and Tom regarding the exposure to the public about SHEALD. They would portray what they did to the people to protect them with the hope that they would achieve recognition. They concluded that by explaining the history of SHEALD and how it began was important and a good introduction. Sara would be designated as the ideal ambassador for this by introducing them to the world through the media. They were all aware that when the time came there would be a frenzy from the press and an interest into the private lives of the protectors. It would be good to have some recognition for those who were no longer with the organization and suffered with their lives at the hands of the aliens but a great invasion into their private lives would begin. For now, they could relax as their secret remained safe though General Jackson believed it was only a matter of time. Most of the staff at SHEALD were content with working in the background and getting on with the job without anyone noticing them. No one did the job for ego or recognition but because they believed in the cause and wanted justice and peace for Earth. They had pride, passion, and courage to do what was right at any cost to themselves, that was what they did best.

Sara woke that morning with cramp pains in her stomach, but as it was mild, she assumed it would fade as the day went on. There had been a security press leak as someone had managed to hack into one of the computers and found images of an autopsy of an alien. This was the first time anyone had managed to break into the SHEALD security system but it had happened and needed to be dealt with immediate effect.

Several Government computers had also had similar hackings recently and the level of security was upgraded and now they would have to retrieve the images and ridicule the ones that had been exposed, as fake.

Sara and Carl were discussing this with Paul when Sara doubled over in pain. Carl took Sara straight to the hospital and Doctor Walker, who was examining her gave a bewildering diagnosis. "You are having phantom labour pains and I suggest that you are taken directly to the laboratory to see your baby at once. The likelihood is that the baby is about to be born." Sara was quickly taken with Carl by her side to the lab and sure enough there was a commotion of activity in the Med 4 Tank. "The baby is on its way" said Vlad in great excitement. Their son had been in gestation for eight months and three weeks and would not require the incubator. A crib was moved into place and Vlad released a lever as the electronic birth canal opened and the baby travelled slowly down and out. As it neared the end of the canal the sac and fluid were removed and the baby appeared in the crib. Vlad disappeared with Tim around the back with the baby and there were a few moments of silence. Sara and Carl lay in anticipation not knowing what to expect and then the most wonderful sound of the baby crying rang in their ears. He was alive!

Vlad brought the baby round to Sara and Carl wrapped in a blanket. "He is perfect," said Vlad and handed the baby over to Sara as she held the baby in her arms and fell in love with the bundle of joy she was holding instantly. Carl looked on, this was his son that he never believed he would see or hold and yet through sheer dedication and hope he was real. Sara turned to Carl "Want to hold your son?" Carl nervously held out his arms, he was so tiny and fragile, and Carl had never held a new-born baby before but he was filled with pride and aspiration for the future of his son. "Hello Harry, welcome to the world and the Peter's family," said Carl. Sara wept with joy at the miracle they had and the love she had for Carl and her son Harry.

Vlad wiped the tears from his eyes as Carl walked over to him. "Vlad, from the bottom of our hearts we cannot thank you enough for what you have done for us. You have made our family whole. You never gave up trying and your devotion has meant so much to us and will go on to help others too. I salute you my friend for your courage and determination." Vlad became emotional again. All he had ever wanted was to be respected for his work and he had always had the drive as a doctor to preserve life at all costs and now he had been part of helping to create one.

The twins fussed over the new baby making Sara happy in knowing that they showed interest in him, since she hoped that they would all become part of their extended family. Their children were their future and possibly they would follow in their parent's footsteps. These children were likely to be SHEALDS legacy and although the twins were nine years older than Harry, she hoped that they would be part of each other's lives long after they had gone. The twins were growing up fast and had recently been attending the Military air force school which Sara hoped Harry would attend when he was old enough, but for now, she wanted to enjoy every moment with her husband and son. She finally had it all and was thankful. "It doesn't get better than this," said Carl and Sara agreed.

Sara had always kept a diary from young. It was one of the important items that she did not want to give up from her previous life and had requested them on her list when the reassignment team had moved into her home to sort out her fake death. For years she had written the highs and lows of SHEALD, nothing was left out. She still used paper to scribe on. After all these years never once had they appeared on the computer. It had started with her mother who had the idea to help her daughter improve on her writing and reading skills.

Though, Harry had not been happy about the diaries about SHEALD believing if they had ended up in the wrong hands, it would have destroyed the organization. Consequently, Sara was careful were she stored them but continued with her diaries in secret. For many years she wrote about the amazing people she had been honoured to work with and their extraordinary adventures. Her hope was that one day her son Harry would read the diaries and in a different society without secrecy would learn all about his mother and father's past and about the amazing work they did. Maybe there would be another Harry Commanding SHEALD to follow on the magnificent work of his parents and bring meaning to the sacrifices they had all taken.

Doctor Ivanov was currently in talks with the Health Organization and his papers on the synthetic womb had been accepted by the highest governing boards and was beginning to attract attention from the media. After many discussions it was agreed that Doctor Ivanov should have the attention he deserved to go forward with his work as long as he kept SHEALD hidden. Carl had vigorously fought for Vlad. He would be perceived as working as a Military Doctor, Psychiatrist, and Surgeon who through his vast experience of war injuries and trauma had brought together a thesis that proved the possibilities for a human embryo to be planted into a synthetic womb and grown without the aid of a human body. He had funded most of this work himself so the organization knew that there would be no comeback on them. Sara, Carl, and Harry would be given anonymity for safety reasons and it would stay classified for as long as they requested. The only lead to them was the naming of his procedure which was called SARA or Simulated Antenatal Reproductive Activator though it's significance to the outside world would have little connection to SHEALD.

Everyone sat around the TV screen in the control room at SHEALD and Lunar base were doing the same to watch Doctor Vladimir Ivanov being interviewed about his groundbreaking work with the Synthetic womb SARA. As Harry Peters was not registered in a civilian hospital it was easy to avoid anyone from unravelling the true nature of his birth. One day Harry Samuel Peters would learn the truth about his birth, but for now he was too young to understand. Doctor Ivanov came over well on TV and there was a profound sense of pride throughout the organization. Tim and Marc were bursting with pride at Vlad's celebrity status and let everyone know. Sara was just happy that Vlad had finally received the recognition he deserved and was no longer seen as the "Weird and crazy Russian doctor who gave people the creeps." He was an intelligent scientist with a passion to bring a positive solution to a sensitive issue plagued by many which caused suffering to so many families. The most exciting news of all was that he was in line for the Nobel peace prize.

Ivanov had also been invited to be involved in Lancaster University and was presented with an honourable degree. They had a picture of him in the hallway at the science block of the University in recognition of his work which was of immense pride to him and Tim. It was hoped that he would inspire future students and they may follow in his footsteps. Vlad was keen to advice the University and its students whenever he could and was a regular visitor and lecturer there.

The satellite on the Saunders project that needed to be installed in the Mars orbit was named SAAM2 (SAM2) and would intercept any UFOs entering the space area. This would alert SHEALD and then Lunar base. However, since the installation of SAAM2 a few months earlier there had been nothing of interest. There were the odd pieces of space juj,nk that had found their way further afield but apart from this it had been questionable whether the billions spent was giving any return. On the contrary the training centre was becoming extremely popular and in constant use. Eventually after a long interval a yellow alert was made by SAAM2 of a possible sighting. It was only just noticeable in the area of Mars but Carl and Sara gathered in the SHEALD control room with Paul to monitor any further approach. Paul checked the radar. "It looks like a UFO but its shape is different," said Paul. "Could this be another alien race exploring other planets?" Suggested Carl. Tom was on Mars base with Leah in their control room. "It's possible Carl, Leah has the speed reading which is much faster than any UFOs we have seen before," said Tom. "Stand down, negative entry," related SAAM2. The spaceship had turned around and voyaged deeper into space in the opposite direction.

They had been concerned that they had been planning a different attack as there were so few. Were they using tactics to give a sense of false security that they were no longer interested in Earth? The last few autopsies from aliens killed showed a much weaker body now that they were unable to get their fresh supply of organs anymore and were most probably dying earlier. The conversations that Marc had during telepathic contact also revealed an aggressive, bombastic nature with a dictating nation that had never experienced any peace in their world. Marc had tried to convince them to work with Earth for a peaceful resolution but they were arrogant and did not want peace, preferring war.

Sadly, the aliens that did survive an attack and were able to communicate were short lived as they were unable after all this time to tolerate our atmosphere fully and died. Yet, their similarities to their own planet and ours indicated that they should have survived. Ivanov assumed that this was due to the long journey in space to get to Earth and the pressure it put on their already weakened bodies. There were lessons to be learnt from this race with their destructive tendencies of rule and conquer until obliteration led to extinction. One can only help if that help was accepted.

# Meeting of the Minds

Once again SAAM 2 gave the yellow alert on Mars and SAAM1 On Lunar base also picked up the link. There were two alien aircrafts that were orbiting Mars with some hesitation. The interceptors lay in wait for the command to attack and eventually SAAM2 went to "red alert" and the interceptors launched.

"Hold it!" said Carl. "Interceptors do not attack, unless I give you the order to, I repeat hold fire." Carl waited, but there was no reaction from the alien crafts. "Interceptor's all stand down," instructed Carl. "But sir," interrupted the lead interceptor, "there are two UFOs in our location, do you want to take the chance of them attacking?" "It's my decision and I will take the responsibility; all interceptors stand down and retreat back to base," ordered Carl. The interceptors obeyed Carl's order and returned. These ships were different than usual and Carl could not be sure they would be aggressive and wanted to give them an opportunity first to see if they were friendly. So far, they had not launched an attack on Mars. "That's a brave move," said Tom. "It may be, but we need to at least try," replied Carl. The two crafts then halted in space just over the Saunders project base and stayed motionless over the base for the rest of the day.

Sara contacted Marc immediately. "Marc your needed on Mars now, get packing," she insisted. Sara and Marc took the next available Mars shuttle and Tom made his way over from Lunar base to Mars leaving Carl at HQ. As soon as the Mars shuttle landed the two UFOs began to move nearer to Mars and to everyone's surprise they landed on the planet. Tom quickly changed into his space suit and helped Marc to get into his. The Mars buggy was already on standby for them and they speedily ventured on Mars towards the alien crafts. The Mars buggy stopped within a short distance of the two

UFOs as Tom and Marc entered out onto Mars moving towards the ships. The UFOs were still at first, but as they neared the ships, they began to show movement and lit up. Suddenly one of the crafts doors slid open. Standing in front of them was the figure of an alien. This was a completely different race altogether than before, even with its helmet on it was clear how these beings were from a different planet. They were Thin and very tall at around seven feet with large oval eyes and two small holes for a nose with two further holes at the side of the head that could be presumed as ears. Their arms were long and their skin had an illuminous glow. There had always been drawings around the Earth over the years of this type some from thousands of years ago on cave walls and more recently from those who had witnessed sightings or believed they had been abducted by aliens. They had no opening for a mouth suggesting similar to other aliens that communication was telepathic.

Tom signalled to Marc to try and make contact. Marc moved closer and closed his eyes. He concentrated on the mind and third eye and as he did his whole body elevated and moved towards the alien. Tom was unsure what he should do at this point. Sara was back at the operation centre in the Saunders Project, listening and watching every move. She realized that by now Tom would be considering the possibility of firing at the alien to release Marc, but Sara could see that Marc was unhurt and in no danger. "Tom, stay calm. Marc is fine just stay with him he is making communication with the alien," instructed Sara. The alien glowed stronger as Marc levitated in the air, Marc looked to be in a trance and said nothing. After some time, Marc floated back to the floor and opened his eyes as if awaking from a sleep. The alien retreated back into the spaceship and the crafts flew off at great speed into deeper space and in a matter of moments the UFOs were gone.

Marc collapsed in a heap as Tom helped him back to the buggy and returned to the base on Mars. On arriving back to base Sara was waiting for them both with medics. Marc was taken to the medical unit with Tom. Carl wanted to know how Tom was. "I'm fine, there was a calmness out there that I can't explain," said Tom. Carl also asked Sara how Marc was after his correspondence with the alien. "It was too early to say for sure but he looked well and the doctor had carried out all the usual tests and could find nothing of worry and all his vitals were good. He did seem exhausted and was in a deep sleep at present, so they were letting him continue his rest for now," replied Sara. These aliens did not want to hurt anyone just to communicate.

Marc, Tom, and Sara all spent the night at the Saunders base on Mars. In the morning Marc was busy writing his report of what he had experienced and seen with the alien. Tom and Sara took advantage of the time and spent it with the new Commander of the Saunders project. Colonel Alex Steinberg was still finding her feet with the new posting as she had only recently taken up her position there. Although the Mars base had been completed nearly two years ago it had taken a while to find and train the right personnel for the job. Before this sara and Tom had commanded the base between them with the help of Ali and Leah. Sara did not wish to be too long away from home these days with Harry needing her and although a live in Nanny helped out whilst they worked Sara did not want to be an absent parent. She also missed Carl too much if she was away for more than one night. Tom was similar and although Fiona was understanding he had a family now and commitments. Late hours were fine but nights away were not and so the posting of Steinberg was a welcome to both Tom and Sara. It was good to have Tom with her and it meant they had time as friends to talk more. "It never bothers you this ESP stuff does it, Sara?" asked Tom. "No, once you understand it, it's fascinating and a wonderful gift to have and for those involved it becomes natural," said Sara. "To be honest, it scares the hell out of me, then I don't understand it, the sooner I do, the better," remarked Tom.

Back on Earth Marc was relating his findings with Commander Peters, General Jackson, and the commission team with his report. Marc explained that the aliens had come in peace and were on an expedition around the Universe which they did often. Their planet was many solar systems away and Marc was shown images of their planet but knew that it would take many years to get to should we want to venture there ourselves. Their planet was called Zyanide which was an oxygenated planet meaning the aliens breathed air, comparable to the human race. Like our world they had plants, trees and water and were surrounded by other living planets with a sun and two moons. It was a fertile land with an abundance of living creatures and a life expectancy extending to two hundred of our Earth years. It seemed that the alien who Marc had conversed with had mentioned that he himself was one hundred and two Earth years old. They were more advanced than Earth people and had previously visited over twenty thousand years ago. However, they had no intention of interfering with the evolution of Earth and so left our world to develop at its own pace.

During their expeditions they had met many other beings from afar and near who they had been able to communicate with successfully and they felt that the peaceful meetings had much to offer with the exchange of useful knowledge that they were able to trade. There was plenty to gain from a peaceful meeting with other likeminded beings. Then the alien introduced Marc to a crystal which glowed brightly and replicated a ball of energy that was freely available on their world and caused no detriment to their planet. This was their source of fuel for their long journeys. The alien also spoke of stations around the galaxy where they could stop off and converse with other extra-terrestrials with some even having the ability to use speech however, everyone could use telepathy if required. There was rarely an occasion when they were met with aggression but they would quickly deal with any negative outcomes. Especially if it could lead to war. They found this kind of conflict intolerable and spoke openly of the previous visitors to Earth who they knew to be aggressive, arrogant, war mongers. Others had tried to reason with them but they were none accepting of support or advice from anyone, which eventually contributing to their own downfall and eventual extinction.

There was, also, a warning to Earth from these beings that "Earth should not destroy itself in a comparable manner to those who had threatened their very existence." They had been monitoring Earth of recent times and were extremely disappointed in its progress and behaviour. They were aware of those scientists who had showed an interest and groups that were forming to fight against this. Still, they knew it needed much more support from the leaders to end the need- less wars with constant fighting and destruction of the planet for the sake of greed. This did not sit well with this new race. "You must learn to honour your world or the same fate will bestow you as did the destructive aliens and you will become extinct." Warned the Zanide's.

They made a promise to return soon with more constructive advice on how to heal the damage of the planet and to bring us news that would incorporate us in the inclusive Universal family. This was an important message with a video showing Marc elevating and connecting with the alien. The Commis- sion was disturbed by the message but at the same time in- spired and promised to take this back to their leaders to de- velop new strategies in bringing this to fruition. The meeting was to be recorded for the world leaders to receive and ab- sorb as this was a critical message that would be life changing and a call that had to be accepted in order to move forward with Earths survival, it was now or never.

# The Cat is Out of the Bag!

All the world leaders were gathering. Many were on a video link but a vast majority of them had made the long trip to New York for this special conference. Personal disagreements between countries were left at the door as this was much bigger than the bickering and tickle tackle that had put a wedge between nations. This was about the survival of man and their habitat. Sara, Carl, Tom, Marc, and General Jackson were also travelling to New York to address the nation of leaders. They had never presented to a conference of this multitude before and were naturally nervous at the thought of being in front of them with this message. Once again, the recording was played for all to see and Carl and General Jackson made their presentation. Afterwards there were many questions to be answered. Some doubted the authenticity of the video but, SHEALD had come prepared. This was the most important message SHEALD had ever been subjected to. The time for NASA to be finally aware of the organization would also now be called upon. It was time for everyone to know about the institute and its true relevance to the survival of their world.

So, it was time to tell the world about SHEALD in order that people would listen to the message and be understanding of the truth. The way that this was managed would be paramount to its success as they did not want mass hysteria of doom, gloom, and extinction. It had to be strong so that people would listen and take heed. This would be a well-organized release that required the utmost sensitivity. It should be a message of hope and unity, after all the people of Earth had only ever wanted to live in peace. It was the evil dictators who had intervened and caused such greed, hate and mass destruction but there was still time to make amends and that time was now! A special team of PRs were brought in from around the world and chosen journalists were recruited for the release of the new message. It would have to be in the right format to encourage the belief and follow the events for the good of the planet. Sara was to be the head of the launch and she had been in conference with several public relations personnel and a trusted journalist who were aiding her in collating her diaries into a book. The full story of SHEALD would finally be told, the highs, lows, the laughs, the tears, and the fears. At last Harry would be known to the world for the hero he really was and General Grant who founded the organization would live on forever. It was frightening and, in some ways, more frightening than anything Sara, Tom and Carl had ever experienced as this was their special story which needed to be told correctly and without prejudice for the sake of humankind.

Guy Samuels was a well-respected Journalist and TV interviewer from Boston in America. He began his career as a war correspondent who moved to England to become a news reader and an outstanding documentary maker. He fought hard for the rights of the vulnerable and exposed many evils in the world. He was enthusiastic about bringing the truth and justice to the people and his latest TV interviews had gone worldwide. People trusted this man and would listen to him so would be perfect for what they needed. He chose his work carefully, not for monetary gain but for the good of others. The PR had set up snippets through the media to entice people in with an important message that would soon be released that would change the lives of everyone forever.

It began with a TV interview from Guy Samuels with Sara. The studio was set and the cameras were in place. The message came through his earpiece "3, 2 and 1, we are live!" "Today, the Governments of the world released information which verifies that for many years we have been visited by Aliens from other planets. The existence of UFOs is real but have no fear, as a secret organization has been working in the background unknown to us for over a decade and a half. The name of this secret organization is SHEALD or the **Special Headquarters for Earth's Alien Legion of Defence**. They have been fighting the cause from a base on the Moon and Mars and right here on our very own Earth. A new book tells of the journey by Colonel Sara Peters which explains how it all began. This extraordinary story involves many heroes, sacrifices, and exceptional technology with aircrafts of which we can only dream of. This is a fascinating look into the lives of the alien defenders. A story of loss, sadness, laughter, passion, and love. It's a love story that will break your heart. It gives me the greatest pleasure; everyone please welcome my amazing guest Colonel Sara Peters. The audience applauded as sara stepped out and onto the TV screens. This was so surreal but she was doing this for SHEALD.

The interview went triumphantly and was broadcast in every country, some had interpreters' others subtitles in every language possible as the message had to get out. Sara felt exhausted emotionally and physically as she had answered and related some of her hardest memories. She also knew that she would never be able to walk in public again without recognition and although she was a bubbly sociable woman, she was also very private too. There was her son too, Harry who would now be named as the first child to be born in the synthetic womb SARA and needed to be protected from any ridicule or bullying. He also needed to know the truth but at the moment he was much too young. One day they would have to sit him down and tell him how fortunate he was to be so badly wanted through love and by the determination and selflessness of a Russian genius and friend.

After Sara left the studio, she felt relieved that it was over though, she knew this was really just the start. Carl was waiting for her in the after-show room, Sara was still shaking as Carl hugged and kissed her. "You were great, I'm so proud of you," he said. "I did it because I am so proud of all of you," said Sara. "Darling let's go home?" requested Carl. For Sara, those were the best words she had heard all day and pulled her coat over her shoulders. Sara Held on to Carl's arm as they left the building but they were met with an array of press with flashing lights and shouts for Sara. As the press closed in on them Carl thought they would be there for the rest of the foreseeable future and never get to the Taxi waiting to take them home. Just then, a car screeched up in front of them.

"Get in quick!"

It was Tom, "I couldn't let you do this on your own so I came down and saw all the press and knew you were in trouble. I think it may be best if you stay with us tonight as I doubt you will get much peace otherwise," offered Tom.

Harry was already being looked after by Fiona so would not need to be uprooted or be involved with the press mayhem. The frenzy had begun, but Tom soon lost the convoy following them. "So, my training did come in useful for something then," said Tom proudly.

The book sold out in twenty different languages in days of sale and every newspaper headlined about UFOs and SHEALD. The media had been primed to give this a positive spin and thankfully they did this without hesitation. A film offer followed the book but this was left to the PR people. Sara was happy to sign the contract as long as it was a true reflection of the book and they had already discussed what would happen to the profits of the film and book.

As Sara, Carl and Tom had wanted it to go to the families who had lost a loved one who had been a member of SHEALD. It would offer funding for any further Education for their children and families who could apply at any time. It was named the Peter Davis funding after the young pilot who was killed with Harry on that terrible day.

When the film was ready for release Carl, Sara, Tom, Fiona, Vlad, Tim, Marc, Paul, Leah, Ali, Jo and Saphy were all invited to the premier. They were not used to all the glamour but Sara did not let them down. She decided to wear the beige and gold dress that she first wore at the Ball all that time ago. She had not been able to let go of the dress as it had so many happy memories and now it would be perfect for this occasion.

"My word, after all these years you still take my breath away with your beauty," said Carl.

Sara may have been in her late forties but she was still as stunning as ever. The press had a field day taking photographs of the main characters of SHEALD and they were more popular than the film stars to their disgust. It seemed everyone wanted to talk to the Earth defender heroes and take their photos and learn all about them.

It was the strangest feeling watching a movie on a large Screen that was telling your story, but it was told well and truthfully. Of course, Sara cried a few times through the film but she was not alone and Carl found it the strangest feeling of all. "We are the people who have travelled through space, fought aliens, relied on a man with ESP to communicate with UFOs, had a baby without being pregnant and yet this is by far the most bizarre thing ever!" relayed Carl.

It was a while before normality was resumed and as promised young Harry Peters was sheltered from the press. He saw his mother's appearance on TV but at the age of 6 years old was not completely aware of the enormity of what his parents had achieved. Mum and Dad had sat down with Harry before the TV interview so that he would have some knowledge before the release of the media frenzy. His comments at the time were, "does that mean I can stay up later to watch Mummy on TV?" Much later in life when Harry had a full understanding, he told them both how proud of them he was and he hoped that one day he could give his parents the same pride in him. Then he had a head start as he had both Carl and Saras compassion and determination.

It was four years since the film premier and people of Earth had taken the story and message to heart. Lessons were learnt and the world did become a better place from those earlier days. Wars had become history that were never to be repeated. Negotiation centres were set up around the world for countries to work together so that disagreements were resolved by talking, not fighting. SHEALD was a much different place from the early days as the attacks from aliens had finally stopped. The evil alien race was gone forever. However, new contact had been secured with the aliens from Zyanide on Mars. These extra-terrestrials advised that soon others would visit from far away planets and they would help with plans for newer and better spaceships to travel at faster speeds and over further distances. Allowing us the ability to travel to other solar systems and beyond the universe.

Harry Peters was ten years old now and had been attending a private Military boarding school for some time. This meant that Harry was away from home throughout term time and only home during school holidays. Sara missed Harry greatly but realized her son's potential was very promising and he was already becoming an excellent student. He had the same cheeky sense of humour and twinkle in his eye that Carl had and when Sara tried to be serious with Harry over some mischief she would struggle, as he would give her a certain look and she would realize it was hopeless. Though Harry was a son to be proud of with his dashing looks. He was Tall with blonde hair and green eyes and with Carl's rugged looks, never faltered for admiration from the opposite sex.

# Adios

The cottage garden was looking pretty with the summer plants displaying the best of their blooms. Sara and Carl were sitting out enjoying the garden in the late summers evening. "You know Sara, I would love to potter in the garden like a normal person instead of having a gardener, do the ordinary stuff that we never have time for. You know Harry will be grown up and leaving home before we know it," said Carl. Sara was confused about where this conversation was going. "What is it, Carl?" asked Sara. "I think I'm getting too old for all this SHEALD drama and all I want is to be with you my darling, hold you a bit longer, walk and talk with you more and love you deeper." Sara smiled "You couldn't love me any more than you already do my dear, but I do understand what you are saying. So, if you are going to retire then I will too, and, we can still spend the precious time we have left together," replied Sara. Carl gripped her hand. "So, its decided then?" said Carl. "As long as we are together my dear, I will always be happy," said Sara. "Ditto," replied Carl and kissed her hand.

In November 2040 Sara and Carl Peters retired from SHEALD. It was an emotional day being surrounded by all their friends, everyone in turn visited the office to say their farewells. It would never be goodbye only 'adios' as they would join the committee that oversaw the funding for SHEALD and there was to be a much happier occasion as Tom would now take control as Commander. He had earned his position as every Commander before him, through sheer hard work and dedication and SHEALD would be in safe hands with Commander Tom Green.

Sara and Carl spent most of their retirement in France. They had bought a holiday place in the south of France but commuted back and forth to England when needed. Harry would join them on holidays and there were plenty of visitors. Especially Tom, Fiona, Leah, and Ali. Life was good and happy and three years after Tom had taken Command, he was joined by the twins Luna and Leo. At twenty- two years old Tom and Fiona were bursting with pride at their achievement. They brought new life into the organization and a new set of eyes to observe and make changes for the better. They helped with the ever-changing technology that came and went as the years passed by and in 2053 Harry Peters also joined SHEALD to his parent's immense joy and Tom took Harry under his wing. His potential at twenty-three years of age for leadership was obvious from the start. Harry along with Luna and Leo spent much of their time in conferences with visiting aliens. They even travelled through the solar systems themselves as they now had the potential for space travel on a much greater level. They had become good ambassadors for Earth and forming strong relationships with those they interacted with.

Tom had seemed different on his visit to France with Fiona this time. He was quieter and looked tired, he had lost his spark and was pale and thinner than usual. On his last visit in 2058 Tom explained that he had been diagnosed with Leukaemia and was now nearing the end. It still came as a shock to everyone when the news of Tom's death came. He was only sixty-four years old and Carl took the news badly. His friend who had been with him through his journey of SHEALD had gone and the Fab Four were now two. Fiona and the twins were naturally devastated and Sara and Carl decided to return to England for good, so they could be near Fiona and the twins and offer any support they needed. It was at this time that the committee wanted to commission a statue for the entrance to SHEALD and they had suggested it be of the four defenders. Sara did not need to think about this, she knew the very Photo that would show all to the world as they were. The photograph that Harry had locked away in his desk that he had treasured and had been displayed on the office wall would be perfect as it showed how they were, Friends to the end. The statue was erected twelve months after Toms death and stood proudly in the entrance to SHEALD for everyone to see. Sara was in the middle with Harry to her right and Carl and Tom to her left as they all stood together smiling with their arms around each other. It was flawless and would stand there forever more. Underneath the statue was a plaque that simply read "The Fab Four."

Although Marc was in his early seventies now, he still had some involvement with SHEALD. By now medicine had moved on and Marc was fitted with a simulated voice box that helped him to be able to speak normally. Doctor Ivanov had made this his next project and had begun research but past the baton to a much younger student at Lancaster University who eventually was able to produce the present model for Marc. Marc had met his partner Emma at SHEALD and they now had two wonderful children Lola and Zac that had inherited Marc's gift. Marc had grown in confidence since his early days and studied a master's degree in Parapsychology so that he could eventually open a gifted school for children with ESP. He wanted them to learn that they had a gift that was not a curse but a useful skill that should be nurtured to its full capacity. He never wanted any child to suffer the fate he had as a child. His papers on ESP and Telepathy were well respected and used often for studies in ESP worldwide.

Marc still kept in touch with his old friends from SHEALD and would visit Sara and Carl at the cottage when he could and he also saw Vlad and Tim regular as they lived close by. Vlad lived well into his nineties and after helping many couples to have children he was able to do the same for himself and Tim with two Sons Alex and Victor who were born with SARA. Both Saphy and Jo had each donated an egg to Vlad and Tim and felt they were doubly blessed to have their friends involved with the parenting. Vlad had continued to adapt his model with one tank instead of the four original Tanks for ease and SARA was now available to everyone who needed it.

As for Paul, he finally convinced Samira at HQ to date him and stayed happy together until his death at the age of fifty. He had received a kidney transplant by a new method of growing organs from personal DNA but sadly his weakened body suc cumb to its pressure. He left no surviving children. Paul had found it ironic that if the aliens were still visiting for organs, they could have been helped to grow their own without hurting or killing anyone but then these aliens were not interested in peaceful outcomes. Strangely, none of the group had moved too far away so they were all still in contact with each other as often as possible. They had shared something incredibly special with SHEALD and the bond of friendship would last forever.

Marc had slept well recently but tonight he had woken from a dream and he knew he had to go to the hospital at once. In his dream he had seen Harry and Tom who were both smiling and happy. They were strong and young as they used to be but they had a message for him that Carl was at the hospital and would be soon joining them and that the Fab Four would be together again once he returned. They told him he needed to go to Sara but for what reason he was not told and although he did not fully understand the message he did not delay. His partner Emma knew that he must go and encouraged him to follow his instincts. When Marc arrived at the hospital Harry and Sara were just leaving and Marc caught up with them in the car park. He was too late to say goodbye to Carl as he had already passed away and although he was sad to have not been able to see Carl, he was pleased to have caught up with Sara.

When Sara saw Marc, she went over to him with Harry. "Oh Marc, he's gone, my rock, my love, I don't know what I am going to do without him," she sobbed. Harry held his mother close to him, he too was still in shock of his father's loss. "I had to come, Harry and Tom sent me, they were expecting him, he will be safe now and with his friends for eternity." Sara was comforted by his words and thanked him. Although he was not sure why he had gone to the hospital he was glad he had brought some comfort to Sara and Harry. He had done as he had been asked and he was sure it had helped in some way. Harry helped his mother to the car and as she turned to get into the car, she shouted to Marc. "Thank you, Marc, for everything you have done, I will see you soon," she smiled. Sara had always believed in him and had brought him to his success which he was eternally grateful for. As their eyes met, he felt a deep connection with the woman who had rescued him from a sad and lonely life and had brought him to his full potential so that he too could help others. He had never had the time before to thank her for the wonderful trust she had placed in him and the gift of hope that she had given. As he stared back at her he felt her whisper in his mind's eye "It was my pleasure my dear old friend, Goodbye" and suddenly he understood why he had to come.

On the 23rd of August 2070 Carl Peters quietly passed away at the age of eighty-four with his wife Sara and son Harry by his side. Sara was distraught and sadly it was the following morning that Sara Peters was also found dead by her son Harry. She had passed in her sleep at the age of eighty-one and had survived her husband by just a few hours before joining him. Her friends believed she died of a broken heart.

Printed in Great Britain
by Amazon

85517399R00131